ADDICTED TO HER

CEDAR HILL DUET BOOK TWO

VM RHEAULT

ABOUT THE BOOK

**Not every addiction is deadly . . .
or so they say.**

Beau

I knew the second I saw Talia Scott I'd want to keep her until death do us part.

Everyone warned me her addiction recovery wouldn't mix well with my past, but I don't learn from my mistakes.

I'm needy, suffocating, and I try so hard to give her space, but I can't stop.

She's going to run, just like my fiancée did so many years ago.

Her addiction didn't kill her, but mine might.

———

Talia

When my sister, Devyn, investigated Rick's accident, she brought a lot of people down.

But not the two who matter most.

When I pick up where she left off, I must face my addiction and prove to everyone, including myself, that I'm stronger than that.

Billionaire Beau Hendrickson doesn't think he's good for me, but what he doesn't understand is, I'm addicted to his love, and that's one addiction I don't want to break, no matter the cost.

CHAPTER ONE

Talia

I made a big mistake.

I should have listened to my sister. She knew I was going too fast, and she was right. I mean, who moves in with a guy you've known for only a couple of days? It didn't help that he swept me off my feet, literally, after Stevie Johansson shot at Devyn at Beau and Rick's construction site and I was too woozy with fear of losing her to walk. I'd gotten caught up in the romance of it all . . . the way he couldn't stop looking at me, the way I could feel his eyes bore into me. It didn't matter where we were or who was watching. He didn't care, and God, yeah, I fell for it.

Fell for the way he'd say my name. Fell for the way he always had to have his hands on me.

Too bad I didn't know the second I moved in, the second Devyn and Rick were back in Old Harbor, he'd turn into a stranger.

We've had our good days . . . Christmas was nice. He made

sure I didn't miss Devyn too much. New Year's Eve was fun. We rode in a carriage and looked at the holiday lights in the city park. Rick and Devyn got back together and flew in from Old Harbor. That didn't last long, though, what with Devyn needing to go back to work and Rick focusing on his branch of M&H Development.

Now I sit alone in Beau's penthouse. I don't have a job. I don't have classes to go to because I thought it was a great idea to blow off a semester.

Beau's at work, and I sit, puttering around with nothing to do and nowhere to go.

I don't have a car, though Beau says I can ask Mack, his driver, to take me anywhere I want. I don't have any money. Beau's paid for what I've needed since I moved in, but I can't go shopping, and I don't need anything anyway.

I've tried to read and lose myself in a TV show, but when I lived with Devyn in Portland, there wasn't time for that. I was in class, doing homework, or trying to work and help as much as I could with the bills.

And therapy.

That took time. Lots of it.

Devyn didn't ask me if I'd keep going while I was living with Beau in Cedar Hill. She treats me like a grownup, like I can make good choices, not like I'm twenty-five and dealing with a past addiction to Sweet.

I love her for it.

And I hate her too, for not seeing that I need more.

I need more than spending my days alone. I need more than Beau coming home, kissing the top of my head, and then locking himself away in his study. Sometimes he'll poke his head out and wish me a good night, but most nights I get ready for bed alone, go to sleep in his guest bedroom alone, and start the whole lonely process all over again.

I thought he was falling in love with me, but that was just a pretty daydream.

I want to move to Old Harbor and live with Devyn again. She would tell me I'm welcome, that it doesn't matter she already moved into Rick's lighthouse. All I have to do is call her, and she would come and get me.

Sitting at Beau's kitchen table, I scroll social media on my laptop. It's all I've been doing lately—reading all the articles that pop up about Devyn being brave enough to figure out what really caused the accident on Rick and Beau's construction site. Sometimes the articles mention me, but mostly they wonder if Neil Simpson was telling the truth in his suicide note when he said that Declan Everett and Stevie Johansson bribed him with Sweet to sabotage the hotel.

It's something we'll never be able to prove, and it bothers Devyn. Rick tells her to be happy with what she's done. He's grateful she found proof that it wasn't his impatience that caused the crane to tip over, but she's wanted to tear Stevie down for years and that was just one more time Devyn didn't have enough to lock her up.

I click out of the newspaper articles and bring up Portland's community college website. I don't have time to sign up for spring semester at a new school, but if I contact the admissions office and beg them to let me register for online classes, I could, just before the deadline. It would give me something to do until . . . until what? Beau kicks me out? I should leave before he does that.

I keep hoping that one day he'll come home from work, carry me to bed, and make love to me. Afterward, we'll be lying there all sweaty, our hearts pounding, and he'll ask me to marry him.

The screen blurs, and I wipe my eyes. That will never

happen. He changed his mind, and he's only being polite until I leave.

I email the admissions office. I have a week before spring semester starts, and if the classes I need aren't full, I won't be too late. It won't matter where I'm living if the classes are online, and I think I'd rather try to find a routine in Old Harbor than hang around here any longer.

I'm packing when Beau comes home at five-thirty the way he always does. He's wearing one of his crisp suits, his shoes stained with salt and melted snow. His briefcase hangs from his hand. He doesn't waste any time locking himself in his office saying he has to work. Well, he can have at it.

"Going somewhere?" he asks lightly, leaning against the doorjamb of the guest room.

"This isn't working out," I say, folding a sweater. I can't look at him or I'll start crying. I don't want to leave. I moved in because I'm falling in love with him, but I can't stay if it's one-sided.

"Can I come in?"

I jerk a shoulder. He always asks, but it's not like he needs permission. This is his penthouse. I'm only a guest—and an unwanted one at that.

He stands next to me and smooths some of my hair out of my face. My cheeks are wet. I don't want him to see, and I turn my head.

"I'm sorry if I've been working too much," he says, dropping his hand and tucking it into the pocket of his slacks.

"It doesn't matter." I step around him and grab a handful of camisoles out of the dresser. Foolishly, I'd unpacked, thinking I'd be here for a while. "I'll go and you can have all the time you need."

He nods. "Did you talk to Devyn then?"

"Not yet. She'll want to come get me as fast as she can, and

I don't want her driving at night." My hands shake. I don't know why I'm trying to fold silk.

"I wish you wouldn't." His voice is mild, like he isn't breaking my heart in two.

"Why?" I ask, finally meeting his eyes. "So you can ignore me some more? So I can feel like you don't want me here? So I can keep going to bed alone? You can tell me you've changed your mind. I already know you have, so you saying it won't hurt."

"I haven't changed my mind about anything, Talia."

Stepping around him again and grabbing a few pairs of panties this time, I drop them into my suitcase. Devyn brought me a few things after she moved to Old Harbor, but I still don't have all my clothes and that's a good thing now. "I've been here for two and a half months, and I thought things would be different. I don't have anything to do, and maybe that's my fault, but you treat me like I'm in your way—so I'll get out of it."

He presses his lips into a thin line. "You don't understand."

"I understand more than you think." I pause. "It's okay, Beau. We haven't known each other for very long, and you decided I'm not what you want. I'm too young, or you don't like that I was addicted to Sweet." I reach out and touch his arm. Even through his suit jacket and dress shirt, I can feel his hard muscles. "It hurts, but I *do* understand."

He reverses our positions in the second I need to blink, and his hand grips my wrist like a vise. "You have no fucking clue what you're talking about." He backs me away from my suitcase, and I run out of room, my head thumping against the wall.

His eyes snap.

I'm not as tall as my sister, and he leans over, his face inches from mine.

"You have no idea how much control I need to be around you. I have wanted you from the second you walked into my office. The need to touch you, the need to be around you . . . You were addicted to Sweet so you know how it feels. I want to fucking *consume* you, but I'm afraid if I let myself, there will be nothing left of you when I'm done. I want to tear the clothes off your body, I want my lips on every fucking inch of your skin. I want to be so deep inside you, I won't know what day it is. But if you think for one second I would let myself do that to you, then maybe you *don't* understand."

Tension crackles around us, and I swallow. I didn't know he felt like that. He's kept his emotions so locked up I thought he wanted nothing to do with me.

"There's only one problem with comparing me to Sweet."

"What?" he grounds out through clenched teeth.

"Sweet doesn't give. It only takes. It ruins your life, it breaks your heart, it destroys your soul. I'm not Sweet, and I want to give those parts of myself to you." I press my mouth to his and nudge the soft skin of his lips with my tongue asking him to let me in.

He stands completely still, and just when I think he's going to push me away, he tangles his fingers in my hair and yanks to tilt my head. He ravages my mouth, our teeth grinding together. Sucking in a ragged breath, he lets go of my wrist and lifts me up. Eagerly, I wrap my legs around his waist.

"You shouldn't start something you can't finish," he says, carrying me to his bedroom.

"Do you mean sex? Or this relationship?" I ask, unknotting his tie.

"Either," he says, skimming his lips down my neck. "Both."

Beau and I haven't shared many details about ourselves during the few short weeks I've been living with him. Maybe Rick warned him or maybe Devyn talked to him, but he knew I was an addict and knows very little about anything else.

He drops me on the bed and goes to work on his tie himself, his eyes smoldering with threats and promises.

I stare at my hands. "You don't know much about my time hooked on Sweet."

I was going to say, "My time on the streets," but unlike a lot of drug addicts who pass out on a sidewalk or sober up only long enough to find a place to sleep in a shelter, thanks to Devyn, Mom and I had an apartment. It wasn't much. When Mom and I were both using, housekeeping wasn't high on our list of priorities. The only thing we cared about was our next score, but we didn't hang out together. She spent a lot more time on the streets than at our apartment, but I knew it was safer to get high behind a locked door.

It's what I did for it that hurts my heart.

Beau pulls his tie from his collar and lets it fall to the carpeted floor in a flutter of black and electric blue. With his eyes hooded, he slides his suit coat off his broad shoulders and starts unbuttoning his black dress shirt. "How long has it been since you were with someone?" he asks.

I've been out of rehab for three years, living one of those years here in Cedar Hill before Devyn was fired from the *Times*, the other two in Portland where we moved when she found a reporting job. Before any of that, I spent three years in rehab. Three years of rehab for a six-month addiction to one of the strongest, most addictive drugs on the planet.

"Six years."

"Do you remember it?" he asks, unbuckling his belt.

Shame burns my cheeks. "Bits and pieces."

"Were you raped?"

I shake my head. I wasn't as bad off as some people. There are addicts like Mom who can barely remember their names, and there are addicts like Neil Simpson who can function, who can hold a job and nurse the addiction on the side. I was somewhere in the middle. I needed it, my grip on normal everyday life slipping with every taste. The day the police arrested me was the day they saved my life. There are women who let sick assholes do whatever they want if they're paid with Sweet. I was close to being one of them.

He kneels between my legs and holds my face between his hands. That's the one thing that always struck me whenever Devyn and I were around Beau—his sensitivity and his vulnerability. He's been hurt, but he's never told me how or when, or who or why.

His light brown hair falls into his eyes, and I brush it back and let my fingers move down his cheek and along the stubble of his jaw. He's a lot more sophisticated than I am, though Devyn would say I have experience of a different kind. That's probably true. I lost most of my innocence going to that party and getting hooked on Sweet. I lost a lot in those six months, addicted and spending every waking second thinking about it. I know I'm pretty—I overheard a dealer say once that I was lucky, but it also made me feel targeted. There are some people who see a pretty thing and want to break it because they can't have it. That applies to everything, even people.

"Do you want to be here? In this room and on my bed?" he asks, lightly rubbing the pads of his thumbs over my cheeks.

I want to tease him or roll my eyes, but if I'm not serious, he'll get dressed and lock himself in his study for the rest of the night. He's kept his hands off me thinking I can't handle what he wants to do to me, but I want it more than anything.

"Yes."

"Okay." He starts to unbutton my blouse, this billionaire on his knees in front of me, belt unbuckled, shirt undone, his hair mussed. We've gone into my sexual history, but I'm too scared to ask about his. He's Rick's age, almost forty. He couldn't have reached that age without being in a serious relationship. Maybe an engagement, possibly a marriage. The first night I stayed here, the day Stevie Johansson shot at Devyn, I looked him up online. There were hundreds of pictures. Women, *goddesses*, walking with him, their fingers linked. It wasn't until I looked again and again did I realize how flat his eyes were, and I wondered how long it would take before he looked at me that way.

Though I don't have anywhere to go during the day, I dressed in slacks and a blouse. It's the only way I feel like I fit into his penthouse . . . and his life. Ratty pajamas wouldn't work, and I asked Devyn to send me my dressy clothes.

He opens my blouse, revealing a teal green bra, and sucks in a breath. I'm glad I'm wearing matching panties.

In Portland, Devyn and I spent a lot of time together. Not just sitting around our rented house, but shopping, lunches, cheap weekend matinées, whatever we could afford. I think it was her way of keeping me busy, but she was also trying to make up for the time we lost while she was building her career. One of our favorite things to do was go to the fancy lingerie store in the mall. We'd splurge on bra and panty sets, lotions and perfumes, lip glosses and body glitter. My sister's gorgeous, and it wasn't a surprise Rick fell head over heels in love the second he saw her.

She said the same for Beau and me, but her relationship is going to last, and ours, well. We've already got a few things fighting against us.

"Can I touch you?" he asks, his hand hovering near one of my breasts.

I don't want him to ask about every little thing, and I say, "You can do whatever you want."

Fire sparks in his eyes. "Don't you ever say that to anyone else. Do you understand me?" He stands and yanks me off the bed. Shaking my shoulders, a growl rumbles from deep inside his chest. I'd be scared if I didn't understand that he's defending me. Defending me against those assholes on the street who used me, defending me against the next man who takes me to bed, who would get off hurting me, even a little.

He takes my blouse off and hauls me onto the middle of the bed. Anchoring himself over me, he covers my mouth with his, bruising my lips. His cock is hard and huge against my belly, and my stomach quivers. He's not going to be gentle, but I don't want him to be. I want to prove I can handle whatever he wants to do to me, just like I said.

His teeth nip under my jaw, down my neck, and over my collarbone.

I twist my fingers in his hair, and his scruff, as he kisses me, burns my skin. I tilt my hips, needing more. It's been a long time, but my body still knows what it wants.

He moves his lips to my breast, and he bites at my nipple. The pleasured pain shoots through me, settling in my core, and I cry out. He tugs harder, and wet floods my panties.

"You still say I can do whatever I want?" he asks, his voice rough.

"Yes," I gasp.

"You won't regret it," he says, inching down my body and pulling at my pants and panties. I'm not wearing the sexy kind of stockings, only the granny knee-high pantyhose with the awful elastic at the tops to keep them in place. I didn't think I'd be going out, let alone doing something like this, and I blush as he rolls the nylon down my legs.

He doesn't care, and he stands and lets the scraps fall on the floor. He unbuttons his dress pants, slides them down his hard thighs, and takes off his boxer briefs. There's nothing left except his dress shirt and socks, his cock thick and long, pre-cum glistening at the tip. I don't care how fierce he's trying to be or how dangerous he wants to pretend he is. He looks adorably intimidating, and I push back a smile, my heart hammering with nervous excitement.

He takes off his shirt and his socks, and when he comes at me, my smile drops.

He leans over me, unhooking the front clasp of my bra. He doesn't waste the energy to throw it on the floor, only pushing it aside and nestling his hips between my thighs. The tip of his cock nudges me. I'm not on birth control, but I'd love to feel him inside me without a condom.

"Do you want this fast or slow?" he whispers.

The question confuses me. I know how sex works, but to be able to choose like a setting on a washing machine is new to me. "I— I don't know."

"Slow, then." His breath is warm against my lips.

He nibbles at my nipple again, this time sucking my skin between his teeth. I have time to only moan once, and then he's moving on, kissing down my belly and settling between my legs.

I've never been eaten out before, and without thinking, I try to put my knees together.

"Stop," he orders, pushing my thighs apart. "A man has never done this for you before?"

"No." My voice comes out in a whimper, though I didn't mean it to. I've never heard of a man hurting a woman doing this, and Beau won't hurt me anyway. If he did, he would do it only to give me pleasure in the pain.

"Relax, love."

I try to loosen my muscles and concentrate on the soft comforter and the fluffy pillow under my head. The room's dark, but I don't worry about what he'd see if there was anything more than the city lights blinking through his windows. I've groomed myself down there, hoping that one day I'd end up in his bed, but I'm worried about how I smell and how I'm going to taste. I'm nervous that he's going to want a blowjob, and I've never given one before.

All these things are jumbled in my head, but his mouth covers my pussy and I can't think of a damned thing. Hot, his tongue nudges my clit, and I buck, my hands clenching the comforter.

"Stay still," he says, putting his arm across my hips and trapping me in place. His scorching mouth covers me again, and his tongue swirls lazily around my clit. He pushes a finger inside me, and I moan.

A stirring of an orgasm starts under his tongue, and despite his arm pressing against my belly, I arch my back, wanting more pressure. In response, he pushes another finger inside me and twists them.

Tears gather in my eyes, and my heels dig into the mattress. I didn't want to tell him that I've never come before, that I didn't know how this would feel.

He adds another finger, the tip grazing that exactly right spot that sends me over the edge. The climax stiffens every muscle in my body and sparks sizzle all my nerves.

I jerk away when he licks at my clit too long and the pleasure turns into an uncomfortable sensation.

He takes the hint and kisses the inside of my thigh. "Is that something you might want me to do again?" he asks, reaching into the drawer of his night table. He takes out a condom.

Wiping my eyes, I say, "I think so."

"That's high praise," he says, chuckling and tearing the wrapper open. He meets my eyes in the glow of the city's lights. "I'm not wearing this because I think you're dirty. I don't want to get you pregnant, that's all."

I let out a breath. "How did you know that's what I was thinking?"

He lies on top of me and props himself up, his hands on

either side of my head. "I'd go without if you were on birth control or if we were ready to have kids, but you're young and still have a lot of living to do."

Lifting up onto my elbows, I ask, "What do you mean?" He sounds so sad.

"I mean, I never want to do anything you're not ready for. Come here." He nudges me backward so I'm lying down again and gives me all of his weight. His breath flutters over my face, and I can smell the tangy scent of my flavor on his tongue. Slowly, he pushes inside me, lightly kissing my lips, a hand under my ass.

My orgasm made me so wet it's not uncomfortable, and relaxing, I wrap my arms around his neck.

"Fuck," he mutters.

"Is that bad?" I ask, kissing under his jaw. He's not as rough as I thought he'd be, letting me settle, gently rocking back and forth and giving me time to adjust to his size.

"You're so tight, so tiny. I don't want to hurt you, love."

"You're not. Beau, you could never hurt me." His weight is delicious, and I tug him farther down on top of me. I want to feel all of him . . . inside me, over me, everywhere.

"I was when you thought I didn't want you. This is all I've been thinking about. Fuck," he murmurs again against my lips.

He starts to move, a deep, steady glide, the tip of his cock hitting my center with every thrust. My body aches, but in a good way. I don't feel like I'm going to come again, but soon Beau's ready, and he tenses. He screws his cock into me as he comes, sweat slicking his skin.

Moments turn into minutes as he calms down. He presses his forehead against mine, his heart thrumming.

"Did I hurt you at all? Be honest, Talia."

I shake my head, my hair brushing against the pillow. "No."

"I wanted to," he says, a shadow flickering in his eyes. "I

wanted to hurt you for trying to leave. Then I started thinking about you and Sweet, and I couldn't. I couldn't take you as hard as I wanted, as fast as I wanted. I'm always going to think of you as a little girl on the street, and you're always going to shred me. Stay here. We'll order takeout and eat in bed. I need to clean up."

"Beau," I whisper, kissing the corner of his mouth.

Brushing his lips over mine, he murmurs, "I know."

He doesn't take very long in the bathroom that's attached to his suite, and he's lying next to me seconds after I take my bra off and settle between his crisp sheets.

"If you miss your sister and want to go, I'll drive you to Old Harbor myself in the morning," he says, propping his head in his hand. "I'd say we could fly, but I want to spend those five hours with you."

"I don't want to go, but I need more. I need to do something more than sit around and wait for you to come home. I don't want to shop. I don't want to wander around the city by myself. I emailed the college in Portland and asked if I could take online classes spring semester. If I can squeeze in before the deadline, the classes and homework will help. I'm not used to so much free time or being on my own." I sit up and tuck the top sheet under my arms. "Devyn warned me I would feel like this, but I didn't believe her. I need to find a new therapist or contact the one she and I were seeing in Portland and ask if I can do virtual sessions. I need more, and it has nothing to do with you." I lean forward and kiss him, resting my palm against his jaw.

"I'm sorry I didn't see it." He sighs. "They let Everett completely off the hook. We heard the news today. There's nothing besides Simpson's suicide note that points at him, and it's not enough. All the charges were dropped."

"I'm sorry."

"I am too. Rick's pissed off, of course. They shot at Devyn and kidnapped her, but no one can prove a goddamned thing. I've been preoccupied with that, but that's no excuse. If you'd be happier in Old Harbor, you should tell me. We can still see each other."

Every once in a while, is what he means. Old Harbor, where Devyn and Rick live on Harbor Lake's ragged shore, is five hours from here, on the road. Beau has the resources to fly back and forth, but he's running Cedar Hill's branch of M&H Development alone now. He might have good intentions and we'd see each other a couple times a month, but that would fade down to nothing by summer. He's too busy, and too much in demand as Cedar Hill's Most Eligible Bachelor now that Rick's gone and Declan Everett is engaged to Stevie Johansson, for a long distance relationship to work.

"Where do you think this is going? If this is a casual thing for you, I should go." I don't want to sound like that, but if he's just going to kick me out in a few months, I shouldn't get my hopes up.

"This has never been casual for me. I wouldn't have asked you to move in with me if I felt that way. I want you here, and now that I've had you, maybe it will take the edge off."

"Yeah?" I ask, sliding down into the soft sheets and cuddling into his chest. He wraps his arms around me, and I let out a sigh of relief. My sister told me that choices can be made and unmade. If I choose to stay here, I can always leave if I feel like I have to. There's no harm in giving us time to see where this will go.

His hand drifts down my back and his fingers dance over my hipbone looking for more. Nudging me onto my back, he finds what he's looking for, and he pushes two fingers inside me. "Maybe not." Rubbing his lips over my cheek, he says, "Tell me if you ever get tired of me."

I pause, thinking that his request is strange. He'd get tired of me faster than I would ever get tired of seeing his handsome face.

"I never will," I say, hooking my leg over his ass and positioning myself over his cock. I slide him inside me. It's stupid, but I don't care if he's not wearing a condom. I want to feel him, feel his hot cum inside me.

We don't end up ordering food.

We feast on each other instead.

CHAPTER TWO

Beau

Sunlight plays across her face as I get dressed for the day.

I don't want to leave her alone after the things she told me last night, but I have meetings all day—some that have to do with the site—and I'm going out there to take notes of what can be done now before the spring thaw. There isn't much, but more than I would have thought, considering it should have been cleaned up better than it was. Luckily for Rick, an abandoned portable outhouse and dumpster were left behind that had helped him find Devyn that night, but things like that shouldn't have been there in the first place.

My only excuse is that I'd been too preoccupied with Rick's recovery to make sure things were done the way they should have been, and trusting that son of a bitch Neil Simpson was another mistake that won't happen again. I may not have the degrees Rick has, but I can supervise what we have left of the build, and I'll watch it go up with an eagle eye.

Fucking Everett.

I sit on the edge of the bed and rub my thumb over Talia's cheek. I can't believe how close she'd been to leaving me. I tried like hell to be gentle with her last night, and it had almost worked. As the clock worked its way to four in the morning, I had her again, and I showed her just exactly what I meant when I said I wanted to consume her. There isn't an inch of her skin my lips haven't touched, there isn't one place on her body that doesn't have my mark, evidence of my hands on her.

Like a forest fire, I destroyed, and left nothing but ash in my wake.

I won't apologize, but I can't let it happen again.

"Talia, love," I whisper.

Her eyes flutter open, the deepest green. I'd fallen into them the day we met, and I haven't found my way out. I don't know if I want to.

She winces as she moves, and my mouth dries. I've been obsessed since the second I saw her, and I want her again. This time slowly, while I look into her eyes and tell her how much I need her, and how scared I am that one day she won't wait until I come home to leave.

"Good morning," she says, lifting up onto an elbow.

"There's coffee, decaf," I correct myself quickly, always forgetting that since she moved in, I don't keep caffeine here. "I need to go in today, but I can take a half day tomorrow, and we can . . ." I stumble. It's been almost a decade since I spent time with a woman simply hanging around. Talia and I did our share after she moved in, but that was during the holidays and activities like decorating the tree and carriage rides were built in. Now they're over and we're back to boring, everyday life.

She nods. "It's okay. Now that I know I'm staying, I'll line up a few things. Maybe find a receptionist's job at a mental health facility that I can put toward my course work."

I don't like the thought of her leaving, even to go down the street for bread. "If you're sure. I don't want you to be unhappy."

"No, I'll be fine. I don't want you to think that I'm bored. I didn't know how you felt, but now that I do, I'm in a better place." She kisses my palm, and old memories of a different woman doing the same come back.

Rick never said one thing about Talia and her addiction. I wonder if I would've listened if he had.

Doubtful. I would have said enough time has gone by, yet ten years have passed in the blink of an eye.

"Why don't we fly out to Old Harbor this weekend? We can spend some time with Rick and Devyn, and I can look at the land he's been buying out there." The trip's a spontaneous idea, but I like it. Rick hasn't been the same since the accident, but traces of my old friend have come back since he met Devyn.

Talia's eyes brighten. "I would love that."

"Good. You'll be okay until I get home?" I ask, brushing my fingertips over her cheek. "You won't try to leave me again, will you?"

Naked, she crawls into my lap, and I cradle her like a child. She rests her head on my shoulder and I gently slide two fingers inside her, my thumb gently rubbing her clit. Mewling, she opens her legs, and I lick at her mouth as I make her come. My cock hardens against her ass, but I'm dressed for work and I have an early meeting I can't miss. I need to control my weaknesses around this little girl in my arms. She's only that—a little girl—and if she decides I'm not what she wants, I'll be fine. I was before.

She skims her fingers over my jaw. "Are you okay?" she asks, her eyes searching mine.

I know she's sore from last night, and tenderly, I pull my

fingers out of her. Wiggling on my thighs, she sucks in a breath. I dry my hand on the comforter, wincing at the sound. "Yeah. I didn't get much sleep last night. I'll see you later. Stay out of trouble." I kiss her forehead, and she snuggles into my chest.

Reluctantly, I nudge her away and into bed, and I leave her dozing, her hair in a tangle on my pillow.

———

Work hasn't been the same since Rick's accident. As the days and months went by, people asked me why I wasn't at the site, why I wasn't there watching the lift. I've always been more active on the paperwork side of things, and when the local news channels caught wind of the accident, I heard the lift went bad along with everyone else in the office. I rushed to the site and was one of the people at Rick's side as the emergency techs argued about the safest way to get him out from underneath the boom.

It didn't surprise me when he decided to nurse his injuries, mental and physical, in Old Harbor, after the accident and his wife divorcing him. Social media called him a beast, and he used that, hiding in an old lighthouse that sits on a jagged cliff, not seeing anyone and telling every reporter who wanted an interview to go to hell.

It didn't surprise me, but it hurt.

It still hurts as I walk into the building where we have our offices, wait my turn to go through security, and prepare to spend another day alone. We have a huge team of people, that's true, but fewer now with Neil Simpson dead, Tony Kelly retired, and Fred McAllister, the dirty OSHA rep, in jail for falsifying reports. Everett bribed him to write off the accident, but the investigators looked for a money trail and didn't find anything. With McAllister and Everett not talking and nothing linking the two, the DA couldn't press charges for accepting a bribe and McAllister's sentence behind bars won't be long enough for me.

I say good morning to Lola, my PA, drop my briefcase near my desk, and hang up my coat. I'll be heading out to the site later, and I ask Lola to bring me a coffee service. I don't mind drinking decaf at home, don't mind putting off my booze until Talia goes to bed. I understand better than she thinks how easy it is to replace one vice for another, and if she needs me to have her back, I will. It may not be convenient, but I'll drink my caffeinated coffee and scotch when she's not around.

I sit through meetings and reach for my phone several times to call Rick. He would answer—he always has whenever I've called to bitch about something—but I let him be. He's tumbled into a quiet life working to build a branch of the company in Old Harbor while Devyn writes for the *Harbor Herald*. I'm happy for him, and I don't want my melancholy to bring him down. We've been friends since college, but that doesn't mean things don't change. Can I be resentful that I miss our friendship and business arrangement more than he does? Well, good, because I am.

By the time I'm able to go out to the site, I need the fresh air and a chance to work off some restless energy. I drive myself, shove a hardhat on my head, and unlock the padlock that keeps the fence door closed. Christ knows what's out here anymore. A fucking sharpshooter, his sight aimed at my head. I'll never forget Devyn's face as she ran toward me, or Talia's as she tried to understand what was happening. I should go over the entire area with dogs and a metal detector. It wouldn't surprise me if Everett boobytrapped this place. The new OSHA rep assigned to the case cleared the site, but that doesn't mean it's safe.

The temperature hovers around twenty degrees Fahrenheit, which isn't terrible considering we're located near the upper eastern part of Minnesota, but the wind has a bite to it and I yank my collar up. It's impossible to write on the checklist I brought while I'm wearing gloves, and I roam the site scratching notes, my fingertips tingling.

This should have been done a long time ago, but Rick hasn't cared, and I had more important things to worry about than a project he didn't want anything to do with anymore. The only reason he cares now is because of Devyn.

Falling in love can change a man.

I'm prying the door of the portable outhouse open when Jasmine walks across the site, her hair blowing around her shoulders. She's not dressed to be out here, and I scowl.

"I heard you're off the market," she says, her hands shoved into her coat's pockets.

"Maybe," I mutter, using a crowbar to force the lock to give. Rick explained how he managed to climb up to the second floor, but because of what happened to Devyn, he forgot all about it. I didn't. I don't want to know what could be locked in a frozen outhouse, either, but we let the site sit for so long and there are going to be a lot of things I'll need to face that I'd rather not. Rick should be here, dammit, but if I don't stop thinking about it, I'll only get pissed off.

"Maybe? Do you mean you *don't* have a cute little blonde living with you? What would Nina say?"

"She wouldn't say anything."

"It was difficult for her to show it, but she loved you, Beau."

"Yeah, she sure did."

"It wasn't her fault," Jasmine says, always insisting, always the best friend. She's been like that for the past ten years, as if I were a priest and had the power to forgive Nina her guilt. Nina's dead, and it's not my decision where she ended up.

I growl, drop the crowbar, and take my hardhat off. Frowning, I push it on the top of her head. There's been enough people hurt on this property, and I don't want there to be any more. "It's not safe out here."

"Then why are you out here?" she asks, adjusting the hat over her hair.

"It's my job. Why are you?"

"Your office told me where you were. I wanted to check in. You've been scarce lately."

I pick the crowbar up. Cranky now, I wedge it into the crack of the door and turn so I can shove on it with my foot. "Step back," I tell her. "I don't know what's in here."

She wrinkles her nose and inches backward. Christ, doesn't anyone listen? Everett could have loaded it with a shit-ton of explosives, pardon the pun. I shouldn't be the one opening it.

The lock pops open, and the door slams against the frozen mud. Jasmine staggers back—finally—and I look inside. A black duffel bag is stuffed into the seat, and I yank it out.

"What is it?"

"I don't know." I put my gloves on and unzip it. I can't count how many Sweet Stuff candy packets are in here. The sugary pink powder and white candy dipping sticks exclusive to Stevie Johansson's candy stores are popular right now. I see an ad for them every time I'm online or open the *Times*. I laugh. Here I thought it would be something dangerous. "Christ."

"Is that Sweet?" Jasmine asks, connecting the name to the notorious drug.

I pull my cell out of my pocket and call the non-emergency police number I have saved in my Contacts list. "Nah. It's candy. Probably some kid stole a box out of a delivery truck and got scared. Decided to dump it instead of going to juvie for stealing."

I talk to dispatch and tell them I found some stolen property, and she says an officer is on his way.

"You should go before they get here." I push the bag away with my foot. "You don't need to be around this."

She lifts a shoulder. "It looks harmless enough. Will you come out with us tomorrow night? For old times' sake?" She steps closer to me, her high-heeled boots unsteady in the frozen dirt.

"What good would that do? Nina's been gone for years, Jasmine. Move on."

"Like you have?" she asks, her hair blowing into her face and catching in her eyelashes.

"I've been trying." I think of Talia soft and willing in my arms, my fingers deep inside her as she moans, arching her back and asking for more.

"She's an addict, Beau. Just like Nina was."

A cop car parks behind my truck, and two uniformed police officers walk across the site, their features hard and their postures stiff. Stolen property can be a serious business in Cedar Hill, the definition of serious depending on which side of the law you're on and just who's benefiting from the fencing. Candy isn't a big deal, but Rick and I run our company on the up-and-up, and we report anything that doesn't seem right. I'm glad I had the brains not to touch it. The last thing I need is to be associated with little punk kids trying to prove how tough they are by ripping off delivery drivers who don't give a fuck.

I shoot a glance at Jasmine. "What do you care?"

Staring at the ground, she passes the hardhat to me. She speaks briefly with one of the officers and then trudges over the site, her head still bowed. I want to call after her, but I'm stuck for the next half an hour explaining what happened and why there's an abandoned outhouse on our property.

My day doesn't get any better when I go home and Talia's

not waiting for me. With my heart racing, I poke my head into the room she's been staying in, but all her things are here. I blow out a sigh. I don't know why I keep expecting her to leave. A therapist would ask me if I want her to, but I don't.

I want her, but like with Nina, the cost may be more than I can pay.

CHAPTER THREE

Talia

I'm stiff, but in a good way, the feminine-pride kind of way. I made him lose control. A man who runs a billion-dollar company, a man who negotiates million-dollar deals on his lunch break. I made that man lose control in bed wanting me, and the bruises he left behind are trophies I'll wear until I can make him do it again.

We kept using condoms, and I know it's smart. Devyn would be so disappointed if I got pregnant before I was married or before I managed to graduate with my psychology degree. I don't want to disappoint her, but I don't want to disappoint myself, either. I deserve a future full of success—professional and personal—and to have children with a man who has made a commitment to me and our family. Beau might have swept me off my feet and carried me to bed, but he didn't tell me he loves me and he didn't ask me to marry him. Even if he had, it's too soon for me to say yes. He hasn't seen much of the world I need to live in since the rehab facility discharged me. He might think drinking caffeinated coffee at work and sneaking drinks after I go to bed is only an inconvenience, but those types of inconveniences are what he'll have to live with for the rest of his life. There's no way he's had enough time to decide if he wants to take on something like that without regretting it.

The hot shower eases the aches in my muscles, and the coffee, despite it being decaf, is still good—hot and strong. I get dressed for the day and do my hair and makeup because that's what I do. Then I sit with my laptop at Beau's dining room table.

Someone in the registrar's office at the community college forwarded my request to my advisor, and he said I could still register for classes and attached a list that will put me closer to getting my degree. Because we were technically low-income, when I applied for financial aid, I was granted a free ride. I accepted gratefully and vowed to never waste it. The grants are still active and will cover the spring semester. I choose four, which is full time at sixteen credits, and as long as I keep a 3.0 GPA, I'll fulfill the financial aid stipulations. My advisor asked me to email him the financial aid award letter for the current year as he misplaced his.

I saved it in the cloud, and I click it open.

Devyn and I have our own master folders, and I open mine and scroll through every file, but I don't find it. I must have saved it in hers by mistake and I close out of mine and open hers. We shared everything when we lived together, though we didn't have much to hide from each other. My therapist always said how important it was to keep communication open, and Devyn has been really good about it. Proof of that is her files aren't password protected, and I start searching through them. Most of the files are full of articles that she'd written, hoping to sell to various magazines and journals. Some files have story ideas and blog post topics, any side hustle she could think of because we needed the cash.

Looking at all the ways she tried to come up with a little extra money brings tears to my eyes. I don't know where I'd be without her.

One file is named "Sweet," and I click on it, already knowing what's inside. My palms start to sweat as I move the cursor around the numerous documents saved in the file. Page upon page is filled with Devyn's resources and sources she gathered while she was researching Stevie Johansson. I knew she'd been digging around every second she could, but what I didn't know until this very second was how often she'd sneak out of the apartment after I went to bed. Me falling asleep gave her the only free time she had. She didn't need to babysit me then, to make sure I didn't relapse.

Snitches, things they said. Time and place.

She spoke with a priest named Father Will often.

Directors of homeless shelters, soup kitchens and halfway houses. Rehab facilities, only the kind that aren't as nice as mine was. Last resort facilities in the crappiest parts of Cedar Hill. Lower than the one Neil Simpson checked himself into to hide from Stevie.

I'm looking at a year's worth of Devyn's sources. No wonder she was devastated when Bill, the editor-in-chief of the *Cedar Hill Times,* fired her. So many hours down the drain. So much effort, hope, and prayers. Gone.

I close out of that folder and scroll, looking for the folder I might have saved my award letter in. I'm about to click out of the cloud completely and do a full laptop search or go through my email for the original documentation, but a folder at the bottom of the screen catches my eye.

Mom.

I click on it, my heart pounding. Since I got out of rehab, our mother has been the one thing that's come between Devyn and me. I want to help her. Devyn says she's a lost cause, and for my own mental health, to leave it alone.

This folder *is* protected by a password, and I try everything I can think of that would work. Her birthday and my birthday. Her name, Rick's name, and my name. Our mother's name and favorite foods. It would be one of those, but I'm not getting the combination right, or maybe she added an exclamation point or a question mark to the end.

It should be enough that she's been keeping track of Mom on the streets, at least, that's what I think this folder is about. That while she was digging for information on Stevie Johansson, Devyn had bumped into her, maybe tried to buy her food or convince her to go to rehab.

I'd never call Devyn heartless—not after all she's done for me. She's the last person on earth I could. She's so passionate about everything around her, but her cold attitude toward our mother has made me angry more than once. I'm glad I was wrong. That she had, in her own way, been trying to help her. I haven't seen Mom since I got arrested six years ago. Devyn's afraid of anything that could make me spiral again, and I'm not sure if looking for Mom is a good idea either, except, what kind of daughter would I be if I didn't try?

I have most of Devyn's research, and she's not here, so . . . what if I picked up where she left off? Even with my classes and homework, that won't take up all the time Beau spends at the office. We might have made some progress last night, but he still needs to work, and if he shuts himself up in his study, that leaves me hours in the evening with nothing to do. I need more than trying to watch a TV series I don't care about. I need to be productive and useful.

We're going to visit Rick and Devyn this weekend, and I can casually pump her for information. She would never let me walk the streets, and Beau would lock me in my bedroom if he knew my plan.

I'll have to keep this to myself.

It's what a good investigator would do.

Devyn didn't get as far as she did telling everyone who would listen that she was looking into the Sweetheart of the Midwest. Stevie figured it out anyway, but not for close to a year. Using her sources, maybe I can find something that will break Stevie Johansson. We know she's guilty. Neil Simpson said as much. There has to be one thing, just one small thing, that will send her to prison.

In some of the most notorious crimes, all it took was one little slip-up for the police to make an arrest.

I need to find Stevie's broken taillight.

Eager now, I copy the files onto a thumb drive.

Mack will be a problem, and I'll need to avoid him. He'll tell Beau my every move.

I step out of the lobby, the thumb drive tucked into my purse, but Mack isn't waiting, and in relief, I blow out a breath. I ride the city bus to the Cedar Hill Public Library, my mind buzzing. When I was taking classes here in the city, we would study there sometimes instead of using the campus library, and I know my way around. They've done some rearranging since I was here last, but I find the public computers without trouble and send everything besides Mom's folder to the printer. It will be easier for me to go through everything if I can read it on paper. At the information desk, I pay the printing fee and renew my library card. Devyn had the *Times'* resources to fall back on, but if I need anything, I'll be depending on the library and what I can find online.

I like the change of scenery and sit at a table, people whispering around me and children running for story time that's being held in a room next door. With Beau working all the time and Devyn living in Old Harbor, I hadn't realized how lonely I'd become. I soak up a girl's laughter, missing my friends and the fun, happy times we had on campus.

Using a pink highlighter I borrow from the woman at the information desk, I sort through the pages, highlighting what seems to be important. I have no idea if it is or not. Devyn didn't tell me anything about the things she found while she was walking the streets. I knew she was asking questions about Stevie, but I was so busy getting used to life outside the rehab facility, a lot of what she did went by me.

It was only after she ran my sister out of town that I fully understood what Devyn had been trying to do, how serious it was, and why she would have done it at all. I hadn't gotten to truly know my sister as a person until we moved to Portland and started spending time together. It wasn't a surprise that I liked her, but actually enjoying her company was something I hadn't counted on.

Now I want to be her when I grow up. She's so self-assured and confident. Smart. People look up to her. I want that charisma, that drive. I want to belong with Beau, not feel like a stray dog whenever we're together.

My muscles are still sore from the way he put his hands on me near morning, his lips leaving a blazing path across my skin.

I don't know what he saw when he looked at me, a vulnerable girl hiding in her older sister's shadow. He saw something, but I'm scared that if he looks hard enough, he'll realize it's fake. Maybe that's another reason I want to help take Stevie down. There's no doubt in my mind that she and Declan Everett kidnapped Devyn and dumped her at Rick and Beau's site. I want him to pay for hurting Rick too, and maybe that will help Beau keep those feelings for me.

It's my darkest nightmare. Not being enough.

I work until the sun sets, and it's past time Beau would be home from work. I can't see a rhyme or reason for some of the information Devyn collected, and maybe she didn't know, either, saving every detail just in case. I spend too much time trying to figure it out, and I leave the library in the dark. I'll talk to Devyn this weekend and maybe she can point me in some direction. I need it. I'll be starting from almost nothing.

A stationery store not far from Beau's building is still open, and I buy my own set of highlighters, pens, folders, and notebooks. When the older woman scanning my things announces the total, I wince, but I pay for everything with my own money.

I clear my mind as I walk to Beau's penthouse and ground myself in the city's energy. I like Cedar Hill, but I preferred the slower pace in Portland. Beau would never move, can't, really, and if we stay together, Cedar Hill will be my home. I need to find a therapist here, or reconnect with Shelby, the woman Devyn and I saw in Portland. I've gone through a lot of changes, and besides some light conversation with Devyn, I haven't talked it out with anyone. She doesn't know how close I was to leaving last night, either, and I need to put that on someone. Preferably not my sister since Rick and Beau are good friends and she doesn't need to be in the middle.

The day I moved in, Beau introduced me to the concierge, who keeps a suspicious eye on everyone, and he nods at me as I walk through the lobby to the private elevator.

It takes a minute to ride to the top of the building, and I'm sweating in my winter jacket by the time the doors open into the pretty foyer.

Beau never told me how long he's lived here, or if a woman besides me has ever lived with him. He hasn't asked me much about anything, our short talk before we had sex last night the closest we've come to sharing real information about each other. I think he's been trying to keep things pleasant, and yeah, some of my past has been very unpleasant, but I try not to feel like he doesn't want to get to know me in case he doesn't like what he finds.

"Hey, where have you been?" he asks, shuffling into the foyer, his hands tucked into his pockets. He does that a lot, hiding his hands, jingling change or keys. He's still dressed for work, and the way he fills out his suit makes my mouth water. As Serena, my friend from college, would say, he's fucking hot.

I hang up my jacket and take my boots off. I look like I've been somewhere important in my black pants and blouse, and I'm glad I asked Devyn to send me my dress clothes. Nodding to my bag on the floor, I say, "I was able to sign up for classes, and I just bought a few things from the stationery shop down the street. How was work?"

He cuddles me to his chest and kisses the top of my head. "Don't go anywhere without letting me know. I was worried."

It's not an unrealistic request. It's what considerate couples do, and I'd sound like a brat if I said I didn't want to do what he asked. "I'm sorry. I stopped at the library and renewed my library card in case I need something for school. I didn't realize how late it was. I'll be more careful."

Beau steps away and skims his thumb over my jaw. He's got that look in his eyes again, the one that made me fall the day we met in his office. Sometimes I study myself in the mirror and try to see what he sees.

I must not be able to, because all I see is a young woman who was hooked on Sweet, doesn't have a job, only a couple hundred dollars to her name, and a monkey on her back that's choking her so tightly, sometimes it's all she can do to drag in a breath.

He sees more, and I wish I could too.
"What are you thinking about, love?"
God, I love it when he says that.
"When you look at me like that. I wonder what you see."
"A second chance."

CHAPTER FOUR

Beau

This weekend trip is as much for me as it is for Talia. She misses her sister, and I need to touch base with Rick.

She's bouncing with excitement on the plane to Old Harbor, staring out the window and pointing to all the trees and the highway below us. I reserved us a suite at a hotel downtown. Rick said we were welcome to stay in his guest room, but I wouldn't feel right if Talia and I were intimate while Devyn slept down the hall.

Devyn's been great not sticking her nose into our relationship, and I have to give her credit for letting Talia make her own decisions. Rick already warned me about her age, and our talk on the site the day I told him I was falling in love with her sticks with me. Last night, when she came home, I wanted to get into it. I'd been waiting, gritting my teeth for almost an hour. I wanted to lay into her for being . . . what? Independent? An adult? Gone? Not where I thought she should be? I wanted to tear into her for being thoughtless, but she's not a prisoner, in my penthouse or in my arms, and instead, I reminded myself she came back and to be happy with that.

I made arrangements for a rental SUV, and it's waiting for us on the tarmac. The ground crew loads our bags into the back as we step down the stairs of the luxury Cessna that Rick and I bought as a business expense. We fly clients in and out of Cedar Hill from all over the country, but lately, because of Rick's accident, we've been using it more for personal trips.

As we drive through Old Harbor toward Rick's lighthouse, Talia peers out the truck's window. I haven't seen any of the small city Rick claimed as his new home, and I'm interested too, from a business perspective. Rick said there's room for growth here, and I want to see it for myself.

"You've never been here before?" I ask Talia. We start up the steep road.

"No, not before we met, and you know I'd already moved in with you when Devyn moved here."

That's something I think about a lot. Something that keeps me up at night. Did we move too fast? Does she have regrets?

History repeating itself, as Jasmine was all too happy to point out.

I fall too hard, too fast, and if I was smart, I'd leave Talia here. But I'm not smart and I don't learn from my mistakes. I don't say anything and pretend I'm dealing with the road. It's slippery, but the truck's tires have good traction and I'm not speeding.

"What about you?" she asks over the silence.

"Rick hasn't invited me, so no. I haven't needed to come here."

She tangles her fingers with mine, and I hold on. "It will be fun to explore then."

"Yeah."

Rick and Devyn are waiting for us as we drive up, leaning into each other. He's dressed in jeans and she's casual in the yoga pants Talia also likes. Both are wearing unzipped winter jackets and snow boots. I didn't tell them we were on the way—Talia must have texted Devyn. I park next to Devyn's car, curious why Rick hasn't bought her something better. She should be driving a truck with all-wheel drive, not her old beater.

Talia flies out of the SUV the second I put her in Park, and they hug like they haven't seen each other in years. If she missed Devyn that much, I wish she would have said something. Maybe I *should* leave her here.

"Hey," Rick says, holding out his hand. He gives mine a firm shake, slapping me on the back. "You two are just in time for dinner. Devyn has a roast in the slow cooker and biscuits in the oven. How was the flight?"

"Good. Smooth. Old Harbor's bigger than I thought it was. Got a good look at her from the sky."

"I told you, there are business opportunities here."

"Speaking of business, is there a place we can talk? In private?" My breath is white in the cold.

"Right now?"

"Yeah."

Rick nods, searching my face. I need to tell him about the candy I found on the site. It isn't a secret, but I want to catch up without an audience.

"We have some business to take care of, you girls good for a little bit?" Rick asks Devyn. I don't miss the way his voice turns scratchy.

No one can keep anything from her, and her eyes dart between us, her reporter's nose twitching. She'll get it all out of Rick later after Talia and I head to the hotel. She'll have to be happy with that.

"Yeah," Devyn says, her arm around Talia's shoulders. "Is everything okay?"

I can't lie. I can never lie, and I don't want to. "Probably."

Talia frowns.

I never gave her any reason to think things weren't okay, and this is the first she's heard about it.

She opens her mouth, but Devyn nudges her toward the lighthouse. "Come on," she says.

Talia's eyes catch mine for a moment and she pauses, though she lets Devyn herd her into the house without a complaint.

"Do you have luggage?" Rick asks.

I slam the SUV's door shut. "Nothing to unload. We're staying at a hotel downtown."

Rick chuckles, and jerking his head, he leads me toward a medium-sized building near the lighthouse. From what he's told me, he works in the cottage and does his laundry there. "You finally did it and don't want Devyn to hear. How long has it been?"

"A couple of days ago."

He whistles and opens the door. The warmth is welcome, and I close it quickly behind me. "Took your time," he says.

"I would have waited longer, but she was going to leave. She thought I changed my mind. It was the only way I could think of to show her I hadn't."

Rick kicks his boots off and hangs his jacket on a coat rack near the door. The large room is decorated with shining hardwood floors, intricate rugs, and lots of rich, dark oak. An L-shaped desk sits off to the side, and a small, but fully stocked bar is set up against the opposite wall. An archway leads to somewhere, but if Rick doesn't offer me a tour, I'm not going to ask.

"Actions speak louder than words, from what I hear," he

says. I take off my shoes and hang up my jacket. I usually wear a suit, but I took this afternoon off to start a longer weekend and the black khaki pants and sweater feel too casual. "But some women need the words," he continues. "Devyn does, because of her work, I guess. Luckily for me, my words still meant something because my actions sucked. Drink?"

"Sure. Thanks. I wasn't giving her the words, either." I lift a shoulder. "Devyn left, and I was scared to be alone with her."

Rick trickles a couple fingers of whiskey into a lowball glass. Passing it to me, he says, "Not much time has gone by. There are days I look at Devyn and think she's a hallucination. Met her four months ago, and I can't think of what my life would be like without her."

I force myself to smile. I wish Talia and I would have it that easy. "I'm happy for you."

"Thanks." He pours himself a glass from the decanter and perches on the armrest of a brown leather loveseat. "What's up?"

"I was on the site the other day, and I pried the outhouse open like you wanted me to. There was a duffel bag full of Sweet Stuff candy in it." I sip my drink.

"That's it?" he asks, his eyebrows raised.

"Yeah. There was a lot of it. Some little kid must have ripped off a delivery truck but decided it wasn't worth the trouble. I wouldn't think Stevie would be too happy with someone ripping her off. Eventually a little adds up to a lot." I pause. "Jasmine was there. She saw it."

Rick skims by that part. "Did you call the cops?"

"Yeah, for what good it did. Never heard anything back. Probably won't. It's only candy, but I don't like that it belongs to Stevie. Don't know why it couldn't have been a hundred packs of Juicy Fruit. Even smokes would have made more sense."

He stares at the floor. "Well, I don't think there's anything we need to do about it."

"No, not from what I can tell, but it would've been nice if Devyn could have found out more." It would have been a relief for all of us if Devyn could have put Stevie in prison.

Rick lifts his head, his eyes flashing, and he snaps, "That's not her job. They could've hurt her worse than they did. I don't want her anywhere near it."

"I wasn't saying what she did wasn't enough, but I wish—" Nothing I say will sound right, and I sip my drink. I wish that what she'd done would have had a better outcome. Finding out the accident wasn't Rick's fault gave him peace he wouldn't have had otherwise, but Everett's free and Stevie Johansson is still selling candy . . . and Sweet.

"Sometimes you have to lose," Rick says, rolling his shoulders. "We're not used to that, but sometimes that's the way it has to be."

"I know. I just wanted that fucking Everett to pay for what he did to you and to our men."

"Eventually he'll get his. We don't have to be the ones to give it to him. Devyn still wanted to go after Stevie, but I was an asshole and asked her not to." He chokes. "I want her safe, and she loves me enough that she's doing what I asked. It's the police department's responsibility now."

"You're not an asshole," I say mildly. "You love her. But I doubt the cops are working on it. No one wants the Sweetheart of the Midwest to lose her crown. No one wants her to go to prison. If they did, Devyn wouldn't have had such a fight. As far as Everett goes . . ." I shrug.

"Devyn wasn't happy, but she didn't argue. She might still snoop around without telling me." Rick stands and pours a little more whiskey into his glass. He offers me another drink, but I shake my head. One is enough, and Talia will smell it on my breath. "If she does, I'll have to look the other way. I trust her not to do anything stupid. What was Jasmine doing on the site?"

"Same thing, different day. Talking about Nina, and she asked me to go out with them. She gave me a little pushback for Talia."

"She thinks you dating her isn't a good idea."

I wander around Rick's office and stop to look at a framed print of the lighthouse. "No, she doesn't, but there are days I don't think it is either. She's too young for me, and I'm not in the right place to handle her history." I twist my mouth. "I was her first real fuck, Rick. It's too much responsibility."

He chuckles, happy and settled in his relationship. "You want her to get that experience somewhere else?"

I scowl. I don't like how thinking of another man putting his hands on her makes me feel. "No."

"Then I don't know what you're bitching for. Teach her what you want her to know. She spook out on you?"

"No. She was fine." Better than fine, she was everything I needed, took every bit of pain as I ravaged her and then begged for more. There's nothing I would change about the night she almost left.

"Then what?"

"Nina—"

"Nina had problems that didn't have anything to do with you. You thought you could save her, and you couldn't. Talia could be the same. You gotta be prepared for that, Beau. If something happens, it won't be your fault."

"Just like if Devyn starts trudging through the muck after you asked her not to, and she gets hurt, that won't be your fault either, right?" I ask dryly.

"We can't lock them up, though God, when I look at Devyn, sometimes I want to. Are you going out with Jasmine?"

"I might, and see some of our friends. I don't know. That life seems so far away now." I clear my throat. "Yeah, so I just wanted to bring you up to speed. A few more weeks, and the sun will melt the snow off and soften up the ground. We'll finish cleanup and get going on the build."

"I'll try to fly in more often. I've been keeping Devyn to myself, but I don't want her poking around Cedar Hill, either. We can't lock them up," he repeats, draining his glass. "She knows how I feel."

"Will that be enough to keep her in check?"

He takes my empty glass from me and puts it on the bar. "I hope so. I can't lose her."

"Yeah." My voice is soft and gets lost in the rustling of our jackets. I can't lose Talia, not after these few short months together, but I'm standing on the sharp blade of a knife, waiting for her to realize I'm not what she wants after all.

The way Nina did.

CHAPTER FIVE

Talia

The faint scent of beef roast and vegetables brings me back to cozy afternoons when we lived in Portland, Devyn working on an article for the newspaper while I did homework. Afternoons like that were something I didn't know I needed after spending three years in a rehab facility eating in a cafeteria with strangers who had turned into more than acquaintances but were less than friends. I needed stability, a place to call home, and love slams into me so hard that I press my face into her shoulder, the rough material of her jacket scratching my cheeks.

I never have to explain what I'm thinking to my sister, and she gives me the time I need by hugging me to her, her lips resting on the top of my head, like the way Beau does when he wants to cuddle me.

"Sorry," I mumble, pulling away.

"You don't have to be sorry," she says, hanging her jacket on a hook attached to the wall. I do the same and take my boots off. "I miss you too."

The entryway is dark until she opens a second door that leads into a large kitchen.

I dressed casually for the flight, in yoga pants and a tank top, with a loose nubby cardigan over it. Devyn's dressed the same, and I find a bit of relief that though things seem like they've changed so much that I don't recognize my own life, there are some things that haven't, and more than likely, never will.

"How do you like it here?" I ask.

"It's good," she says, blushing. "I went to the doctor last week and had my IUD taken out. We're trying for a baby."

I swallow. This is something I should be happy about, and I am. My sister looks so blissfully content I would never wish anything less for her. But I'm afraid, too. I'm afraid that she'll have a baby and a family with Rick, and she won't have room in her life for me anymore.

Forcing myself to sound cheerful, I ask, "You don't want to wait until you get married?"

"We will in the spring, something small. I doubt my cycle will be back to normal before then. I've been on birth control for so long she said it could take months, maybe years, to get pregnant. Right now, we're just enjoying being together, but if it happens, it happens." She smiles, but she looks at me and it fades. I must look hurt. "This doesn't change anything. We'll be even more of a family with a baby. You're not losing me. You know that, right?"

"Yeah, sure." I look around, faking interest in the kitchen appliances and the elegant picnic table that stands in as a dining room table.

She opens her mouth like she wants to press the issue, but she says, "Do you want to see the rest? Go up to the top?"

When Devyn was snowed in, she sent me pictures, but I *do* want to see the top in person, and I nod.

I wish she wouldn't have told me about trying to get pregnant. Now I'm going to feel like she's trying to replace me, even though I know that's stupid. She's always been very careful not to act like she's my mother, and it's something we talked about in therapy. Just because she stepped up in the exact way I needed her to, that doesn't mean she doesn't want her own kids.

"That'd be great," I say to fill in the silence.

She sighs, relieved the awkward moment is gone.

I've never been in a lighthouse before, and I look around with interest. It's a beautiful building, and knowing my sister, it's not a surprise that she likes living here.

I'm struggling to breathe by the time we reach the top, but the view steals my breath in a different way. "This is amazing," I say, turning in a circle.

"It really is. I love it, but I don't come up that often. Rick can't handle the stairs unless he's having a good day. He hurt himself looking for me, and he has a surgery consultation next week for his shoulder. He doesn't want to, but I'm making him go."

"I'm sorry." Rick wouldn't be looking forward to another surgery—I bet he's had enough of doctors and hospitals to last the rest of his life. But it's not only that. Rick broke up with Devyn because he felt guilty that he didn't keep her safe from Declan and Stevie, but Devyn would never blame him for something he had no control over.

"It's okay, but it's another reason we decided not to wait. He already hurts, and it will only get worse as he gets older."

"Yeah, I get that." And I do. I can't be selfish, and I'm more than old enough to take care of myself.

"How's it been going?" she asks, leaning against the

window, Harbor Lake stretched out behind her in a churning sea of angry grey.

I sit on the metal floor and the cold seeps into my yoga pants. "Good. We finally did it."

Devyn presses her fingers to her lips. "How was it?"

How do I explain that every time we make love, it's like he wants to consume every cell in my body? How do I explain he devours me to the point I have nothing left, and I lie there in a heap of cum and sweat, barely moving until he nudges my thighs apart to do it again? How do I explain that he goes at me all night, but I only want to give him more?

Shrugging, I say, "I feel like I'm not enough for him."

She nods and sits next to me. "If you love him, you'll always feel like that. You'll always feel like you want to give him everything you possibly can so he doesn't leave. That's insecurity, and you can't let it control you. If you're not enough, if what you give him isn't enough to make him happy, then he's not the man for you. I didn't say much about your ages and what that could mean for you, but I hope, that you two are enough for each other because you deserve to be happy too."

We did talk about that a little while we were looking through the accident's paperwork. Devyn seemed to think his age would do more good than harm. I hoped, maybe, she'd be right, but that was before I lived with him, before his sophistication dripped all over me and I feel like a drowned rat whenever I'm around him.

It's not that I don't think that I'm out of his league because of his money. Beau's about as down-to-earth as anybody can be, but it's his charm, his sexy appeal, the way women look at him like he's chocolate mousse they want to lick out of a dessert dish, that makes me feel inferior. He handles himself in a way I could only dream of, like Devyn and her take-charge attitude. She belongs with a man like Rick, waltzing into Cedar Hill and snapping their fingers, and everything they want falls into their laps.

And I skulk around, hoping no one notices me.

Sometimes I wish Walt had never sent Devyn to interview Rick for the *Pioneer*. That we still lived in our small house in Portland, scraping together enough cash to order pizza because Devyn's paycheck hadn't cleared in the bank yet.

Now I feel homeless. Beau asked me to move in with him instead of with Devyn and I was stupid and said yes.

I don't answer her, and she gently holds my hand. "Do you want to move here? Rick said you're more than welcome."

It's tempting, but I can't lie. I'd rather miss Devyn and see Beau than live in Old Harbor and miss him. I'd be caught up with going to class, doing homework, and working a part-time job somewhere, and he'd be busy with the hotel's construction in the spring. It wouldn't be long before he forgot all about me.

"No. I emailed the college in Portland and registered for spring classes after all. I snuck in just before their deadline. That will help, and I'll look for a job. I think once I have something to do, I'll feel better about living in the city without you."

She smiles, and I can see the relief all over her face. Not because I turned down her invitation—Devyn would never not want me around—but she thought dropping out of school, even for a semester, was a poor choice, not that she would ever tell me that. "I'm glad. You've worked so hard since getting out of rehab. I don't want any of that to go to waste."

"I should have listened to you in the first place. After I registered, I felt a lot better. I had to look for my financial aid award letter, and I found some of your files on Stevie. Now that you're trying for a baby, you're going to stop looking into her, aren't you? Rick won't let you if you're pregnant."

She stands up, tugs her cardigan around her, and leans against the glass. She speaks to the lake, her voice soft. "He asked me to leave it alone, and that was before we decided to try. The night he asked me to marry him, he said he understood why I wanted to keep pushing, but he didn't, not really. He doesn't want me poking around anymore, not after what happened, and it was hard for me to give in. I've wanted to take her down for so long." She sighs and glances at me. "But how can I choose between the man I love and my own needs, beliefs, and values to always do the right thing? She's guilty—that's clear—but it can't be my fight, not anymore."

She wants it to be, though. It's not that she'll never tear Stevie's Sweet empire down, it's that Rick's asking her to push aside a part of who she is. I wonder how happy she'll be after a few years of reporting traffic violations and the high school hockey team going to regionals. Inwardly, I wince. That's not fair. I'm sure she and Rick have talked about it to the point where she probably never wants to talk about her career ever again.

But if he won't let her snoop around anymore, it gives me a way in. Again, I think about picking up where she left off and finishing what she started.

"If you could go back to it, what would you do first?" I don't know where to begin. I'm not an investigative reporter, and I'll be stumbling around hoping I find something, literally, in the dark.

She wrinkles her nose. "I haven't looked at my notes in such a long time that I'm not sure. I'd gotten to know a couple of the gang members who helped Stevie distribute it around the city, and some of the dealers. Hookers, strippers, night club owners. They all said it came from Stevie. I mean, not blatantly said, 'Stevie Johansson supplies Sweet to Cedar Hill' but they called her Sweetheart, and who else could that refer to? I know she uses the postal service and the delivery companies. She uses her own trucks. I *know* that, but it's like a ghost is supplying Cedar Hill with Sweet. When Barney and I talk about it, we go back to her stores. She launders her money through her candy stores, right? She has to be." She sighs. "Her stores do well, but no one wants to ask if she's *really* making millions of dollars selling licorice."

"You'd start with her stores?" I ask, confused. If the people she talked to on the street are a dead end, then what?

Lifting a shoulder, she says, "I couldn't get near one of her stores in Cedar Hill, and I've never been to the one here. I bet all of her employees have been told to watch out for me. If Barney's theory is right and you and his niece got hooked because you bought candy from one of them, I don't want anything to do with her stores even if I could sneak in. No," she muses, thinking. "Maybe I'd see how many of your friends at that party ended up hooked on Sweet. It's an interesting theory, but her drug ring has many spokes. You'd need to follow one and see if you can find the center of the wheel. If that didn't pan out, I'd go back to snooping around on the street. Maybe there's been some turnover and I'd find a kid who'd rather tattle on her than deal. She must pay well. I've never come across such loyalty."

"Maybe she pays them with Sweet," I say.

"No. Dealers aren't hooked. They'd use the supply, not sell it. None of the dealers I talked to were addicted."

I shiver. I didn't think my addiction would be part of finishing Devyn's mission, but that was stupid. Even talking about Sweet now, as far off the street as I could possibly be, still brings the sugary taste to my tongue and the craving stirring in my blood. Everybody thinks that staying away from booze and caffeine helps me, and it does, a little, but Beau didn't think, and Devyn sure as hell didn't think, that he and I having sex would create a different kind of addiction.

I need the intimacy with him. Is that addiction, or am I looking for proof he loves me?

I'm not an idiot. I know sex isn't love, but when he holds me as I catch my breath and whispers kisses across my face while he praises me, that's love. At least, that's what I want it to mean.

Swallowing, I focus on Devyn's face. "You'd find the kids who were at the frat party." It's not as much as I thought she'd give me, but she's right. She's been off the streets for over two years now, and I know that dealers come and go. They may never rat Stevie out, but they're dumb in other ways. They skim off the top or give their friends deals. Stevie Johansson wouldn't put up with anything that would cheat her out of her money. No one knows what happens to the dealers who play with their lives. Like with most things that concern her, no one dares to ask.

I realize that I have something Devyn didn't have while walking the streets. She's always been on the wrong side. She's never been hooked, never had sex with another addict hoping he'd share his stash. Never crawled in an alley, literally crawled through puddles and trash at three in the morning, praying to find a dealer. That was my life, and I thank God every day it wasn't for that long. Six months is nothing compared to some. Compared to Mom.

"Yeah. That's the newest information I have. To get back into it again, I think I'd be starting over. I didn't have that much, even after a year of digging. I hit a nerve though, to make her that furious. I was close. I really think that." She tilts her head. "Why?"

I pretend not to care. "No reason. I'd never looked at your research before. You have so much of it to have so little."

"Yeah, well, that's how it goes. Maybe if the police cared and had helped me, but I was working on my own."

I want to ask about our mom, but that's a conversation for

another day. We always end up fighting, and I was just fishing for information. She'd think when I'm back in the city I'll look for her, and if she and Rick are trying to get pregnant, I don't want her worried about me.

Groaning, I stand up. My butt's numb from sitting on the hard floor. I step into her arms and rest my head against her shoulder. I miss her hugs, and soon she'll be giving them to her children instead of me. "I'm happy for you guys," I say. "You'll make a great mom."

"Thanks. I'm old though, and I'm not looking forward to the pregnancy part of it. My body isn't what it used to be. Come on, let's go downstairs. I hope Beau didn't have bad news. Do you know what he wanted to talk to Rick about?"

She leads me down the stairs.

On the way up, I was too distracted to count them, but now I don't bother. "No. He doesn't talk business with me."

"Rick doesn't tell me much, either, but I don't mind. He seems happy with the office space he bought in town, and that's all that matters to me."

I wish I could say Beau's happiness is all that matters to me, but I need a lot more than that. I need to find my own happiness, too, and that feels really far away.

———

We eat dinner and chat about how Rick and Devyn like living in Old Harbor. Afterward, Beau and Rick hide in Rick's office for another quick meeting before Beau and I check into the hotel.

Devyn puts on a fresh pot of coffee and grabs her purse out of the entryway. "Here, I have something for you." She opens her wallet and wiggles out a blue debit card. "I don't need my paycheck from the *Herald,* so I opened a checking account in your name. My paychecks will be direct deposited into it on the first and third Friday of every month. My salary isn't that much, but I don't want you to have to ask Beau for spending money. I'm sure he'd give you money whenever you asked, but that's a tough position to be in, and you'll feel better if you have your own cash. Call the number on the back and activate it, set up a PIN, and you can use it at any ATM. There's no withdrawal fee."

I don't want to cry over a debit card, and I skim my finger over the thin piece of plastic, the name of the credit union and a lighthouse logo at the top. The chip is shiny and silver, and my name's a flat white. "Are you sure? Are you sure you don't want the money for yourself?"

"Rick and I have a joint account set up. I didn't want to at first, but he talked me into it. I don't want to say that you and Beau aren't as close as Rick and me, but I think you're still treading water and I don't want you to have to use him as a life preserver. You'll have more fun learning how to swim if you have your own floatie."

I laugh. "Wow. You thought of that before we got here, didn't you?"

She blushes. "Maybe. But it's true."

"Yeah. Thank you. I still have a little from my job in Portland, but it's running low."

"When I opened your account, they gave me instructions on how to set up online banking, and I'll email them to you. Then you can check the balance whenever you need to. They have a cell phone app, but you'll be on your laptop all the time for class, so you might not need that."

"I don't think I'll need to use it very much, but having some spending money will be nice. Thanks." It will also help me pay for taxis and a new bus pass. Beau lives about as far away from where I need to go as he could possibly get, and there's no way I want Mack driving me to that part of the city. He'd tell Beau in a heartbeat. I know Devyn paid people to talk to her, and if I need to buy information, now I'll have the money to do it. She said her paychecks aren't very big, but she supported us in Portland on her salary. I won't need nearly that much, and the money will add up faster than I can spend it.

We chat while we sip coffee, and Rick and Beau come in not much later. He presses his cold lips to my cheek, and Devyn serves more coffee and chocolate chip cheesecake.

I love how she's settled into her life here. She settled in a lot faster than I have, but she knows this is permanent, and I don't feel like that about living with Beau. Even though we're finally sleeping together, he has a hands-off attitude he can't hide, and I don't know where it's coming from and if it's my fault. I'm still waiting for him to come home from work one day and tell me that he's changed his mind.

"Ready to head out?" he asks as Devyn and I finish putting our dessert plates in the dishwasher.

"Yeah, sure," I say, drying my hands on a paper towel.

"We'll come back in the morning. Rick and I are going to get some weekend meetings out of the way. We thought you two could keep yourselves busy."

"We'll do a little shopping, right?" Devyn asks me, brushing her fingers through my hair. That's another thing I miss, and I happily agree to spend Saturday shopping and having lunch.

Rick hugs me on the way out the door, and it surprises me. I've always thought of myself as a plus one in their relationship, but maybe he has softer feelings for me than that. I return his grip to thank him for making my sister so happy.

In the truck, I lean my head against Beau's shoulder, the wool scratching my cheek.

"Have fun?" he asks, using the truck's GPS to find the hotel downtown.

"Mmm-hmm," I mumble sleepily, the city's lights flashing through the windows.

"Good. Let's get you up to the room so you can go to bed. We'll sleep in and order room service. I told Rick we wouldn't bother them for breakfast. This is kind of a vacation, and I want you to enjoy it."

I like the idea of sleeping in and waking up in his arms. He's usually out the door before I wake up, but spring semester's starting soon and that will change. I intentionally signed up for an 8 AM class to make myself get out of bed and take advantage of the day.

He parks in the parking ramp attached to the hotel, and he carries our suitcases inside. The front desk clerk checks us in and slides a slim envelope over the counter that has our keycards in it.

Because he's carrying our suitcases, I hold on to the envelope, and we stand quietly in the empty elevator. We reach our suite on the thirtieth floor, and I unlock the door, nudging it open for him. The room is scented with the usual hotel fragrance, and we step over the plush carpeting into a sitting room.

I haven't stayed in a hotel very often. The last time I did, I was still in high school and traveled across the state with my speech team where I shared a tiny room with three other girls. I could get used to it, I think, stepping into the bedroom and falling backward onto the bed still wearing my jacket. It's been a long day, and I'm tired.

He laughs and brushes my jaw with his finger. "You'd be more comfortable if you changed into your pajamas."

"I will. I was just thinking that I'd like to travel. I haven't stayed in a hotel since high school. Do you travel a lot?"

He disappears for a second and then steps back into the bedroom without his coat. "Not since Rick's accident. I've been keeping the company together. When he told me he was going to ask Devyn to marry him, it pissed me off and we got into a fight." He takes his shoes off and pulls his sweater over his head. He balls it up and tosses it on a loveseat that's underneath a large window. The drapes are closed, and the only light is coming from a lamp in the sitting room. Wearing only his pants, he yanks his suitcase onto a wingback chair and pops the clasps.

"You don't want him to marry her?" I ask, rolling onto my side.

"I was happy he found someone. Renata left him and he convinced himself he'd be alone forever. No, it was that he said they were going to live here. After the accident, I was doing the work of two people, and I still am. I wasn't doing so much work to only keep my hands off you. I've had to."

"Can't you find a happy medium?" I ask. He shoves his slacks down his legs and puts on a t-shirt and pair of flannel pajama pants. He looks sexy, like a male model for loungewear.

"Maybe after the hotel's built. In a couple of years. You wanna go somewhere?" he asks. "Any place you haven't been?"

"I haven't been anywhere." I finally scoot off the bed and take my jacket off. "I haven't been out of Minnesota," I say, stepping out of the room. I hang my coat next to his in the little closet by the door and backtrack to my suitcase.

"That won't work. I'll talk to Rick. How about this summer we go to Hawaii for a week? We'll rent a private cabin on the beach and you can swim naked and look for seashells." He nuzzles my cheek.

I dig through my suitcase for pajamas. I want to ask him how many women he's taken on a romantic vacation like that. How many women he's had sex with on a private beach. Maybe we won't last until summer, and I force a smile. "I would love that."

"Good. I want to give you whatever you want, Talia. Anything at all."

Love? The way I love you? It's on the tip of my tongue, but I was a beggar once and I won't be one again.

"Some of the things I want can't be bought."

He scoffs and walks into the bathroom gripping a black toiletry bag so hard his knuckles are white. "Then I guess that's a problem because all I have is money."

He shuts the door, and the click echoes through the silent room.

———

Shaking, I use the other bathroom to brush my teeth. When I come out, he's lying in the dark near the edge of the mattress with an arm over his eyes.

I crawl onto the bed. "Beau . . ." I start, but I don't know why he's so mad.

"Go to sleep."

"But . . ." On my knees, I move across the bed. I lay on his chest and push his arm off his face. "Why won't you talk to me?"

His eyes snap open. "What do you want me to say?"

"I don't know. I don't know anything about you. When was your last relationship? I don't know if you've ever been married, or if you have any kids. I don't know who your friends are besides Rick. You said we'd have a party to celebrate the New Year, but I thought you meant with more people than just him and Devyn. What did you do before I moved in with you? Who did you do it with?"

"I worked. I have a group of friends from college who still live in the city, and when Rick was married to Renata, we'd all go out. I haven't been in a serious relationship for a long time.

Years. I've never been married, and if I have a kid out there, I don't know about it. I doubt his or her mother would let that slide, right?"

I'm relieved he's talking to me, but this isn't the direction I thought our conversation would go. His money doesn't mean anything to me. I'm a broke, uneducated girl who used to be hooked on Sweet, and that might not sound true coming from me, but I know how to live paycheck to paycheck. I know how to count coupons and buy things on sale. I could love a poor man . . . I know how to be poor too. "Is this about money?"

"I don't know, Talia. Are you making this about money?"

I rub my thumb over his lips. "No."

He swallows and looks away.

"Why don't you go out with your friends? You haven't gone out after work since I moved in. That's been months. You must miss them."

He sighs and wraps his arms around me. "Maybe. What about you? Do you have friends?"

I wiggle, happy he's holding me. "I used to, in Cedar Hill. Devyn thinks I should look up some of the kids I went to college with. She's always encouraging me to branch out."

"She doesn't want you seeing me, does she?" he asks, skimming his fingers up and down my spine.

"She doesn't want me to have *only* you, but she was like that in Portland, too. She wanted me to go out with the kids from school and make friends with the people I met at work. She wants me to be well-rounded, I guess. The more people I have in my life, the less empty I'll feel."

Beau props his head on his hand. His eyes bore into mine, and I realize this is what I've been missing. Quiet moments in the dark, talking. In Cedar Hill, our time in bed is always so intense, but I like this too, maybe more.

"I want that for you, too." He pauses. "I'm sorry I was a

dick earlier. I didn't know how it would affect me, seeing Rick. I was holding out hope he'd come back to Cedar Hill, but he's too happy to do that now."

"I was thinking that too, about Devyn," I say, grateful Beau and I are on the same page . . . about something. "I'm afraid she won't have room in her life for me anymore."

He threads his fingers through my hair, his thumb brushing my cheek. "She'll always love you, Talia. You're her family. And I meant what I said earlier. I want to give you whatever I can. I'll have Lola call the airport on Monday, and whenever you want to fly here for the weekend, call and make the arrangements. I might not always be able to go with you, but if Devyn picks you up, you'll be fine flying alone."

I love the sound of it, jetting off for a weekend getaway, even if it's only to Old Harbor, but I say, "I wouldn't want to come without you."

"Yeah?"

I force a laugh, the disbelief in his voice heartbreaking. "Yeah."

He hides his face against my neck. "I care about you so much. So fucking much."

I want to say I love him back, but I don't, my intuition warning me with a quiver in my stomach. If I had known how things would play out, I would have said it, and I would have made him believe me.

CHAPTER SIX

Beau

Monday morning I step into my office and feel something different for my desk and the conference table in the corner. For the windows that look over the city and the shelves filled with books. Rick's never coming back. I thought he and Devyn would eventually move back to Cedar Hill, but he's happy where he is. Talia told me they're trying for a baby, and a pressure built up inside my chest. I had to force myself to smile and say that I was happy for them.

Talia isn't the only one who feels like she's losing a sibling—Rick's been like my brother since we were freshmen in college. As his makeshift younger brother (by a few months), I really am happy that he found Devyn after his ex-wife left him. The accident almost killed him, and he deserves to be happy. It's my own issues that make it feel like he's abandoning me.

The rest of the weekend went by in a pleasant haze of Talia's kisses, Devyn's cooking, and exploring Old Harbor. Rick and I also planned where we were going to start steering the company. Usually, I get excited when we have those kinds of meetings, but we started talking about how we'd split things down the middle, working each side together but separately, and I lost all interest. I wasn't working with my friend anymore. We were business partners and nothing else.

I sink into my chair and ignore Lola who pushes in a coffee service. I've gotten used to drinking decaf, and the scent doesn't perk me up like it used to.

On the flight back to the city, Talia curled up in my lap and put her head on my shoulder. While we were in Old Harbor, I found out a lot about her, like that she enjoys thoughtful conversation, and for a woman as young as she is, she's knowledgeable about quite a few subjects. Both nights we talked until late, and she had me laughing more than once. I knew she was intelligent, but she's whip smart and has a sense of humor she hadn't let out.

She stayed in the guest room last night and I went to bed disappointed, but when I woke up this morning, her body was wrapped around mine. While I was getting dressed, she told me her classes start next week. With Devyn's encouragement and my . . . she didn't say permission, but it's what it felt like she was asking me for . . . she's going to look up some of her friends and see if they're still around. Without a hint of jealousy, she told me I should do the same. When she asked me about my past relationships, I should have told her about Nina, but Talia doesn't have any exes to talk about, and I don't want to drag Nina into our relationship. She's been gone for a long time, and I'm over it.

I don't know why I brought up money. She and Devyn are probably the two most down-to-earth women I could ever meet. Devyn cared more about nailing the bastard who hurt Rick to the wall than she ever did about his money, and Talia's the same way. Money was my insecurity, and I was lucky Talia let it go as easily as she did.

The meetings take on a new slant too, and I explain Rick won't be back in an in-person capacity. Everyone's heard about Devyn—some of them met her when she and Talia used Rick's office to go through the accident reports—and they weren't surprised, but it caused a bit of a wave. We had the same vision for the future of the company, but we headed different projects. He enjoys the commercial side of our business, like the hotel, and I'm more at home with projects like golf courses and the butterfly garden I completed last summer.

No, prying outhouse doors open isn't my thing, but we didn't make our billions building city zoos and museums. Rick knows that's what I like best and let me head those types of projects. It didn't hurt that it put us in good standing with the mayor of Cedar Hill.

I'm in a piss-poor mood all day, and stepping into the penthouse where there's nothing but silence makes it even worse. I've asked Talia to tell me if she's going somewhere, and yanking off my tie, I check my phone in frustration. There *is* a text from her, and I must not have heard the chime. She said she's looking for an old friend and to eat dinner without her.

Great.

I want her to live a full life . . . I know I'm not enough. Nina hammered that into my head like a battering ram, but my relationship with Talia still feels too new for us not to spend our evenings together. I wanted to eat dinner with her and bitch about my day. I wanted her on my lap, my cock buried so deep inside her I didn't give a fuck about anything else. I wanted my fingers tangled in her hair, my mouth at her breast, her cute mewling sounds coming from the back of her throat as I sucked. She's a wild little thing, and I never would have known just by looking at her.

It's still early, and I can't be angry, not yet. I'm not her dad, and I can't set a curfew. If I could, she wouldn't be out past seven, but that wouldn't fly, and it would make it damned near impossible for me to go out too.

Talia's not here to see it, and I gulp a whiskey. I lean against the kitchen counter and try to think about what else there is to do other than locking myself in my office and doing more work. My phone chimes, and gratefully, I reach for it. I wanted it to be Talia, but I know it's not. I assigned her number a dreamy bell/flute thing Rick would give me shit for if he ever heard it.

Jasmine's text pops up. *Come out with us. It's been a shitty Monday.*

I can't argue with that. It *has* been a shitty Monday, and it got worse when I walked into an empty penthouse.

Where? I text back.

I probably gave her a heart attack. Since Talia moved in with me, I haven't gone out once. The only time Jasmine has seen me was the day she stopped by the site.

Gretta's.

Of course she'd want to go there. It's been our regular hangout place since we went to the U of M. A few years ago the owner passed it down to her daughter and we were glad nothing changed. The same decorations, the same 1920s music. No TVs on the walls, only conversation, lots of booze, and an art deco feel that was Nina's favorite.

All right. You there now?

ETA: 10 minutes, she types back.

She'll beat me there by five minutes since the art museum Jasmine curates is two blocks away from Gretta's, but that's okay. I don't feel like calling Mack, and still wearing the suit I wore to work but without the tie, I hail a taxi.

On the way to the bar, I text Talia, practicing what I preach. *Meeting up with a friend for a drink. Won't be out late.*

She sends back a quick, *Have fun!*

I want to reply with something other than "Thanks!" like "Be safe," or "I miss you." Or better yet, "Talia, I love you so much I don't know what I would do without you in my life," but no one has to tell me that's a ridiculous thing to say to a woman I've known for only four months.

I step into Gretta's, and Jasmine, Bart, and Kindra are sitting at a hightop in the corner. The white and black checkered floor brings back memories of dancing with Nina after too many drinks, as do the waitresses dressed like classy flappers who danced with us, enjoying our playfulness and hoping for huge tips.

This isn't the first time I've been here since Nina passed away, but it has since I met Talia, and I wasn't prepared for the punch in the gut I'd get as Jasmine notices me and waves.

Bart twists to see who she spotted in the crowd, and he hollers over his shoulder, "Hey! Look what the cat dragged in!"

On a Monday night, the bar isn't as full as it could be, but several people turn to look, and a couple of the waitresses lift a hand, the ones who have hung around recognizing me.

"Hi! It's nice to see you out and about," Jasmine says, leaning into me as I slide into a seat.

"Thanks for the invite. My Monday was shit too," I say and kiss her cheek. I shake Bart's hand and brush my fingers over the soft skin of Kindra's wrist. She tugs on my fingers and smiles faintly.

"We waited for you to order," Jasmine says, tilting her head toward a waitress wearing an emerald green sequined dress that reminds me of Talia's eyes.

"Thanks, but you should have gone ahead. You know what I like."

She shrugs, her shoulder bare besides a thin spaghetti strap. She's still wearing the clothes she wore to work, like we all are, and a blazer and winter coat are draped over the back of her chair.

"Maybe I don't know anymore," she says as the waitress approaches us, her heels clicking against the marble.

The jab stings, and I give the waitress my order, what I always drink in defense of what Jasmine said. Sensing the tension, Bart asks about work and Rick's defection, I mean, his branching out to another city.

Bart's a hedge fund manager in his father's firm, and Kindra's a fashion buyer at the largest luxury department store chain in the United States. We've all landed on our feet, though they would say not as well as I have, and that's only because I've worked with Rick since we graduated from the university.

"Tell us about your little cutie," Jasmine says.

We've already finished our first drink, but the alcohol hasn't done much to relax her. There's an edge to her voice, and I clench my teeth. "It's not like I haven't dated since Nina's death, Jasmine," I say, waving at the waitress to order another round.

"He has a right to see people," Bart says. We were never as close as Rick and I are, but Bart had my back when Nina passed away, protecting me from Jasmine and her grief.

"He's more than dating," she says, glancing at me out of the corners of her eyes. "She's living with him."

"Oh, yeah?" Bart says, sounding surprised. "Good for you. I want to meet her. You should have brought her out."

Kindra squeezes my hand to tell me she's on my side, and I squeeze back.

"She's a Sweet addict," Jasmine snaps.

"Used to be," I murmur, the wail of a clarinet almost drowning me out.

"So what?" Bart says, his hand tightening around his glass

of rum and Coke. "We all have something, and you aren't perfect."

Jasmine blushes.

I'm missing something, and I shoot Bart a confused frown, but he shakes his head. "Forget about it. Where'd you meet her?"

I explain while Jasmine ignores me, hostility radiating off her body. I'm glad I didn't invite Talia along. In fact, if Jasmine's going to keep acting like this, Talia might not meet any of my friends. We would have to go to dinner instead of meeting at a bar, but if Jasmine can calm the fuck down, there's no reason why Talia can't hang out with us. Unless they all thought she was too young for me and didn't want to get to know her simply because she's not our age.

We decide to head out a lot sooner than if Nina would have been with us. She was a partier, but when she passed away, I didn't stop. I went out with a different woman every night, though how I partied turned more sophisticated the richer and older I became. Instead of dive bars, we went to the symphony, the opera, a play. Afterward, we'd drink in expensive, classy restaurants. I kept it up until I couldn't keep it up anymore, much to Jasmine's disappointment.

Bart and Kindra say goodbye, and his shoulder brushes hers as he holds the door open for her. "Did something happen there?" I ask Jasmine who finally loosened up after a couple more drinks.

She shakes her head and puts on her blazer. "Not sure. They look cute together, if they are."

"Yeah." I pay the tab, putting two one hundred dollar bills under her glass, and help her with her coat. "Do you want to share a cab?"

We step onto the sidewalk, and the frigid January evening freezes us. It's not windy, and that helps, but it's not the kind of weather for a stroll downtown. Still, she says, "Do you mind if we walk for a bit?"

She stumbles in her heels, and she links her arm with mine to steady herself.

"No, I think some fresh air will do you some good."

The sidewalks are busy, and I miss the quiet of Old Harbor. Rick's newly adopted city has the same energy, the same bright lights, but on a much smaller scale. A much more manageable scale.

"If I ask you a question, will you be honest with me?" I ask.

We walk past a restaurant we've been to a handful of times, and I wish Jasmine would have chosen a place that served food. I'm starving, and all the whiskey I drank is churning in my gut. We don't have anything to eat at the penthouse, and even with Talia living with me for the past few months, I'm not used to stocking the fridge and pantry, preferring to ask her what she wants to eat and calling for takeout instead.

"Yeah, sure. I thought we were friends. Why would you ask me something like that?" She peers up at me, her deep brown eyes liquid in the streetlights.

"What do you have against Talia? How did you know about her?"

"Gossip rags, mostly," she admits, shuffling along, her high heels scratching against the sidewalk. "When her sister was in the news for blaming the city's Sweet problem on Stevie Johansson. All that broke, and there were a few articles about her. How she spent time in rehab, some of the nasty ones betting on how long it would take her to relapse. I don't read stuff like that, but I saw pictures of the two of them, and I gave in. She's pretty. At least I didn't say she's too young for you."

"Do you think she is?"

We keep walking, and she rests her head on my shoulder. "No. What she's gone through probably makes up for it, but I just thought, with the way Nina died, you would stay away from that. Partying is one thing, but dealing with addiction is another. We know which way Nina went, and it was hard on you."

"That wasn't the only thing that happened. She must have told you."

She laughs, but the sound's scratchy. "She told me, and the stupid thing is, I didn't care about that. All I could think about was if she got her way, I'd never see you again."

I stop and nudge her into an alcove. "What do you mean?"

Her mouth turns into a disappointed frown. "You just don't get it, do you?"

Talia would because she has street smarts I don't have. Devyn would because she's shrewd and can read a person in five seconds and know what's what. Even Rick would because he's sensitive, and after the accident has a compassion that you can only get through experience.

I don't have any of that, and Jasmine's going to have to do better if she wants me to understand. I bite back a curse. "No. I don't get it. You're going to have to spell it out."

She leans into me and looks up, her lips parted. She's beautiful, but she's not my type. I prefer blondes.

"It's been ten years, Beau."

"Yeah, it has. I'm moving on. You should too."

Tears fill her eyes. "I can't."

I step out of the alcove and hail a cab. "I'm not letting you drag me back there."

A yellow taxi stops next to us, and I open the back door for her. Without meeting my eyes, she slides in, and I give the driver a fifty. She stares out the window as I slam the door shut, and leaning against a parked car, I watch the cab melt into traffic, the red and green intersection lights glaring too brightly in the cold.

What does she want from me? I've lived in the past for ten years. Why does she want to keep me there? It would have been helpful if she had actually talked to me and told me what she was thinking, but all I know is that she misses Nina. We all do.

Ten years is a long time to mourn someone.

I trudge back to my building wishing like hell I could make a cup of coffee and a ham and cheese sandwich. Christ, I'd take peanut butter and jelly at this point.

I step inside the dark penthouse. Talia's still out.

I take my jacket off, hang it up, and kick off my shoes. I'm more than ready to change out of my suit now, but I go into the kitchen anyway, thinking maybe there will be a box of overlooked crackers I could chew on while I change.

I open the fridge door and blink in surprise. It's full of food. I do the same with the walk-in pantry, and that too, is stocked.

Talia's been a busy girl, I think gratefully, my eyes greedily scanning the cans of soup, boxes of pasta, and jars of sauce.

I open the fridge again, and yep. There's meat in there. Packages of ground beef, a whole chicken, and pork chops and steaks.

Now if I only knew how to cook.

CHAPTER SEVEN

Talia

I ask Beau to kiss me properly before he heads off to work. Mondays, he's said, are especially busy, and I'm going to take the opportunity of his long day to do my own work. Classes start next week, and I won't have much time for anything else.

He chuckles, low and gravelly, and leans away, smoothing my hair away from my face. Even though we made love all night, I want him to crawl back in bed. He's more relaxed after the weekend in Old Harbor, but there's something sad underneath too. He didn't want to say goodbye to Rick and Devyn, and I hadn't either.

I wait until the elevator doors slide shut and then get out of bed. I put on a pair of panties and a tank top, and fill a mug with coffee. The empty shelves are sad. I poke around for a forgotten bagel or a stale piece of bread to make toast. Now that I know I'm going to be here for the next little while, I should do something about it. This might have been okay when Beau lived alone, but I'm getting tired of takeout.

I shower, do my hair and makeup, and get dressed for the day. I make a list of the things I want and call in a grocery order to a small store a few blocks away. For a week's worth of food, the total comes to over five hundred dollars. I'm stocking the kitchen from scratch, and the large sum isn't surprising. I can use the debit card Devyn gave me, so the amount doesn't give me a sick feeling that it would have, but it turns out it doesn't matter. I give the grocery store clerk the address, and she says Beau already has an account and I can add the charge to his bill if I want. I don't think he'll mind paying for food, and I say okay.

I tell her I'll be here when the delivery men come, and I settle behind my laptop with a cup of coffee to wait.

Devyn gave me a few ideas to work with, and I grab a notebook that I bought as part of my "school supplies." I'll need them for school, yeah, but today I'll use a notebook, a pen, a pink highlighter, and sticky notes to plan my attack against Stevie Johansson.

I look over my sister's notes that I printed off at the library.

The names and dates are over two years old, and she's right, for her it would be like starting over. Her notes might not be as useful as I thought, and I set them aside.

She said she'd start with the kids at the frat party I went to, but at parties like that, no one knows each other. The U of M campus is huge, and hundreds of guys are members of that fraternity.

I knew Serena, Tasha, and Jessie. They were the girls I went to the mall with the day we stopped at Stevie's store.

I met Serena's sister and parents, but she never met my mom. Mom's been hooked on Sweet for a long time. For a while she was able to hide it and keep her job as an accountant at a car dealership, but by the time I met Serena on campus during orientation, she'd started the not-so-gradual slide into caring about nothing except the next lick. I stopped bringing my friends home.

Using the White Pages online, I search for Serena's parents' phone number. Taking my therapist's advice, I wrote her letters and we kept in touch even though we were in different facilities. But she was discharged before I was and I lost track of her. I was lucky. My therapist supported and advocated for me, and I'd been allowed to stay. Three years in rehab. Three years for a six-month addiction.

Sentenced for the rest of my life.

I didn't know Serena was on the streets again until I bumped into her sister one night while Devyn and I were shopping here in the city. Standing near a pallet full of soda, Brenna told me what happened, and I can still feel the texture of a case of Mountain Dew under my fingers. Devyn always brought me with her. One, to keep an eye on me, and two, to keep normalcy in my life. I never thought shopping was boring. I cherished every sober second I had.

Even today, I liked ordering chips and dip, tomatoes and lettuce, meat, pasta, coffee, orange juice, and eggs. I don't think there's a second of any day that I take for granted.

Cell phone numbers aren't listed, and I call a landline number that pops up in the search results. The number matches the address where I knew Serena used to live. I thought her parents were nice people and it broke my heart when I heard Serena didn't have anywhere to go after rehab released her.

That would have been my fate if Devyn hadn't taken me in.

She held me for a long time after we came back from the store, my tears wetting her shirt in gratitude and shame. We sat on the floor in her kitchen with groceries scattered around us, her leg anchored over my hip and my face buried in her shoulder as I cried.

The memories make me even more determined to rip Stevie apart.

Mrs. Feeley answers the phone, her voice clipped and angry. "Hello?"

I swallow. It's difficult for me to deal with conflict, hostility, and anger. It's something I worked hard on in therapy. I never wanted Devyn mad at me for something I did, and I lived with her for months before finally understanding that even if she got frustrated because I forgot to put laundry in the dryer, it didn't mean she didn't love me anymore or that she was going to kick me out.

Living with Beau has been an adjustment as well. But an easier one because when he asked, he told me there weren't any strings, and I believed him. He took his hands-off approach a little too far, but I'm comfortable now that we found a compromise between him giving me space but not so much that I feel unwanted. It also helped Devyn let me choose and didn't pressure me one way or the other.

"Mrs. Feeley, I don't know if you remember me, but this is Talia Scott—"

"What do you want?"

I plow ahead, even though my first instinct is to hang up. I'll never find out what I need to know if I can't talk to people.

"I'm wondering if you know where I can find Serena?"

"No. Her sister might."

She quickly rattles off a number, and I'm thankful that I had my notebook and pen ready. She hangs up, not giving me a chance to double check that I wrote it down correctly, and with my fingers trembling, I dial her sister's number.

I get her voicemail, but these days, no one answers a number they don't recognize. I'm not surprised I have to leave a message asking Brenna to call me back, and I give her my phone number even though it will show up on her phone.

My cell rings almost immediately.

"Talia! Oh my God, it's good to hear from you. How are you?"

I relax into a puddle in my chair. I hadn't realized how much her mother set me on edge until I heard Brenna's friendly voice. "Good. I called your mom, and she gave me your number. I hope you don't mind."

"God, that old bat talked to you?" Brenna laughs. "Take that as a compliment."

"I'll try, but I don't think I want to do it again."

Brenna stops laughing. "What happened with Serena hit her hard. They don't talk anymore."

I can't blame Serena for avoiding her mom, and I feel guilty about my own mom. Family should support each other.

"I'm sorry."

"It is what it is. Mom blamed her for fucking around. She should have been studying instead of looking for trouble. You were there, so you know. What's up?"

"I was wondering if you know where she is. Serena, I mean."

Brenna sucks in a breath. "She calls me every once in a while. I'm going to the U of M now, and she says she doesn't want to drag me into her crap. The last I heard, she was an outreach director's assistant at a little church near Camden Way."

I wince. I know Camden Way, but if I'm going to do this, I can't let that part of Cedar Hill scare me. "Do you know the name of it?" I ask.

"Haven Presbyterian, I think? It's not a Baptist church. I'm sorry. She told me, and I forgot."

"No, that's okay. It's great, in fact. Do you think she'd mind if I went to see her?"

"I dunno. She doesn't talk about the before stuff very often. Before she went to rehab a second time. Doesn't hurt to try, I guess."

"She went to rehab again?" I ask, straightening. I don't know what I was picturing when I thought about finding her, but I didn't think she'd be sober.

"Yeah. I don't know where or how long, though. You'll have to ask her. Like I said, she doesn't talk about that much. Not with me anyway."

"I get it. Thanks for letting me know. Call me sometime, and we'll get coffee. I'm going to school too. We can bitch about homework."

Brenna laughs. "Sounds good. Where are you living? Are you here in the city?"

"Yeah. I'm staying . . . downtown," I say, reluctant to tell her my exact address. I know how lucky I am, and not because Beau's rich, either.

She whistles. "Nice. Made a decent life for yourself. You were always gorgeous, so I guess it's not a surprise. I gotta go. If you find Serena, tell her hi from me. I miss her."

Her voice cracks, and she hangs up.

I clear my throat. There's no reason to cry.

Okay. I have a place to start. I try to remember some of the guys' names we partied with, but it was so long ago and I had a lot to drink.

The concierge rings the penthouse's phone and asks if I ordered groceries, and I tell him that I did and that the delivery men can come up. Using a cart, they roll in several crates and I help empty them onto the kitchen floor.

They turn to leave, and I say, "Thank you so much. I added a tip when I put in the order."

One of them smiles and says, "Thanks. Enjoy your day."

"Thanks. You too."

Quickly, I put the food away, and by the time I'm done and have eaten lunch, it's after one.

I can't go out dressed the way I am, and I search through Beau's front closet and find a dirty work jacket he must wear to construction sites. It's too big, but it just adds to the illusion that I either stole it from someone, bought it for cheap at a thrift store, or it was given to me during a clothing drive. My jeans, sweater, and boots are new, but there's nothing I can do about that. I don't want to trick anyone, but I put my hair in a messy ponytail and scrub some of the makeup off my face. I'll never fit into that part of the city again, not unless I'm addicted to Sweet. Devyn has too much class and style, and it rubbed off on me.

Nervous, not knowing what I'm going to find, I head out. It's been years since I've been in that part of the city, and I wait at the corner for a city bus, my heart thrumming.

I might be able to find a cab with a brave enough driver to go out that way, but it's not worth it. I wore flat boots for a reason. I'll be doing a lot of walking.

At another bus stop, while I wait for a connecting bus, I use the debit card Devyn gave me and withdraw some cash. I didn't bring a purse, just my ID and debit card that I tucked into a pocket inside Beau's jacket. Carrying a purse is the fastest way to get mugged. I've known women who were almost beaten to death for what little they had in their wallets.

The change from the "nice" part of the city to the "bad" is gradual, until it isn't. You can check your cell for the time in a perfectly good part of town, but when you look back up, it's no place you'd want your car to break down. As people get off and get on, they grow sadder and more hopeless. No one lives around here if they don't have to.

An old woman catches my eye and tries to smile. God only knows what she lives with, and I smile back, hoping a kind face will perk up her spirits. It's all I have to give her.

Nothing but my fight to survive without Sweet is mine.

The bus route ends a mile from Camden Way, and I have no choice but to get off unless I want to turn around with the driver. It's tempting, but I slide out of my seat and step into the aisle behind the old woman. The sidewalk in front of a pawn shop is covered in a layer of deep snow. It hasn't been shoveled, and my boots sink to my ankles.

The fierce wind cuts through my jeans, but Beau's jacket is lined, and the material smells like him.

He said he sees a second chance when he looks at me, but I don't understand what he meant. A second chance at what? Family? Marriage? He never talks about other women. He might have been bitter, but I agree if he had a child somewhere, a woman wouldn't let him get away with not paying child support. Beau's practically famous. Everyone knows how much money he has.

Another reason I didn't want to tell Brenna where I lived, or who I lived with. Rick lives like he doesn't have money. Beau does not.

The snow crunches under my boots, and the wind whips at my face and stings my ears. I was lucky, if you can say anything about my time addicted to Sweet, that I was hooked during the summer months. I didn't have to freeze to death looking for a dealer, or try to find a place to get warm. Shelters fill up and will turn you away. It's not that they don't care what you do after they lock the doors, it's that they can't.

A heavy beat thumps from a bar, and the neon lights glow weakly in the setting sun. It will be dark soon, and if I find Serena, I'll have to keep an eye on the time. The city buses stop running at ten, and there's no way in hell I'd ask Beau to pick me up. When I told him I was looking up old friends, I doubt he thought I meant this.

Two men sitting near the window drinking beer leer at me as I walk past. I don't meet their cruel gazes through the dirty glass and I hide my face, hunching into my jacket.

I want to stop and see if Mom's inside. I want to go in and ask if anyone has seen her around. Maybe someone knows where she is or where she's been sleeping. I should have asked Devyn, but there's no faster way to make her stop talking than bringing up Mom. I understand Devyn's fear. I really do, but if I can do something, then I should.

The lights blink on as the sun goes down. It's too cold for her to be out here, but I look anyway, searching for a figure huddled in a storefront's doorway, hoping for a little warmth hiding from the wind.

Camden Way is up ahead, but it's a long street, and I'll be walking for a lot longer than I want if I choose the wrong direction. Churches here don't look like churches in nice neighborhoods. Their entrances look like storefronts, places to meet and have coffee while you pray. There are no steeples, no lawns for children to play on after services. I bet this church doesn't have pews, maybe metal folding chairs in a tiny sanctuary. I don't remember Haven Presbyterian, but I probably walked by it a thousand times without noticing, too eager to go home and get high off my purchase.

I walk east, the cold seeping into my bones. The walk back to the bus stop will be miserable, but maybe the wind will die down and I can stay out a little longer to look for Mom.

The stores start to look familiar in a way you'd remember a movie you watched years ago. The dealers and the druggies might have changed, but the streets stayed the same. Businesses struggling to stay open—a daycare, a hair salon, a DVD rental, more pawn shops. A lone barista is working in a café by herself hoping no one walks in wanting more than a cup of coffee. There are more closed than open, For Rent signs taped to the windows with bars protecting the glass.

I would have walked right by Haven Presbyterian if an old man holding a Bible hadn't pushed out the door and murmured, "Bless you," as he passed me.

"And to you," I say automatically, skidding to a stop in front of a whitewashed brick building next door to a Salvation Army.

Like I thought, the inside doesn't feel like a church. There's no one around, but I catch the scent of stale coffee and sugar cookies and my stomach grumbles. I stand in the small lobby thinking about my next move, and my phone chimes the generic sound I left attached to Beau's number. I hope he's not texting me to ask where I am. I don't want to lie. I don't want to start our relationship on lies, but I can't tell him the truth or he'll never let me out of the penthouse.

I owe it to myself, and to Devyn, to finish what she started.

Meeting up with a friend for a drink. Won't be out late.

I wait for more, but he's not going to ask when I'll be back. Thank God.

Have fun! I reply, but I don't say anything else. I shove my phone back into my pocket and look around.

A large bulletin board is hanging on a wall: help wanted, daycare openings, AA meetings and other fliers attached to the cork with brightly colored pins. The door wasn't locked so there must be someone around, and I step farther into the church. A laugh floats from a room down a set of thinly carpeted stairs.

The sanctuary's dark, but I peer inside for my own curiosity. They have pews, and an altar stands in front of a large wooden cross.

I turn around and go down the stairs, the wood creaking under my boots. I walk by a large room that's used for childcare. Toys are scattered on the floor, and two playpens are pushed against a wall. Across from the nursery is an equally large kitchen that looks like it's used to feed several people at a time.

Serena's giggling, and I knock on a door that's half open. My friend is sitting on a worn desk chair in front of a desktop computer that has seen better days. A man, not much older than we are and wearing a dress shirt and tie, is nibbling her neck.

They both see me at the same time and straighten. Serena staggers to her feet, her eyes wide. "Talia?" She looks me up and down, and a tear drips down her cheek. "Jesus Christ, look at you!" she exclaims and yanks me into her arms.

She's bony, her hair shorter than I remember, but she's sober and her eyes are clear.

"What are you doing here?" she asks, letting me go.

"I'm living in Cedar Hill again," I say.

She frowns. She doesn't know I left.

"Brenna told me where I could find you. I hope you don't mind. She says hi."

"No, I don't mind, but why?" The man behind her clears his throat. "Oh! This is Aaron. He's the outreach director here, and my boyfriend," she tacks on, blushing.

I reach out my hand, and he shakes it with a firm grip. "Nice to meet you."

"Nice to meet you too. Talia. Talia Scott? I've heard a lot about you." He kisses Serena's cheek. "I'll give you two some privacy. I'll be upstairs."

"Thanks."

He shuffles out the door, leaving it cracked, and Serena pulls me into the little office, gesturing for me to sit on an old loveseat.

"You look good," I say, code words for sober, happy, and settled.

She nods, understanding the shorthand. "I am. I relapsed

the second I got out of rehab the first time. If Mom and Dad would have—" She stops and shakes her head. "Anyway, one night Aaron was walking home, and he saw me huddled on the sidewalk a few blocks away. He found a safe place for me to stay and paid for another stint in rehab. I don't know how. Donations, maybe. He gave me something to get clean for, you know? I was hooked on Sweet, but he told me he loved me anyway. Said I was a little lamb that lost her way. It doesn't sound romantic, not like that, but he . . . I wouldn't be here without him."

"That's great, Serena, it really is. I'm happy for you."

To find someone who can love you even with your crap, someone who's willing to stand by you no matter what. That should have been her parents, but God. Karma, Fate, they gave her someone else instead. Maybe someone better.

"Thanks. We're getting married soon. When it warms up and we can have the ceremony outside. I work with him here, but we don't have much money. Tell me about you," she says, grabbing my hand. "I got out and let you disappear. I'm sorry I lost touch, but Mom and Dad didn't let me move back home and I was so lost."

"I get it, and it's okay. I've been good," I say honestly. "I spent a lot of time in rehab, and when I was well enough to leave, I called my sister. She's been a blessing. She took me in and made sure I had a goal, something to work toward, like Aaron does for you. I'm in school. Taking classes to be a psychologist."

Serena smiles. "You would know a lot about that."

"It's one of the reasons why I chose it. Empathy matters." I pause. "Do you remember any of that stuff about my sister a while back? Were you seeing Aaron then?"

She leans against the cushion and bites her lip. "Kind of. She was looking into Sweet. Where it comes from, right?"

"Yeah. She saw what it did to me and wanted to get it off the streets."

Serena wraps her arms around herself. "I wish she would have. It's hurt so many people."

"I know. She gave up after Stevie Johansson got her fired from the *Times,* but after talking to someone, she had an idea. You don't mind talking about this, do you? I don't want to trigger you."

"No." She closes her eyes and drags in a deep breath. "You can still taste it though, can't you?"

"Yeah." I think about Beau instead of the pink powder. I have someone too.

"What did your sister find out?"

"She said something about how the day we went into Stevie's store in the mall we might have bought tainted candy. You brought dipping sticks to the party. Do you think that's how we got hooked?"

"God, Talia, that was so long ago. Anything's possible, you know? But the candy from her store? That doesn't make much sense. Maybe? Why would she do that to her customers?"

"To get them hooked so they have to buy Sweet from her?" Devyn was so sure that's what Stevie's doing, but while Devyn usually isn't wrong, the theory isn't sounding right to me either.

"That seems so risky, but if that's true, then I feel doubly guilty—" She stops, her voice breaking, and she presses her hands to her eyes.

"Why? What are you talking about?" I tug at her wrists, but she won't look at me. "What do you mean?"

She drops her hands, and she links our fingers on her thigh. "I feel so guilty for bringing you to that party. I wanted to go, but I had no idea something like that would happen. I've wanted to apologize, but I was scared you hated me."

"I never blamed you. Not once. I was excited to go. It's not your fault. I've talked to Devyn about it a lot, and she doesn't blame me." *Not like your mom blames you.* "She said we were doing what normal girls our age do."

Rubbing a tissue under her nose, she sniffles. "Then you forgive me?"

"Yes, I forgive you." There's no point in telling her there's nothing to forgive. She won't believe it, and that's not what she's looking for. She needs me to tell her, needs to hear the words, and only that will let her move on.

"Thank you."

"You're welcome. Do you know who else was at the party? I want to see how they're doing too. Jessie and Tasha? They never got hooked that night, right? Do you know if they ate any of your candy?"

She shakes her head. "I have no idea. There were so many people there, and when I was passing it around, I lost track of who wanted some. You'd have to ask. Let me write down a few names for you. I knew a couple of the guys from class. They were pledging."

"Thanks."

More digging. I have a new respect for what Devyn does. Did. Does. I don't think she'll be able to stop investigative reporting even if Rick asked her to.

I put Serena's list with my cash, debit card, and ID, and she leads me up the stairs. As we walk through the dimly lit lobby, I zip up Beau's jacket. We stop near the glass door, and it's black as pitch outside. I'd be scared to leave if the streets weren't so familiar.

"Thank you for coming by. It means a lot that you still think about me," Serena says, gripping me in a fierce hug. "I run an NA support group here, and I see a therapist. Your forgiveness will go a long way."

"You didn't do anything except buy me a dress. You have

always been a kind, caring woman. Don't let Sweet ruin what you can have with Aaron. It's already ruined so much of our lives."

"It has, but Aaron has faith in me and he loves me. I hope you find someone too."

I nod and push the door open. A blast of cold air hits me in the face. "I have, but sometimes I wonder what he's doing with me." My voice wavers.

"I ask Aaron that all the time. Do you know what he tells me?"

"No."

"He says that he didn't save me, that I saved him. He was looking for something, needed a sign, and God put me right in his path. I don't know if you believe in God, but I believe what Aaron said is true. You stepped into your guy's path when he needed you. The best thing you can do for yourself is not let him down. Come to an NA meeting and share your struggles. Tell people how far you've come. We have the times listed on our website. Goodnight, Talia. Thanks again."

"I will, and thanks for inviting me. Goodnight."

I step into the cold, the weight of Serena's words heavy in my heart. I don't want to let Beau down, but sometimes, in the middle of the night when I'm close by his side, it feels inevitable.

———

Letting the tears come, I walk back to the bus stop. They trickle down my cheeks as I ride to a part of the city that most people who live near Camden Way will never see. I need to purge now. I don't want Beau to see me cry. If I cry in front of him, he'll want to know why, and this is part of my life I can't share. Not yet.

I step into Beau's foyer and kick off my boots. The tangy, sugary scent of something cooking hangs in the air.

Dressed in plaid lounging pants and a t-shirt, Beau's standing at the stove stirring something with a wooden spoon. From behind, I wrap my arms around his waist and rest my cheek between his shoulder blades. He feels so strong, so safe, like nothing will ever go wrong as long as he's with me.

It's not true, of course. I have the potential to fuck this up so terribly he never wants to see me again.

I need to have faith that I won't.

He taps the spoon on the edge of the saucepan and twists in my embrace. Hugging me just as tightly, he kisses the top of my head. "You look good in my jacket. Did you have a nice day?"

"I wanted—" Tears clog my throat. I thought I got them all out on the bus. "I wanted something of yours with me." It's only half a lie. It was comforting to have his jacket and scent wrapped around me while I walked the streets.

"That's sweet. Keep it. It's yours."

I look up at him and blink away my tears. He looks so good with his scruff, his eyes filled with humor, concern, and what I hope is love, even if he doesn't say it. He rubs his thumbs over my sticky cheeks. It will be a miracle if I can keep anything from him. "Then it won't be yours."

He chuckles. "Fair enough. Are you hungry? Imagine my surprise when I opened the fridge looking for a beer and moldy cheese and instead, I find paradise."

I shrug, faking a lightness I don't feel. "I was tired of you starving me, and I decided to take matters into my own hands. The woman I gave the order to at the grocery store said I could bill it to your account. I hope you don't mind."

"We haven't talked about—" he starts.

"No, we haven't, and we don't need to," I say, looking around him to the pan on the stove. "What are you cooking?"

He drops the money talk and I'm glad. We're both too tired to get into it now anyway. "Something called Perfect Pasta. It's not bad."

I laugh. Beau Hendrickson, the richest man in Cedar Hill now that Rick moved to Old Harbor, eating a ninety-nine cent box of Perfect Pasta. "Devyn and I used to eat this if we were low on cash. I can't guarantee you'll like it, but it's an adventure." I bought it mostly for the memories. Missing Devyn and loving Beau butt heads when I least expect it.

"I had a taste, and it will go okay with a bottle of Perrier." He rubs at my cheeks again. "Are you okay, love?"

"I am now that I'm home," I say, not realizing what I said until the words came out of my mouth. How entitled I sound, thinking of Beau's penthouse as my home.

"I'm glad you feel that way. Take *my* jacket off," he says, teasing, "and let's eat. I'll tell you about my day if you tell me about yours, and then we can fall asleep watching a movie. Sound good?"

I hug him again, not wanting to let go. "Thank you."

"I'll always be here for you," he says softly.

"Why do you sound sad when you say it?"

"Because I know one day you won't want me to be."

———

He doesn't give me a chance to ask him what he means. He nudges me toward the foyer, and I hang up his work jacket where I found it. I'm not wearing my usual dress pants and blouse, but he doesn't comment on my jeans and sweater.

I butter slices of bread from a loaf I added to the grocery order along with peanut butter and strawberry jelly, and he dishes us up our food.

"What's that?" he asks.

Of course he wouldn't understand, and I try to push back a grin. "We didn't always have dinner rolls."

"Oooh, right."

We sit in the living room to eat our dinner. My laptop and notes are still on his dining room table, and I try to glance at them out of the corners of my eyes to see if he's ruffled through anything. I can't tell, and I'll have to be careful not to do that again. I was so excited to find out where Serena was, I forgot to clean up.

Beau sits on the couch and sets our bowls on the coffee table, and I put our slices of bread next to them and sit across from him on the floor.

I spoon up a bite of the hamburger and pasta meal, and the tangy sweetness takes me back to evenings at home with Devyn. While she cooked, I'd sit at the tiny kitchen table and watch. It was so important to her that we spent time together the first year I was out of rehab, and she didn't let me out of her sight if she wasn't at work. Well, except for the nights she snuck out and I never knew.

"You go first." I push a piece of bread toward him. "Wait a second," I say, bouncing back up to grab two bottles of Perrier out of the fridge. "Okay. Sorry." I'm curious if he'll start with work or going out with his friend, and he starts with work.

"I let everyone know Rick won't be back. That was fun," he says, unscrewing the cap off the bottle I put near his bowl.

I know how much it hurts him, and I quirk my mouth in sympathy. "I'm sorry."

"No, it's my own damned fault. I saw it coming, and I ignored it. I spent all afternoon going over our business plan for the next five years. I don't like where it's heading."

"What can you do to fix it? You don't need the money."

"No, but it's nice to be able to pay our employees," he says. "We'd put hundreds of people out of work if we shut down."

"Right," I say, a little embarrassed I didn't think of that myself.

"I shouldn't let it bother me, but I put so much heart into my side of the company and now I'm going to have to start planning with my head. It won't be a big deal, just an adjustment I didn't want to make. How about you?"

I shrug. "I ordered food, stayed here until it came, and then I looked for a friend of mine. I called her parents, and her mom gave me her sister's number. Her sister doesn't talk to her very often and she could only , , , point me across town. I have a new respect for what Devyn does."

"Did you find her?"

"Yeah." I bite my lip. I can't hide everything from him, and the more I tell him that won't get me in trouble, the better. "She was hooked on Sweet, and she was at the same party I was when the cops busted it. But she didn't have someone like Devyn to help her, and after rehab, she started using again. She's doing okay now, but her life hasn't been as easy as mine."

"You have good people looking out for you. I hope you count Rick and me as part of that."

"Yeah, I do."

"Good. Are you going to see her again?"

I poke at a crumble of hamburger. "I don't know. Maybe. She runs an NA support group—"

"NA?" he interrupts.

I grimace. "Narcotics Anonymous."

"Oh. Right."

"She asked me if I'd go and talk about my experience, but I can understand if she decides seeing me would put her in a place she doesn't want to be anymore. Sometimes it's better to move on, no matter how much you'll miss that person."

Beau nods, a shadow fluttering over his face, but I pretend I don't see it.

"We talked about a few other people we went to school with, and I'll look them up, but we might be in different places now and past the point where we could still be friends. This can be a closure of sorts, then I'll put it away and make new friends." It sounds good in theory, but it's not good that I felt just as comfortable walking Camden Way as I did stepping into the lobby of Beau's building.

He lifts a piece of bread to his mouth. "Do you think that's a good idea?"

"What?" I swirl the hotdish around in my bowl. The next time we have something like this, I'll make it with real ingredients.

"Finding your other friends. Maybe you should leave it alone."

I could. I could forget about this whole plan, except, Devyn worked so hard to put Stevie in prison, and she never forgot it. There will always be a chance Stevie will go after her again. I love Rick and all he's done for my sister and me, but he's proven he's not always going to be able to keep her safe. It's a shitty thing to think, but there's truth to it too.

"I would at least like to see them and say goodbye."

"Okay. Just be careful." He pushes his bowl away. "This isn't very good."

I laugh, relieved he's going to let me do my own thing. "It really isn't."

"Let's order pizza."

I get up off the floor and throw myself into his arms. "I love you, Beau."

He wraps his arms around me and says the sweetest words I'll ever hear. "I love you too."

CHAPTER EIGHT

Beau

I shouldn't have said it, but like a dumbass, I said it anyway. I don't fucking learn, and Talia's going to stomp all over my heart, just like Nina did.

Fuck.

I throw my jacket on the coat rack near my office door and drop my briefcase on my desk. To make matters worse, no, we didn't eat pizza, I carried her to bed, and I didn't use one fucking condom all night. I wanted to mark her, brand her, and yeah, I want to knock her up. I want her carrying my baby, but I know that won't stop her when she wants to leave.

It didn't stop Nina.

Christ. Why can't I *learn?*

Lola pushes a coffee service into my office. I frown, and she backs out and closes the door.

Angrily, I rake my fingers through my hair and pace around my office. I can't be here, and I put my jacket back on and slam my way out to the truck that I use to drive out to construction sites.

I need some air.

My knuckles are white from gripping the steering wheel, and my hands are aching by the time I reach the property. The hotel's skeleton is still beautiful in a sad, depressing way, though I have managed to clean up a little more since I pried that outhouse open.

An Aston Martin DB11 coasts to a stop behind me, and Declan Everett climbs out of the elegant car, not a hair out of place.

The smug son of a bitch.

He caught me at the wrong time.

Without thinking, I stride over the pavement, and before he can say one goddamned word, I punch him with a hard right hook to his jaw. He staggers backward, a hand to his face and his eyes flashing hot.

"You're a fucking psycho," he yells, spit flying out of his mouth. "Fucking idiot."

"How *dare you* try to talk to me after everything you've fucking done to this project, to Rick, and to Devyn. If I had *any* way to prove it, your ass would be in jail, and you wouldn't risk taking a shower ever again."

I'm shaking with rage, and it's stupid, but tears burn my eyes. If it wasn't for this asshole, two men wouldn't have been killed, Tony Kelly would still be operating a crane, and Rick wouldn't be in constant pain. *And he'd still be in Cedar Hill*, I think, but I push it back. He never would have met Devyn, and I can't wish her away for my selfish reasons.

Everett wiggles his jaw and adjusts his cashmere coat.

Pansy.

"That was Stevie. I don't give a shit about Devyn Scott."

"Great. Fucking say that again and let me record it. What

the fuck do you want?" I turn my back and flex my hand, my knuckles bruised and bleeding. I hope I didn't break anything. I take my keys out of my pocket and cross the street. I shouldn't let him on the site, but if he's done anything, maybe I can read it on his face.

"I heard through the grapevine that Mercer isn't coming back to the city."

"So the fuck what?" I jerk the padlock off the chain and shove the fence door open. The first thing I did after finding out that Devyn was going to be okay was repair and reinforce the entire fence. I added security cameras too. Something else that should have been done a long time ago.

Everett follows me in without a care in the world.

Jesus Christ.

"Just wondered what your plan is, businessman to businessman."

"Why, so you can get one up on me? I'm sure you'll have no problem doing that since commercial property isn't my wheelhouse." I shuffle over the frozen mud.

"That's why I'm here. What's the plan for M&H now that Mercer's out of the picture?" He follows me across the yard.

"He's not out of the picture." Fuck. I forgot hardhats. Maybe something will fall on Everett's head and smack some smarts into him.

He laughs. "Yeah, sure. He's still hiding in Old Harbor with Devyn sucking his dick every night. You think he cares about you and this dump?"

I don't defend either of them. It's something I told Rick not that long ago. I wasn't interested in running M&H alone, and that hasn't changed. It doesn't matter that he said he'd open a branch in Old Harbor. He said it to shut me up and give himself something to do, but all it does is drop more paperwork on my desk. Devyn would never stop working, and he'd feel like an asshole if she went to work every morning and he stayed home in his pajamas.

"What's it to you?" I mutter, looking for a calm I'm not going to find. Not here, and not with Everett breathing down my neck.

Ten more weeks, then we can get going on this fucking thing. I hate looking at it.

"Actually, a lot," he says sincerely, and I shift my gaze from the building's support beams to his face.

A bruise is already blooming along his jaw.

Good.

I scoff and turn back to the building. There's nothing more I can do now until the spring thaw, and I won't be working on the site like Rick used to. I manage projects from my desk unless I'm needed for the obligatory photo-op like a breaking ground ceremony. This building has already been there, done that. The project's tainted with blood and death, and there will be no more celebrating.

"Mercer doesn't give a shit about your half of M&H," Everett presses, and I grit my teeth. "Ask him to buy you out and come work with me."

"You're kidding, right? Why the fuck would I want to do that? You're mixed up with Stevie and Sweet, and I don't want to be anywhere near it."

"Eh," Everett says, rolling his shoulders. "No one will ever prove she's doing anything. If there was something to find, they would have found it by now."

"Who's they?" I ask, walking deeper into what will be the lobby.

"DEA, Devyn Scott, the cops. I don't stick my nose in her business."

"No, not unless you want to bribe my foreman with drugs. Then you're all over it."

He follows me like an annoying pest. "You don't have any evidence. And Neil Simpson was an idiot."

"It's convenient for you that he's dead. You should get the hell out of here before I call the cops and throw you off the property for trespassing."

Everett laughs. "All's fair in love and business. You know that. Besides, you never enjoyed the perks of a relationship? Devyn's sister moved into your penthouse. You tell me you're not tapping that on a regular basis. Cute little thing."

I pass the section of concrete where Rick pounded the hell out of his and Renata's initials. It was a good day for Rick, but not such a good day for me. I pushed him toward Devyn and away from our partnership and the company.

"Are you threatening her?" I ask mildly, noticing that the crate I took the hammer out of is gone.

"No, why would I? You deserve to be happy after that Nina mess. You waited a long time."

Suddenly, I am so tired I can barely stand up. I miss Nina and what we could have had if we'd wanted the same things, but she hadn't. Far from it. She taught me I was a needy, smothering SOB, and I haven't learned. I haven't changed. I'm going to do the same thing to Talia and she'll get sick of it and leave. Then I'll be alone because Rick and the friendship that I've depended on for most of my life has already disappeared.

I speak against a ball of misery and anxiety gathering in my chest. "You know what? Fuck it. Send me a contract. Show me what kind of deal you can give me. I have to finish this godforsaken thing, but then I can do what I want."

Everett grins, the shark coming out in his expression. "You'll have it no later than Friday. Times they are a-changing, my friend. You don't want to get left behind."

Rubbing his jaw, he ambles toward his car, and the fence door squeals as he walks off the site.

I dig my phone out of my pocket and bring up Rick's number.

"Beau. What's up?" he answers after the second ring.

"I'm putting in my notice," I say, my throat raw. "I'll get the hotel built, but then I'm done."

"Hey. What's going on?"

"I told you. I don't want to work in Cedar Hill alone. I'm getting out. I'm done. Buy my half or sell it off, I don't care." I should hang up, just hang up and let him deal with it, but I wait to see what he'll say. I shouldn't have bothered.

He blows out a breath. "Okay. I knew this was coming, but I didn't want to see it. It would be better if we could talk in person instead of deciding this over the phone."

"Nope. You knew how I felt, and we've had plenty of time to talk."

"You and Talia were just here," Rick says, his voice rough with frustration. "Why didn't you say anything then?"

I decide to tell him the truth. I don't have anything to lose. "Something came up this morning and I'm following a lead. You and I have different goals now and I'm going to see what else is out there."

"Is this about Nina? Valentine's Day isn't that far off, and I know—"

"It's not about Nina. Not everything I fucking do is about her. I asked you for help and all you did was open another branch that makes more work for me. I've worked my ass off for you since the accident, and I was happy to do it while you were healing. But you're settled now, and I still do most of the work. I'm done. If you don't want to work in Cedar Hill anymore, sell my half."

"Okay, but—"

I cut him off, my finger jamming on that little red circle so hard I'm surprised the phone doesn't fly out of my hand. I don't care what else he has to say. He's said enough. Enough for me to realize that once again I've put more time and energy into a friendship, into a relationship, than anyone has ever given me.

I throw my phone and it hits a support beam and falls to the snow-covered foundation. The screen lights up, and I assume it's Rick calling me back, but I don't care anymore. I sink to the ground and press my fists to my eyes. I'm too old to cry about something so ridiculous.

Once Talia decides she's had enough, I'll shuttle her little ass to Old Harbor and go somewhere warm for a vacation that's long overdue. I'm so fucking tired of the cold.

I can't go to Hawaii, not after talking to Talia about it. All I'd do is think of her lying naked on the beach, the sun tanning her skin.

I sit here until long after dark, and as the stars glint in the sky, I heft myself up and pick up my phone.

Rick knows not to bother me, and besides the one I missed, there are no other calls.

I drive the truck to the penthouse instead of swapping vehicles. I just want to lock myself in my study with a bottle and hope to God I feel better in the morning. Maybe I won't go to the office. I'll sleep in and make love to Talia if she lets me. Eat breakfast in bed and ask her what she does all day while I'm gone.

Take the day off.

I step into the foyer, and the delicious scent of roast chicken permeates the air. I pause for a moment, my lips pressed against a sob because I don't have to be alone tonight.

Talia's here.

For the next little while.

CHAPTER NINE

Talia

I'm eager to talk to the people on the list Serena gave me, and in the foyer, I put on Beau's work jacket. My cell rings, and I take it out of my pocket. Devyn's name glows on the screen. For a protective sister, she doesn't call me that often, which has been both pleasant and disappointing. I love talking to her, but if she called me any more than she does, I would have accused her of not trusting me to live on my own. It's something my therapist warned us about. I can't make Devyn feel like she can't do anything right. It's not fair to her, and how I process her actions is my problem, not hers.

"Hey, how are you?" I check the inside pocket that has my cash and ID in it. I'm not bringing my purse with me again, even if Jensen Anderson lives in a not-so-bad-part of Cedar Hill. Well, not so bad compared to Camden Way, but still nowhere I would consider safe.

"I'm okay. Rick and Beau had a fight this afternoon. I

wanted to give you a heads up in case he goes home in a bad mood."

"About what?"

She sighs. "Beau doesn't want to work in Cedar Hill without Rick."

I scowl. "We knew that. Beau hasn't talked about it much since I moved in, but we knew that."

"I think Rick was hoping things would calm down."

"You don't just 'calm down' when you're missing a friend," I say, defending him.

"I know. Anyway, Beau said he wants out and Rick's not taking it well."

"He should have thought of that when he moved to Old Harbor."

"He was hurting," Devyn says, defending her own man.

"I get that, but life keeps going, right?"

"Yeah. Yeah, it does. Rick's finding that out the hard way. I have to go. I'm at work. He stopped by to tell me about it, and I thought Beau might need you."

"Thanks. I'll talk to you later, okay?"

"Yep," she says, forcing a little cheer into her voice. "Have a good night."

"You too."

Whenever I would have a bad day and we could afford it, Devyn would cook all my favorite comfort foods, and that's what I do.

A few hours later, the elevator dings and Beau steps into the foyer. Chicken is roasting in the oven, and I have a pan of whipped potatoes warming on the stove with gravy, and there's a bowl of broccoli with cheese sauce in the microwave.

He steps around the corner, and I tilt my head, asking him to kiss me. I don't think it's a good idea to mention their fight since I doubt he'd be happy Rick and Devyn are talking about him behind his back. He brushes his fingers over my cheek, and I don't miss his bloody knuckles.

"Hi," I say, trying to act as if there's nothing wrong. "How was your day?"

"Shitty, but it seems to be getting better. I'm surprised you're here. What's going on?"

I try not to let my gaze slide to his hand. "I thought I'd make up for Perfect Pasta."

"No offense, love, but that wouldn't be too difficult."

I laugh and wrap my arms around him. "Take your jacket off. I was waiting for you."

"Yeah, sure."

He shuffles down the hallway toward the bedroom and comes back wearing only his dress slacks and dress shirt, the top three buttons undone and his sleeves rolled up to his elbows.

I set the table as he stares into the fridge.

"Are you looking for something?" I ask.

He shrugs and closes the door.

I realize what the problem is. "You can have a drink, you know." Three months hasn't been long enough for him to break his after-work habit, not that he needed to and not that I asked.

"It wouldn't bother you? I don't want to make you uncomfortable."

"No, go ahead. I was addicted to Sweet. I'm not an alcoholic."

He slides a lowball glass out of the cabinet along with a bottle of Glenlivet. "I've never seen you have a glass of wine."

I open the oven door and peer inside. The chicken's done, and I grab the oven mitts off the stove.

"Here," he says, setting his glass down, "let me do that."

"Thanks." I lean against the counter and watch him take the glass dish out of the oven, his hands steady. "Some people have an addictive personality, right?"

"That's what I've heard, but I don't know much about it." He takes the oven mitts off and pours whiskey into his glass. He sips and his shoulders loosen. It doesn't bother me to watch him. It really doesn't.

"My doctor and therapist don't believe that's me. If I did have an addictive personality, I would have been addicted to something before I got hooked on Sweet, or I would have replaced my addiction to Sweet with something else. Smoking, drinking, other drugs. Food. Gambling. Sex. Compulsive shopping, or shoplifting. It doesn't matter what you're craving because what matters is the feeling you get from giving yourself what you want. Like, I could take a sip of your drink and experience what you're feeling. Relief. Warmth. Tension fading away. But I could stop. And so can you because if I asked you not to have another glass, you wouldn't."

I stop to put the potatoes in a serving bowl, and Beau does the same with the gravy. It's nice to have an evening to talk to him. I'm glad that Devyn called.

"Then why do you stay away from caffeine?" He's genuinely curious, and I'm grateful he's interested. I don't pretend I'm not a lot to handle.

"We thought it was a good idea until I was on my feet, as a precaution. It doesn't matter anyway. Decaf tastes the same to me, and any café will make what you want decaffeinated. I don't feel like I'm missing out." I take the bowl of broccoli out of the microwave and put it on the table. "But I need to get in touch with my therapist and start sessions again. It's not drugs I'm addicted to."

"You're on something now, Talia? Do you need help?" Beau asks, grabbing my elbow, a frown wrinkling his forehead.

"No, but after living here with you, I realized that I could have a real problem while I'm in this relationship. Being addicted to love has turned into a joke, but it's not for me. My mom is on the streets, and I haven't seen her in years. Our dad took off a long time ago and he hasn't been a part of our lives since I was little. Devyn's not here. Falling in love made me realize that I need to feel loved, and that's a different kind of addiction. When you would change yourself to be whatever that person needs you to be so they don't stop loving you."

He rests his elbows on the table and clasps his hands, the food forgotten with our conversation. "I never thought of it like that."

"Most people don't until they go through a break-up and they can't function. It's like a physical withdrawal. When we hug, when we kiss, when we make love, every time we do those things, you dig deeper under my skin. My therapist never thought of it while I was in rehab, and I didn't think of it until we met and the only thing in my mind was the next time I could see you. I'm going to be in a bad way if we ever break up, and I don't want to be desperate enough to fill that emptiness with something else."

He stares, his eyes boring into me. I had to be honest. It might sound like I'm using my mental health to blackmail him into staying with me, but at least after our conversation, if he ever decides we aren't working out, he'll understand what it will do to me.

Rubbing his thumb over my jaw, he asks, "Do you ever really get over someone?"

"I don't know. I've never been in love before. Have you?"

"I think if you love someone that much, they're always with you."

My hand trembles as I reach for a serving spoon to scoop potatoes onto my plate. "Then I hope I'm strong enough to try to move on if we don't work out."

"Why do we break up?" he asks, picking up the carving knife.

Spooning gravy onto my potatoes, I say, "Why does anyone? You get tired of that person, or you naturally grow apart? By chance, you meet someone else? You realize you have different goals?"

He lays a slice of chicken breast on my plate. "You feel smothered?"

"Thank you. People smother because they're insecure. We talked about that in therapy. If someone is smothering you, they feel powerless in the relationship, and unbalanced power isn't healthy. If I get too needy, you have to be honest and tell me. If this isn't working out, you need to say something as soon as you know."

"I promise. I've been lied to in the past, and I won't do it to you."

"Thanks." I don't focus on that. "Eat your food before it gets cold. I peeled potatoes, and I made the gravy from scratch."

Beau digs in, and I enjoy watching him eat. I'm glad I was able to take his mind off Rick, even if it was to talk about my, well, they aren't problems, not yet, but those things needed to be said. I don't want to be fragile or weak, but my past has made me that way, and there's nothing I can do about it. Fighting it won't help, and not falling in love won't help.

We need open communication, but that benefits every couple, not only us.

Finishing our dinner, we chat about little things. He doesn't mention who he punched, and the comfort food doesn't chase the weariness from his eyes.

He helps me clean up, and he relaxes as we do the dishes together. I know so little about his past relationships. Has he done this with another woman? I'm already living here, so I'd have to deal with knowing if another woman has slept in his bed. He's almost forty. There's no chance he hasn't lived with someone before.

"Do you want to soak in a bath?" I wipe down the counter, and that's the last thing that needed to be done. Later, I can get the coffeemaker ready, and Beau will only need to press the button in the morning to start a fresh pot.

He pauses.

"I bought some bath salts from the store. Bring your drink."

He doesn't move, and I tug on his hand.

Finally, he follows me into his bathroom. I try not to compare, but the living room in Devyn's walkup across the city would fit in here. The garden tub is huge, and I've wanted to take a bath since I saw it, but I never felt comfortable enough to ask. Until now.

There's no need to wash it out—Beau showers in a separate stall, and I plug the drain and add the lavender-scented bath salts I put in his cabinet.

It will take a few minutes for the tub to fill, but I reach for the hem of my sweater. "You've never seen me naked in the light before."

He smiles, but there's more sadness than happiness in it. "I'm sorry. When you moved in here, I didn't know what to do. It's been a long time since I've been with someone. I mean, *really* been with someone. I almost made you leave, and I'm sorry."

He looks so miserable that I turn away. He's going to make me cry, and then he'll think there's something wrong.

I take my sweater off. "I should have said something way before that. I thought you regretted asking me to move in, and I didn't want to hear it."

"We moved quick, but it feels right, doesn't it?" he asks, his eyes searching my face.

"Yeah, it does," I say truthfully. I've wanted every second since I said goodbye to Devyn in Beau's foyer and she left to pack up our house in Portland.

Sighing, he says, "I'm glad you think so too."

He gets undressed and steps in first. He forgot his drink, and I set the glass on the edge of the tub. He sinks into the steaming water, leans back, and closes his eyes.

I slip out of the rest of my clothes and dim the overhead light. Carefully, I get in, turn the water off, and sit between his legs.

He shudders and wraps his arms around me.

"Are you going to tell me about this?" I ask, brushing my fingers over his bruised knuckles.

"It's nothing."

It's clearly not, but I can't force him to talk to me. I have the patience to wait him out. "Okay."

I wiggle a little closer and kiss his chest, his heart beating heavily under my lips. His warm skin tastes slightly of lavender and sweat.

"I told Rick I want out."

I pause to pretend I'm thinking through what he just said. I don't want him to know I already know. "I'm sorry. I know how much you miss working with him."

"Nothing lasts forever, right?" he asks bitterly. His eyes are still closed, and disappointment and anger tighten his jaw.

"No, but it helps to believe that when something ends, there's room for a new beginning."

He scoffs.

"What? You don't think that's true?" I lean back, and the tub is so deep the water laps at the tops of my breasts.

"It sounds like bullshit on a motivational poster, or something stupid someone says to make you feel better." He cracks his eyes open and glares at me.

I'm not offended. He's hurting and taking it out on me. I may not have ever been in a serious relationship, but I can understand how they work. Beau needs a safe place, someone he can talk to who won't get angry or hurt by what he says. Devyn and my therapist were my safe places. They still are, but things change. Maybe Beau and I can be each other's safe places.

"I'm a lot younger than you are, but I've had plenty of endings in my life. My dad left when I was little. I guess that wasn't the beginning of anything except Devyn, me, and my mom learning how to live without a man around. Sweet was an ending of sorts, you know? My entire life as I knew it ended the day I got hooked."

Beau grabs a hold of my wrist and squeezes. I press a kiss to the corner of his mouth, thanking him for his show of support.

"The day my therapist said I was ready to go home, I almost broke down, but I knew she was right. I was allowed to stay longer than any client they ever had, but stepping out of that building for the last time, even though Devyn was waiting for me, that scared the fuck out of me. She moved to Old Harbor, and what I found with her after rehab had to end so I could begin this, with you. Maybe you ending your partnership with Rick is a good thing. Maybe it's not, but I know it won't be if you don't try."

Blowing out a breath, he says, "It's not even about the company."

"Do you think after all these years you won't be friends anymore?"

He doesn't respond, and I know that's exactly what he thinks.

"Beau."

He turns away, his lips pressed into a firm line.

"Beau. Will you look at me?"

"What?" he snaps.

His bluster doesn't scare me. I hold his face between my

hands and brush my lips over his. "If you miss him that much, move to Old Harbor."

"What the fuck would I do there?" he asks, but he pauses, thinking about the idea.

"Rick must think there's business opportunities there, or he wouldn't have stayed. Keep this office open and work out of it part-time. It's a thirty-five minute flight from here to there. You have enough money you could even work here full-time and fly home every night. You can do whatever you want."

He's shaking his head before I'm even done speaking. "No. He doesn't want me there, or he would have asked me to move too. I'm not a little kid, Talia. I don't need to chase after him. He chose to leave, and that's a decision we'll both have to live with."

"Okay." I don't want to argue, and I don't know enough about their friendship to give him any more of my opinions. There could be other reasons Beau doesn't want to move, like his other friends. Maybe family I know nothing about. For all I know, his parents live in the city. There's so much about this man that I don't know.

I wanted to ask him about his past relationships, but he's done talking for the night. Soaking didn't help him relax like I hoped it would, and he stands up only a few minutes later.

He yanks a towel off the heating rack. "You don't have to get out. I'm going to get dressed and look over some paperwork. I told Rick I'd finish the hotel. I owe him that much at least." He wraps the black towel around his hips and steps out of the bathroom, taking his glass with him and leaving me in the dark.

I don't want him to be alone, but by the time I put conditioner in my hair, rinse it out, and dry myself off, he's already locked in his study.

I think about going in, straddling his lap, and asking him to make love to me, but I don't want to smother him. That's what his last girlfriend must have done, and he brought it up at dinner to warn me not to do the same. I can imagine her fear, and it's something I've felt myself. Beau's rich and sexy. He can have any woman he wants. How easy it must have been for her to start keeping track of him. Maybe tracing his phone or going to his office to make sure he was at work. Paranoia would set in, and every woman he spoke to would turn into someone he could be sleeping with.

Before I go to bed, I check my email. My professors are starting to send us class material, and I spend a few minutes skimming. I write down a list of the books I'll need. Virtual classes don't require you to have them, providing everything students need online, but I like holding the real thing, and my financial aid covers them if I want them.

I'm done half an hour later, but Beau still hasn't come out of his study. I want to wait up for him, but I should start getting used to waking up early. I brush my teeth and crawl in his bed. I almost went to the guest room, but Beau and I are still figuring out who we are as a couple, and I can't do that whenever we have a disagreement. I want to sleep with him every night, and I should ask him if I can have closet space in here. My suitcase is still in the guest room, and all of my clothes are hanging in the closet and folded in the dresser.

I'm not a guest, and he doesn't treat me like one. At least, not since he found me packing. That night, we both learned how to use our words.

Past midnight, Beau stumbles into the bedroom and takes off his pajamas. He slides into bed wearing his boxer briefs.

I curl my body around his. "Beau," I whisper in his ear.

"Hmmm?" He's already half sleeping.

"In your room? Can I have closet space?"

"Hmmm?"

"Closet space."

"Whatever you need, love," he mumbles, turning his head so our lips meet.

Wiggling out of my panties, I take what he offers.

———

I get up with Beau, and I'm showered and dressed by the time he's leaving for work. He gives me a kiss, tells me to have a nice day, and asks if I'll be home later.

"I don't know," I answer honestly. I'd like to be. I would like to start an evening routine where we cook dinner together and decompress, but evenings are the best time to look for Mom and ask around about Stevie Johansson and Sweet.

"Okay. Be safe, for me?" he asks, cupping the back of my neck with his warm hand and kissing me on the forehead.

"I promise."

"Thank you."

That's all he says, and he steps into the elevator, preoccupied with his busy schedule.

Spring semester starts in a few days, and the time I have to myself is running out. I'll still be able to dig into Stevie and Sweet, but not as much. Classes take up a lot of time: homework, online study groups, and participating in the Young Psychologists Association. I don't want to waste my financial aid, but it's more than that. My degree will mean something to me. Helping people will mean something to me. I want to pay forward everything anyone has ever done for me since going to that frat party.

It's too early to go to Jensen's. If he's living the kind of life I hope he's not, he won't be awake until Beau comes home from work, but there are other things I can do while I wait.

Devyn doesn't want me to find Mom. I know it's for my

own mental health she told me to leave it alone, but I can't. If she finds out, she'll just have to understand.

I ride the bus to the neighborhood where Mom, Devyn, and I lived after Dad left. I don't remember much about those years. I remember feeling sad we moved, and we had to give up our yard and the swing set where Devyn would push me if she wasn't with her friends. Our thirteen-year age difference made growing up together almost impossible. When I was small, she would play dolls with me, but after she graduated high school, she moved out to go to the university and I didn't see her much.

Mom made good money as a senior accountant, and the apartment we moved into after she sold our house as part of the divorce agreement was a spacious three-bedroom and two-bath. To my delight, Devyn always stayed with us during the holidays and summers because the dorms were closed.

I was sixteen when Mom had her first taste of Sweet at a dinner party. She hid it well, and she kept her job at the dealership for a couple of years until she started missing work.

It didn't take long for the money to run out, and the property management evicted us when they realized she was unemployed and couldn't pay rent.

The bus lets me off a block from that building, and I shuffle through the snow, the wind not as bitter as yesterday. Walking the streets, even in a nice neighborhood like this, I miss Beau.

By then, Devyn was making a name for herself at the *Times,* and she lived in her own small two-bedroom apartment. She rented us a tiny, clean place in a building quite a few blocks from here. I wanted to walk and see for myself just how far we fell because of Mom's addiction.

Devyn tried to talk Mom into going to rehab, but Mom insisted she didn't have a problem.

Busy at the newspaper, Devyn let her be.

I was old enough to take care of myself, and I finished high school and enrolled at the U of M on my own. I tried to hide how bad Mom was from Devyn, but I think she always knew. She had groceries delivered on a weekly basis and paid all our bills.

She took care of everything—and as a self-centered kid ignoring the world around her, I didn't know how thin that stretched her every month.

I didn't appreciate what she did for us, and shame burns my throat.

It's why I can't be angry she wants me to leave well enough alone. Mom hurt her so much.

I remember one evening she stopped by to check on me. Mom was gone, looking for a dealer, and I was doing homework in the kitchen.

"Come with me," Devyn ordered, throwing my things in a bag. "You can live better than this."

"No. I don't want to," I said.

Devyn froze, and blood drained from her face. "You're choosing this over me?" she asked, knowing exactly why Mom wasn't home, spending money she didn't have on Sweet.

"I'm choosing to take care of Mom over throwing her away like a dirty paper towel."

She dropped the bag. "Fine. Have it your way, but don't say I didn't tell you so."

I waited for her to stop paying the bills we needed her to pay, but she never did. Every month we had everything we needed, and I never once said thank you.

When the court sent me to rehab, I fought. I fought so hard because I knew Mom would be on her own. I wanted to hate Devyn, wanted to hate her for not paying the rent if I wasn't there, and I think I did, for a long time. I gave my rage and my hate to my therapist who would nod and listen, and then she would quietly ask, "What do you want her to do?"

"Something," I'd scream. "Something." And I'd collapse in a heap of tears on the floor.

Until one day we went through it all again, and she asked, "What do you want her to do?"

That time I didn't yell, didn't scream, didn't collapse in a pile of angry tears. I finally realized there wasn't anything more Devyn could do. She couldn't force Mom to go to rehab. She couldn't force Mom to clean up or love us more than she loved Sweet. Devyn had done the best she could, and I was hating her for it.

The day she picked me up from rehab, I had never felt so small.

Now it's not Devyn who needs to do something, but me. I can try and help Mom. I'll try and maybe learn the same thing Devyn did, but it will be my lesson and I won't stop until I know for sure she's a lost cause, just like Devyn keeps calling her.

The apartment Devyn rented for us wasn't as nice as the one we lived in after the divorce, but she'd done the best she could. When I moved in with her after rehab, I found out she lived just as poorly as we had to make ends meet, and that humbled me even more.

I walk up the four flights of stairs to our old apartment, but I don't know why. Mom and I haven't lived here for years, and I'm sure the apartment has seen many tenants come and go. The scent of rice and soy sauce permeates the air, even this early in the morning, and my stomach rumbles. I could get in trouble for hanging around where I don't belong, but I lean against the wall across from our door and suck in a shuddery breath. This place holds so many memories. Bad ones and good ones.

I wasn't prepared for how much I'd miss her, but I should have been. Because of Sweet, I lost my mom at sixteen, and I've been selfish with my grief. Devyn lost a mother too, but because she's older, I thought she could deal with it better. You don't get over something like that.

"Talia Scott! My word! I never thought I'd see you again!"

A large woman wearing a black muumuu covered in brightly colored flowers steps into the hallway from an apartment a few doors down. Her salt and pepper hair is wrapped around pink foam curlers, and a light layer of makeup covers her doughy face.

"Mrs. Otto. You still live here."

Mr. and Mrs. Otto were the caretakers when we lived in the building. Devyn paid the rent and I kept our apartment clean for inspections, so no one bothered us. Mrs. Otto knew what was going on, and from time to time she'd ask me if there was anything we needed. I never knew if she did that because she wanted to or if Devyn asked her to.

"Of course, child. Where else is there to go? I was just checking on an empty. You looking for a place to live? I'll give you a good deal."

I can just imagine Beau's face if I told him I wanted to live here. He probably doesn't even know this street exists.

Pushing away from the wall, I say, "No, thanks, but I appreciate it."

"Oh, then what are you doing here? You lookin' for your mama? She hasn't been around for the past couple of years." She shuffles across the dirty carpet in fuzzy slippers, and I can smell her perfume before she's halfway to me.

"No, I know— Wait. A couple of years? Do you mean two?"

"I'd watch her stumble out of here, and she'd be gone days at a time. Then she'd be back, sleep it off, then go right back out again."

I blink in confusion. "But I thought Devyn stopped paying the rent when I . . . started school."

Mrs. Otto clucks and shakes her head. "Your sister paid that rent every month until the *Times* fired her. I watched the whole disgusting thing on the six o'clock news. I can't believe they'd do her dirty like that, but there's no loyalty in this town. That fucking Bill Newsom, he's a slimeball if there ever was one. Crooked as my husband's teeth, he is. I didn't trust nothing that paper printed after your sister left. What's she up to now, anyway?"

"She works for a paper in Old Harbor," I say faintly. She hadn't given up on Mom. She hadn't until she had to, and she never said one thing. She let me say all those nasty things, and she never said one thing.

"Good for her. That Stevie Johansson bitch isn't as innocent as everyone says. I've had my share of Sweet addicts come in and out of here, all those fucking candy wrappers. They drive me batty. I don't have no tolerance for it, not anymore. The second I see 'em, I call the cops. If we don't fight back, the city will never do anything."

"Don't buy anything from her stores. Devyn thinks there's a possibility people are getting hooked from candy there."

"I don't give that bitch a penny of my money. Not that it does much good."

Nodding, I say, "I never thanked you for everything you did for us. I'm sorry." I wrap my arms around the woman. We're the same height, and her lush boobs press against my chest.

She leans away and grabs my chin. "You turned out all right. Was worried about you for a while, but you turned out. Your mama, now, I don't know what happened to her. Devyn called me in tears saying she couldn't pay the rent anymore and asked me to call social services. I did what I could, but sometimes, Talia, you can lead a horse to water, but you can't make 'em drink. That's what my husband's always saying, and it's true. You think about that the next time you try to make somebody do something they don't wanna, you hear? Put me on your Christmas card list. I wanna see them beautiful babies when you start poppin' 'em out. You know the address."

Patting my arm, she lets me go. She shuffles down the hallway in her slippers and turns a corner to go up to her own apartment.

I stumble down the stairs, and in the lobby, lean against a row of broken mailboxes. Devyn will be at work, and I'll be bothering her, but I don't care.

I'm about to connect the call but Beau texts me, and I jump guiltily. He probably wants to know where I am, what I'm doing, and when I'll be home, but if he's checking up on me, it's because he's worried. I shouldn't blame him for that, not when I need it so desperately.

I read the message, and I feel guiltier.

What did you mean, closet space?

His question brings tears to my eyes. He remembered.

In your room, I answer. *I want to move my things out of the guest room. Please.*

Of course, love. You never have to ask me something like that.

I wipe the tears off my face. I have no reason to cry. Beau is my home, my safe place. This building, this apartment, has never been my home. It was a place for Mom to crash, a place for me to sleep, do homework, and try to live the life of a normal teenager. Rehab wasn't a home, and neither, really, was Devyn's shabby apartment. The most recent home I've had was when we lived in Portland, and Devyn tried so hard to help me feel secure, wanted, and loved.

Now I have Beau. I will always have somewhere to go as long as he loves me.

Thank you. I love you.

I love you too, he texts back.

I send two hearts and close our messages.

Mom tried hard to make a home for us after the divorce, and I owe her for that. She could have given up the second Dad left, but she fought for us and now I need to fight for her.

With my fingers shaking, I connect to my sister's number.

She answers on the first ring. "Hey, honey, how are you doing? How's Beau? Rick's still moping around. He flew into the city today hoping he could get Beau to talk."

I ignore all that. "You paid Mom's rent while I was in rehab and while I was living with you." I make it sound like an accusation, and maybe it is. She could have told me.

She pauses. "How did you find out?"

"I'm here. At the building. I just talked to Mrs. Otto. Why would you do that?"

Devyn sighs. I'm giving her a good reason to get annoyed with me, but since I got out of rehab, she's been an expert at controlling her emotions. "Why *wouldn't* I do that? I still love her. She's still our mother, but since I picked you up from the rehab center, all I've cared about is you. You were so scared, and I only have so much energy, Talia. I wanted to keep you safe, and I didn't want you looking for her. If you're going to blame me, go ahead. I made the best decisions I could at the time, and if you think my best wasn't good enough, then so be it."

"I wish you would have told me. I worried about her, and maybe my recovery in rehab would have been easier. How she was doing, how she was fending for herself, there were days it was all I could think about."

"You can worry about her now then, because she's in the same sorry state she was in when you were arrested. I'm sorry I couldn't help her more after the *Times* fired me. I am really sorry about that. But it doesn't matter where she's living, she's not going to get better. Her addiction is eating her alive, and there's no stopping it. But you can try. You can try, and I hope to God it doesn't kill you too." She pauses. "Talia&Devyn1234."

"What's that?" I ask as an old man with a little dog pushes through the door and lets in a burst of cold air. The dog yips at me, and the man grabs it off the floor and creaks his way up the stairs without giving me a single glance.

"It's the password for the folder labeled 'Mom.' I know you saw it if you were looking at my Sweet research. If you want to know what's in it, that's the password. Talia&Devyn1234. The 'and' is an ampersand and our names are capitalized. If you go look for her, don't tell me. I couldn't bear it if anything happens to you."

She chokes on a sob, and she hangs up before I can tell her I'll be careful.

Sighing, I put the password in my Notes app. I could look through the folder now, but I'll wait until I'm at home. I like thinking of Beau's penthouse as my home, though I'm not quite there yet. A lot of his furniture isn't anything I would have picked out, and I don't have all my things, either, but moving my clothes into his bedroom will help. Devyn still has most of my stuff from our rental house in Portland—she put it in a storage unit in Old Harbor. If I can tear down the wall Beau built to keep himself from getting too close to me, I'll ask if I can have it all. I'm slowly creeping past his defenses, and I'll take my time. I have a lot of patience.

Taking a chance, I head toward Jensen Anderson's apartment, though it's just past noon.

An internet search didn't give me anything except an address and a spotty work history that could either be someone who didn't know what he wanted to do with his life or Sweet addiction. Not everyone my age knows what they want to be when they grow up, but I didn't find his name on the university's graduation list. If he's older than me, he's had plenty of time to graduate, and that doesn't give me hope he's doing much.

His building isn't located in the poorest part of the city, but it's close enough. Someone shoveled the sidewalk though, and the small entryway is scented with lemon cleaner. The security lock on the door works, forcing me to ring Jensen's apartment. I didn't look for his phone number to call ahead, too afraid he'd tell me to fuck off.

The security system buzzes, and the lock releases. I open the door and clomp up two flights of stairs.

The only building I've lived in that has an elevator is Beau's. It will most likely be the *only* building I'll ever live in that has an elevator. Not because I think Beau and I will make it, but because psychologists aren't rich and I didn't choose to become one for the money.

I reach the second floor, and Jensen's leaning against the doorjamb, glaring down the hallway. Sharply, he looks me up and down. Even from here, I can tell his eyes are bloodshot, and God only knows how long it's been since he showered last.

As I get closer, I can smell it, and saliva pools in my mouth. Sweat breaks out along my skin, and I inhale the sugary, addicting, and dangerous aroma of Sweet.

I stop five feet away from his apartment door.

"Who the hell are you?" he asks.

"My name is Talia Scott, and six years ago, you and I were at the same frat party on campus. I got hooked on Sweet that night. Serena Feeley was there—she said you know her."

"So what?"

I swallow.

If you've never been hooked, smelling Sweet is like walking

through a bakery. Nothing more, nothing less. But if you've been addicted, the sweet and saccharine scent sets off a craving that will drive you crazy.

My fingertips tingle, and my heart races.

I lick my lips.

He could French kiss me, and the traces left in his mouth from his last hit would send me right back to where I was six and a half years ago, crawling through an alley, begging for just a taste of Sweet.

"I was wondering if you knew you tried Sweet at that party, or if you woke up addicted like me and Serena."

Jensen steps aside and opens the door wider, inviting me in.

Every cell in my body screams at me to turn around and leave, to find Beau and ask him to hold me and remind me that I put all this behind me.

Instead, I follow Jensen into his apartment, and he closes the door.

CHAPTER TEN

Beau

I step into my office, and two things are waiting for me.
One I didn't expect.
One I didn't need.

"What are you doing here?" I scowl. Rick's standing by the window, staring across Cedar Hill as the citizens of this godforsaken city scurry to work like little ants.

Rick and I purchased this building and refurbished all eighty floors, and the day I chose this office, he couldn't tear me away from the view. It didn't take long for the shine to wear off.

"I thought we could talk like adults, but I see you've already moved on." He tilts his head.

Dropping my briefcase on the floor, I walk over to my desk.

A courier delivered Everett's contract, and his name is written in bold black letters on the front, upper left of the envelope.

I mutter a curse.

Backtracking, I hang up my jacket on the coat rack. "Don't bother with coffee," I tell Lola and then slam the door shut.

Rick's comment hurts. I thought him letting me out of our partnership with barely a "See ya" was the worst it could get, but I was wrong. So fucking wrong.

"Are you seriously doing business with that scumbag? After what he did to us?" *After what he did to me?* I can hear him add, even if he doesn't say it out loud.

"You must think I'm a real fucking chump," I say, swiping the manila envelope off my desk and dropping it into the empty trash can with a *thud*.

Rick catches my knuckles that are bruised and scabbed over, and I cover them with my other hand. He doesn't need to know I was angry enough to beat the shit out of Everett.

I was lucky that Talia left it alone last night. Our stupid conversation ruined what could have been a perfectly enjoyable evening in the bathtub. Then she was whispering something about closet space, and I have no idea what the fuck she was talking about.

"When did that start, huh?" I continue. "When did you start having such a shitty opinion of me? It isn't because of Devyn. She's been great, keeping her nose out of Talia's and my business, and I know if she didn't like me, she'd be all over you like flies on shit. It's not her, so what the fuck is it?"

His face heats.

Christ.

"If all you care about is the company—" I keep going because apparently he doesn't have anything to say (so why the fuck is he here?)— "I told you I'd stay until the hotel's done. That's plenty of time for you to replace me. If that's all, I have work to do. You know your way out."

I fall heavily into my chair and wake up my computer. The hotel isn't the only thing we have going on, and I'll be seeing more than the hotel to completion before I'd feel good enough to walk away.

Uncertainly, Rick steps toward me. "I'm sorry I let you down."

I open the schedule Lola sent me for the day. Meetings, back-to-back, as can be expected, and Everett is slotted in at 4:30. Fabulous. I can pound the shit out of him some more and then go home to an empty penthouse. I doubt Talia will be there—at least she was honest with how she's spending her time. "I have no fucking idea what you're talking about. Just go. Fly back to Old Harbor where you're happiest, hiding from the world with Devyn." I think of Everett's crude description of their relationship, and I grit my teeth.

He ignores me. "When Nina passed away. I should have been there for you, but I was just getting into it with Renata, and I didn't support you the way I should have. I'm sorry."

Pain hits me, swift and sharp. The black days after her death, Jasmine constantly crying on me. I couldn't eat. I couldn't sleep. I couldn't move—too drunk to stand up, too drunk to do anything except crawl to the bathroom to puke and then drink some more. I don't know how long my bender lasted. So much of that time is lost.

"There was nothing you could have done," I murmur, leaning back in my chair, my schedule forgotten. "She was breaking—" I stop.

"I knew you were having problems," Rick says, hoping I'll keep going.

I never talk about Nina, or why we were arguing that night. I don't talk about any of it. I haven't for ten years. Not to Rick, not to Bart or Kindra. Not to Jasmine. Jasmine knows—Nina must have told her everything. But she's never heard my side, will never hear my side of the things Nina said about us.

"If I had just let her go, she'd still be alive, but I couldn't.

Talia explained her addiction to me. She said she could be addicted to love, and to do it gently if I ever break it off. When she said that, it all made sense. I was in love with Nina, too much. I was addicted to her, and when she died, I went through withdrawal. Like a real addict, maybe I'll never get over her." I rub at my heart, the low, dull ache still there. I can picture her so clearly, as if it were just an hour ago I'd seen her last. Her ash blonde hair pinned in a sloppy bun on the top of her head, her brown eyes sparkling with booze, her lips shining with frosty pink lipstick. Her perfections hid her flaws. Maybe I never would have seen them . . . I was too blinded by love.

"I'm sorry. I wasn't there for you the way you were for me after the accident. After Renata left me. And I did it again when I met Devyn. I've been a shitty friend, and you're right. About all of it. I should never have moved to Old Harbor. I should never have let the site sit the way it is. You could have found a lot worse than a bag full of candy. I'm sorry. I really am."

I straighten. "What good is that now? Your apologies don't mean jack shit to me. I told you I didn't want to work here without a partner. You brushed me off hoping I'd forget or that it would blow over. You walked away from our friendship just as much as you walked away from the site. If I mean that little to you, keep walking. I didn't ask you to come here."

"Then you don't accept my apology. There's nothing I can do. You won't talk this out?" Rick shoves his hands into the pockets of his dress pants. I bet he thought I'd drag him to meetings all day, but he's not a part of this branch anymore. There are no meetings now that require his attendance.

"I *am* talking this out. You're here, aren't you? We're talking, aren't we? You're only here because I threw a tantrum and Daddy's coming to the rescue. If I wouldn't have said anything, you still would've been happy as a clam in Old Harbor while I worked my ass off trying to keep the company together. I understand you almost died. I understand you live with pain every day. I understand you hate Cedar Hill, and as long as Stevie's out there protecting her turf, Devyn shouldn't be here. I understand all that. So what I don't understand is why we're having this argument. I. Am. Fine."

"You didn't throw a tantrum, and that's not why I'm here. I'm here because you need me and I've been too stupid to see that. Meeting Devyn blew me away, but that's no excuse. You didn't take the time I offered when you met Talia, so yeah, let's blame everything on me. That's fair. I don't want to dissolve our partnership, Beau. We've worked together for twenty years, and I was hoping to work together for another twenty. What do I have to do to make this right?"

I press my lips together. I put up a stink, and that *is* the only reason he's here. Rick's saying everything I wanted him to say . . . two years ago. Even a year ago would have been better than now.

"You need to admit you're here because I bitched. It has nothing to do with our friendship. People grow apart and they go their separate ways. No one is to blame, and if you want to leave M&H, then be adult enough to tell me. I'm not the one leaving. You left a long time ago."

We sound like a couple of bickering women on one of those daytime TV talk shows, and it's enough that I get this from Talia every night.

Closet space.

I take my phone out of my pocket. *What did you mean, closet space?* I text her.

Her answer pops right after I press Send.

In your room. I want to move my things out of the guest room. Please.

Of course, love, I reply, the sad "please" breaking me. I can feel it in her words, her misery seeping out of my phone. She's hurting, and I want to call her instead of text, but I'm trying to learn. Jesus Christ, am I trying to learn not to crowd someone (I'm doing a fine job with Rick standing in my office), and I can't let my need push her away. *You never have to ask me something like that.*

Thank you. I love you.

Anything else would sound dumb. Ditto. Back at ya. She said it to me, and there's nothing I can do but say it back. *I love you too.*

She sends two red hearts in response. I ignore Rick and wait for her to say something else, but she doesn't, and I toss my phone on my desk.

"I thought I killed two people and hurt Tony Kelly," he says when I finally meet his eyes. "I thought that was me, and now that I know it wasn't, I've been trying to move forward. If you thought you killed someone, you'd walk too. Don't deny it."

I blow out a breath. I already know what I'd do if I killed someone. I killed Nina, simple as that, though the cops said it was an accident and that no one was at fault. Whether Rick remembers it or not, he was there for me. He supported me as much as I'd let him.

He keeps going. "I'm willing to spend more time in the city if you don't leave M&H, but in exchange, you need to spend time in Old Harbor."

"Why?" I ask, Talia's suggestion we move there coming back to me.

"Because if I'm going to help you run your half, then you're going to help me run mine. Compromise has to happen on both sides. You'll like Old Harbor. And if there's something you want that it doesn't have, build it."

I scoff. "Right. Did you just come up with this idea? You'd better talk to Devyn first. Talia said you and Devyn are getting married in a couple of months." I don't let that bite me in the ass either. I suspect from now on I'll hear a lot of things secondhand.

"We talked before I flew out. She said whatever I needed to do to get us back on track. She *does* like you, a lot. She admires how you treat Talia, and she said if Talia had to fall in love with anyone, she's glad it was you."

That means a lot to me, though I would never tell Rick. I admire Devyn as well. I believed for two years the accident was just a freak thing. I never had even the slightest thought that it was sabotage. We owe Devyn the future of this company, and Rick owes her his peace of mind—something it seems he's finding again. I might be bitter, but I'm still happy for him.

"What else do you have to do here? You wouldn't leave Devyn and fly to the city just to talk to me. You'd sit on it until Talia missed her sister and we made the trip out."

He winces. "You know me too well. I have a consultation with the surgeon to see what's going on with my shoulder."

"You still haven't taken care of that?"

"No. I've been avoiding it, hoping it would heal, but they think I did something to my rotator cuff and it probably needs surgery."

"When's your appointment? Do you want me to go with you?" I heave a silent sigh. I cannot learn. I just cannot stop forcing myself onto people. Rick's not a little kid and he can go to a doctor's appointment by himself. I pushed Nina to the point she ran away from me. *Literally* ran away from me. I couldn't give her an inch of space, and I suffocated her. Now I do it to everyone else I care about, and God, if I do it to Talia and she leaves . . .

He lifts his eyebrows. "Yeah? Do you mind? It's in forty-five minutes. I don't want to go, but I can't put it off. I'm so sick and tired of doctor's offices."

My heart lightens. Maybe Rick and I will be okay after all. "Then it's a good thing you're going to the hospital. I hear they heal sick people there."

"When did you turn into a smartass?" he asks, shuffling toward the door.

"I always have been. It's what keeps this company going," I say, knowing that's not entirely true. Up until the accident, Rick and I were equals.

I step from behind my desk, push my phone into my pocket, and at the coat rack, reach for my jacket.

Rick juts his jaw at my hand. "You get a good lick at him then?"

"I clocked him pretty good," I say, sliding my arms through the sleeves. "Everett's always been a pansy. He'll have a bruise for a while."

"Christ. What do you say to lunch after? I'll need a drink by then, and you can tell me about it."

"Sure," I agree as we head toward the elevator, "and you can tell me why I had to hear from my girlfriend that my best friend is getting married."

Rick laughs, and for the rest of the morning, things feel like they used to be.

That night, I help Talia move her things into my bedroom. Seeing her dresses hanging next to my suits shoves a fireball down my throat the size of Alaska, but I'll never admit it to anyone.

Not even her.

CHAPTER ELEVEN

Talia

Jensen's apartment is a pigsty, and I don't mean any offense to pigs. After living in Devyn's clean apartment, our house in Portland, and Beau's penthouse that his housekeeper cleans once a week, I'm used to sparkling bathrooms, kitchens where appliances aren't covered in grime, and carpets that are vacuumed on a regular basis.

I would bet all the money Devyn put on that debit card for me that Jensen doesn't own a vacuum.

Garbage is scattered everywhere, and it really is garbage. Old and crusty food containers, empty pizza boxes, and fast food soda cups that are tipped over, spilling their gooey, sugary contents. There isn't an empty surface anywhere.

And the candy wrappers. Jensen's addicted to more than just Sweet. All the sugar he eats will rot the teeth right out of his head. He can't stop sucking down the powdered sugar in the Sweet Stuff dipping stick packets.

The apartment's tiny, the kitchen and living area together

in one room. A short hallway leads to a bedroom, and through the open door I can see a bare mattress lying on the floor and a dirty blanket balled up at the end of it.

A whimpering comes from behind a couch that doesn't look like it's good for anything except the city dump. A small black dog mournfully peers at me, her sad brown eyes full of fear and hopelessness. Who knows when the poor thing ate last, and my visit suddenly turns into a rescue mission. I'm not leaving that little baby here to fend for herself.

"Who the hell did you say you are again?" Jensen asks, kicking at an empty chicken nugget box. He flops on the couch and turns on the TV. There's no way he'd spend money on cable, and the picture's fuzzy, proving me right, a local channel that barely comes in with a wish and a prayer. Outlines of football players run across a field.

I kneel and hold out my hand for the little dog to sniff. I hope Jensen doesn't notice when she's gone. Though, I'm not sure what he'd do. I doubt he'll remember talking to me.

"Talia Scott. I'm friends with Serena Feeley. She brought candy to the frat party. Did you try some? Do you remember Jessie Norton and Tasha Landry? We went to the party together."

He scoffs. "I don't fucking know anybody. I don't even know what fucking party you're talking about. Do you know how many parties were on campus every night? Jesus Christ. When was this again? A couple of months ago? I wasn't in school then."

I sigh. He's not going to be able to tell me anything. He doesn't know me and doesn't remember Serena. It was stupid to think I'd get anywhere talking to him, and more than likely, if Tasha and Jessie aren't clean, I won't get anywhere talking to them, either.

"Six years ago."

Grease and the scent of Sweet tangle in a sick aroma that's both mouthwatering and nauseating, and my stomach growls and churns. I'll need to eat something soon, but I can't go back to Beau's. If I do, I won't look for Mom. I'll stay there safe, while she's on the street.

"Fuck. Do you know how good I had it six years ago? I was king of the world. Going to school, had a new chick every night. Getting straight As."

The dog crawls over to me, her belly low to the ground.

"Then what?" I ask to keep him talking. He sounds like all the frat guys I used to know my first and only year at the U of M.

"I don't know, man," he says, burying his face in his hands and moaning. "I don't know. It was at a party. This goth chick and I were screwing around, totally not my thing, and she made me eat her out. I didn't want to at first, but fuck, she tasted like heaven. I woke up fucking sweating, and I felt like I was going to have a fucking heart attack. I asked her what was happening to me, and she said she put Sweet in her pussy. I didn't know what the fuck it was. I asked a buddy, and he gave me more." His voice turns into a miserable squeal and breaks on the last word. "I wanted it so bad."

"Do you still talk to her?" I ask, rubbing my fingers over the dog's head.

"Fuck no. She could be dead for all the fuck I care. She ruined my fucking life."

I heard stories like his in group when we were asked to share how we got hooked. It was part of our therapy, part of learning how to forgive ourselves. We were victims, and some had stories like Jensen. Women getting hooked giving blowjobs, or people dumping the sugary powder into their friends' drinks as a joke. That's why I always blamed myself for my addiction.

I shouldn't have gotten drunk. If I'd been sober, maybe I would have paid attention and protected myself . . . somehow.

That could have happened to Jensen at any party. Even the one I was at. He doesn't know it, but he gave me the information I wanted. He didn't get addicted eating the dipping sticks Serena brought with her.

The dog crawls into my lap.

I feel like I owe Jensen something for talking to me, and I'm going to steal his dog, after all.

"Is there anything I can do for you? Do you need money?"

Sadly, he shakes his head. "Ever feel like there's nothing to live for?"

"All the time."

I turn my head and take a deep breath of Beau's cologne that's lingering in the jacket's material. I have something to live for now, and in a couple of hours he'll be waiting for me to come home.

He said I could have closet space.

"Do you want some? I'll share it with you. It's my last one," he says, holding up a package of Sweet Stuff.

I've always preferred salt over sugar and will choose chips over candy every time. "No, thanks. I'm not a sugary type of person."

He uses the white candy dipping stick to scoop up some of the bright pink powder. "I wish I wasn't."

Addicted to Sweet, he's got more problems than diabetes and cavities.

Casually, I cuddle the dog to me and tuck her into Beau's jacket. I'm drowning in it, and there's more than enough room to hide her. I zip it up and get to my feet.

Jensen doesn't notice, lost in the football game.

"Thanks for talking to me, Jensen. I wish you the best."

I sound lame, but he's not listening anyway. I back up, stepping on an empty pizza box, cheese congealed at the bottom.

Sweet Stuff candy wrappers are scattered around his kitchen. He must crave it when he's high.

When Mom would get high, she'd eat through bags and bags of chocolate kisses, and by the time she came down, our floor would be covered in silver foil. If I could get my hands on Sweet, I gorged on salt and vinegar potato chips.

I can't stand them now. I can barely look at them without having flashbacks, but I don't let myself miss them. I have a new favorite kind.

I slip into the hallway, close his apartment door, and lean against the wall. I didn't consider how draining it would be to see who I used to be reflected in how Jensen is now.

The dog pokes her head out of Beau's jacket and licks me on the chin. "Yeah, I feel that." I'm relieved to get out of there too.

Jensen wasn't creepy—God, I've met creepy—but druggies have an edge they can't hide, and being alone with him wasn't the best idea. I promised Beau I'd be safe and the first thing I do is willingly go into an apartment that belongs to a man I don't know. Well, second, but Mrs. Otto isn't dangerous. Jensen could have done anything to me and I wouldn't have been able to stop him.

I wonder how many times Devyn put herself in danger looking for information. Thinking back, she wasn't that rattled the day Stevie shot at her on Beau and Rick's site. I've been around my share of guns and violence, but I was either high and nothing fazed me, or I was hoping to score and I would have done whatever it took to find enough Sweet to make the craving stop, even if it was only for a few seconds.

I don't want to hang around long enough for Jensen to realize I took his dog, and I hurry down the carpeted hallway, but she's so skinny maybe he never will. There's one more thing I want to do before I go home, but I pause outside Jensen's building. He didn't take me up on my offer of help, but I still can. I take my cell phone out of Beau's jacket pocket.

"Cedar Hill Police Department, how may I help you?"

"I'd like to request a welfare check at 2234 Carver Boulevard, apartment 208. My co-worker's name is Jensen Anderson. He hasn't been to work for a few days, and he told me he doesn't have family in the city. I hope he's okay."

She asks me a few questions as I walk down the snowy sidewalk, my arm under the dog's butt to keep her from sliding to the ground, and I answer them the best I can. Hopefully they'll arrest him and send him to rehab. That's the best I can do, and walking toward Camden Way, I try not to think about it anymore.

I inhale the cool air to get the smell of Sweet and grease out of my nose. Stepping into Jensen's apartment was dangerous in more ways than one, but I'm stronger than I thought or Beau made me that way. I'd never do anything to risk what we have.

Not even for Sweet.

It's not that cold, but the tip of my nose and my cheeks are stinging by the time I reach Serena and Aaron's church.

A bell attached to the door that I didn't notice before jingles as I step into the warm foyer. The scent is still the same, stale coffee and staler cookies, and the same notices are pinned to the cork board, but Serena's smile is brighter than the last time I saw her. She holds out her hands and says, "Talia, I'm so glad to see you again. Who do you have with you?"

"I rescued her from Jensen's apartment. I had to call the police and ask them to check on him. He's not doing very well. Jensen, I mean, but probably the dog too," I explain as I unzip my jacket. "I'm bringing her to the animal shelter . . . unless you want her?"

Serena lifts the puppy out of my arms and snuggles her against her chest.

"We welcome all lost souls," Aaron says, stepping up behind Serena and wrapping his arm around her and the dog. "We're just starting a meeting. Come and sit."

It would be rude to turn down an invitation to listen in on their meeting, and they don't have to tell me what kind it is. But I'm still hungry, and my stomach chooses that exact moment to growl.

Serena laughs and lets the dog lick at her lips. "There's pizza, and we'll see if we can find something for this little girl. She's skin and bones."

"Okay, thanks."

I follow them into a room that I missed the first time I was here, and I sit next to a man who has sad and tired eyes.

In the semi-circle, we take turns, and the words come easy. "My name is Talia, and I'm a recovering Sweet addict."

"Hi, Talia," they all say back to me.

There are others like me, Sweet addicts in recovery. Some were hooked on coke, others heroin. One woman was addicted to prescription painkillers after back surgery. We all share a little about ourselves—how we cope and who we have supporting us. The woman doesn't have anyone. Her husband left her and took their kids. She lives in her mom's basement and tries to go to work every day, but her back pain is still bad and her doctor said there's nothing else they can do.

The man sitting next to me lost his family because of Sweet and lives in a halfway house not far from here. I hold his hand to support him while he speaks. That could have been me. If I hadn't had Devyn, that *would* have been me.

The dog sniffs at our feet, lightening the atmosphere. We nibble on pizza between stories, confessions, and tears.

"Does anyone want to say anything before we close for the evening?" Aaron asks.

"I do," I say, surprising myself. I've never been one to volunteer information, my therapists always having to pry everything out of me. "For a long time, I blamed myself, and maybe where you come from in this life, you deserve that blame. We're adults, and we made our choices. You made bad ones, having to be here, but you make good ones too, because you're here."

A couple people in the group laugh.

"You've heard this all before, probably a million times. I know I have. You have to forgive yourself for being human. I put my sister through a lot of pain, and I can see it in her eyes. I have to let that go. I don't want to hurt her anymore, and that's all I'll do if I can't move forward. I met a guy, and I want to be able to say that I deserve him. So I'll keep that in the back of my mind, and maybe that will help me make good choices too."

Everyone stares at the floor, some nodding and mulling over my words. The man next to me wipes tears off his cheeks.

"Thanks, Talia," Serena says as we get ourselves together. "Thanks for coming, everyone, and Aaron and I will see you next week."

We all stand, and the metal chairs creak. The woman who has the bad back rises slowly, and it reminds me of Rick and the careful way he moves. I'm glad he has my sister. He'll be okay as long as she's watching out for him.

I leave behind the people who linger, reluctant to step out of the safety of that little room. For many, they'll go home to an empty apartment and pray until the sun comes up.

I have one last thing to do, and then I'll go home too.

"You're welcome to come back," Serena says, standing at the door with me. The sun set, and the streets are dark.

"Thank you." I unzip the inside pocket of Beau's jacket and

pull out the cash I didn't need the first time I looked for Serena here. "I want you to have this. It's not very much, but I know someone who might be able to donate on a regular basis. You and Aaron are doing good work, and I hope you can keep it going. There are people who depend on this place."

Serena doesn't want me to see how eager she is to count the bills I nudge into her hand, and she tries to push back an excited smile. I didn't give her hundreds of dollars, but in a place like this, every penny counts.

"Thanks. You did good for yourself, didn't you?" she asks, tilting her head.

"I did, but I owe it all to my sister. I'm so sorry, Serena. I'm so sorry your parents wouldn't help you." I hug her to me and cry into her shoulder.

"Shh," she says, smoothing my hair. "I made peace with it a long time ago. You said a lot of things those people hear all the time, but you know what else?"

I shake my head against her thin sweater.

"You can choose your family. Aaron's my family now, and so are those people. The pastor of this church. The director of the Salvation Army next door. We're family, and I'll count you as my family too. Come back when you're ready. I have a feeling there's a lot you can offer anyone who comes here."

Sniffling, I lean away. "I will."

"Be careful going home. It's cold, and the wind's picking up."

"Thanks. Say goodbye to Aaron for me. And thanks for keeping Jensen's dog. I didn't want to take her to the shelter."

"She'll be okay with us. Come see her anytime."

"Thanks. Goodnight, Serena."

"Goodnight."

I step into the dark, but my heart is light.

It's not dinnertime yet, but the sun has completely disappeared. In the darkness, the frozen streets are heavy with hope-lessness, but I've been on these streets in the summer, and still, that feeling never fades. It's not only the season or the time of day that strangles you—it's the place and what happens here.

I walk down block after block, my face tucked into the collar of Beau's jacket in a poor attempt to keep my cheeks from freezing. No one is on the streets, even the prostitutes have found a place to go. It's too cold to walk to Arrowhead Alley tonight—where my mom probably is. The Alley's full of home-less people who take shelter in the dead end and warm them-selves with barrel fires. I haven't been down that alley since I was one of them. Addicts who stick together.

You can choose your family.

The addicts of Arrowhead Alley have chosen theirs.

I go back the way I came, walking past the bar. Tired and run-down, people sit hunched on barstools sipping cheap whiskey, but I don't see them. I see myself in the window's reflection, a girl who belongs on these streets, but at the same time, doesn't.

Beau would say I belong with him, in his penthouse, and with the way he holds me at night, I believe it.

On the bus ride going downtown, I stand for most of the way. The bus is full of people, but most of them don't have anywhere to get off. They'll sit until the driver parks at the bus station, and they'll sleep inside until the buses start running again.

The doorman opens the door for me, and stepping into the building, I see Beau striding through the elegant lobby. The concierge nods, and I lift a hand. I scoot into the elevator just before the doors close and stand next to Beau. He's so hand-some dressed for work, his briefcase hanging from a gloved hand.

"Going up?" he asks, amused.

I push back a smile. "Yes, please."

"Live around here?"

"Yes, I do." I stare straight ahead. If I look up at him, I'll start laughing and spoil his game.

"With a boyfriend?"

"Yes."

"He's a lucky guy."

"Thank you."

"Do you love him?"

There's something in his voice, and we're not playing anymore.

"Yes."

"Does he love you?"

I answer honestly. "I think so."

"Why do you only think so?"

I put my hand in his. "He's afraid to get close. I think someone hurt him, and he doesn't know me well enough to know that I won't."

"Are you strong enough to convince him?"

I look at him as the elevator doors glide open revealing a foyer that I've come to call home. "I made it through six months of Sweet addiction and three years of rehab. I'm strong enough."

Beau meets my eyes. "He's going to need that."

I squeeze his hand. "Then I'm ready."

———

His mouth quirks. "Hi."

I let out a laugh then, our game over. "Hi."

"I'm glad you're home tonight."

"Me too."

He drops his briefcase and kisses me, holding the side of my face with his hand. I breathe him in, the scent in real life that kept me going all day, and my lips tremble under his.

"I'm going to change and make dinner. What do you think about grilled cheese and soup?" I have no idea if he eats grilled cheese sandwiches and soup. It used to be one of Devyn's and my regular meals. Not only was it cheap, but in the wintertime, it was comfort food. Tonight, the bread is a twelve-dollar loaf of multi-grain, the cheese gourmet, and the soup a fancy brand I've never heard of, but it will work. I want Beau to feel cozy and loved in a penthouse that has felt empty for so long.

"Sounds good. I'll change too."

"Tomorrow we'll change in the same room."

"That's right," he says, helping me take his coat off and hanging it up in the closet. "Closet space."

"I'm not letting you back out."

"I wouldn't dream of it," he murmurs, his gaze following me as I round the corner to the guest room I won't be using anymore.

I change into lounging pants and a tank top, reveling in the warmth of the room and the soft material of my pajamas. I'm done first, and in the kitchen, start buttering bread and slicing cheese. He walks into the kitchen dressed in a pair of lounging pants and a t-shirt and pauses. He looks at me out of the corners of his eyes and reaches for his whiskey bottle, but after the day I've had, I could watch him guzzle the whole thing and be nothing but thankful for where I am right now.

"Rick came to the office today. Did you tell Devyn what we talked about, by chance?" he asks, leaning against the counter.

I lay the pieces of bread butter-side down on the griddle. "No. That might get a little tricky sometimes, huh?" I ask, glancing over my shoulder at him. "I always think before I tell her something because I know it will get back to Rick. I *did* call

Devyn today, but not about that. Did you smooth things over with him?"

"Some. I wanted to be sure he came to me on his own, that you didn't tell Devyn I was having a hard time."

I'm glad I was smart enough to stay out of their business and that I can tell him the truth. "Nope."

Slowly, he nods, finding what he needs to believe me. I'm not hurt. I could have easily called Devyn the way she called me. I'm sure she doesn't tell me everything that she and Rick talk about, and I don't want to know. Just like I'll never tell her everything that's between Beau and me.

"What did you do today?" he asks.

I finish putting the sandwiches together and pour two jars of tomato and basil soup into a pot on the stove. "I went to our old apartment. The one Mom and I lived in when we were both addicted."

"Why? What were you looking for?"

Using a spatula, I lift the corners of our sandwiches. I don't want to burn them. I'm not a very impressive cook, and Perfect Pasta is proof of that, but I don't want to ruin what little I know how to make. I shrug. "I don't know. I talked to our old land-lady. She told me Devyn paid for Mom to live there the entire time I was in rehab and the year Devyn and I lived together before we had to move to Portland. I spent years hating my sister, thinking she didn't love our mother as much as I did. It made me feel like a real piece of shit." I stare at our sandwiches, ashamed.

"I've felt like that, a time or two," he murmurs. "That's what you talked to Devyn about today?"

"Yeah." I flip our sandwiches over. They're perfect. With a wooden spoon, I gently stir the soup and say, "All she said was that she was doing her best and that she wanted to keep me safe. She's had so much on her plate for the past few years."

"Rick will take care of her now." He rubs the nape of my neck with his warm hand.

"If Stevie Johansson's out there, he'll always have to."

"That's true," he murmurs. "Those look good. Let's eat in the living room."

"Yeah. Help me dish up the soup, will you?"

"Sure."

We settle on the couch, and I nibble on my sandwich, my feet wedged between his thigh and the couch cushion. Since he started opening up, I feel more comfortable around him. I wiggle my toes and he smiles around a mouthful of melted cheese.

"What else did you do?" he asks.

I decide to skip the part about going to see Jensen and being alone with him in his apartment. It was stupid, and I won't do something like that again. "I went to see Serena and stayed for an NA meeting."

"How did that go?" he asks, trading his empty grilled cheese plate for his soup bowl.

"Good. Strange, in a lot of ways, but good. She asked me to come back, and I probably will. Would you want to go some-time? Meet Serena and her boyfriend?" The invitation slips out of my mouth, and I feel just as stupid as when I learned Devyn hadn't kicked Mom out on her ass. Beau's not going to want to go with me. There's nowhere he'd fit in less.

He pauses, the spoon halfway to his mouth. I stiffen and wait for him to say no, but he says, "Yeah? You'd share that part of your life with me?"

"We can't have a relationship if I don't," I point out. Being a recovering Sweet addict is seventy-five percent of who I am. We wouldn't be able to survive as a couple if I was only willing to give him the twenty-five percent I was okay with. "But you don't have to do something like that. It's all right."

"No, I want to." He sets his soup bowl aside and puts my empty plate on the coffee table. "You were right, in the elevator. I don't talk about her. With anyone. Not even Rick. She was an alcoholic and was rarely sober, but she was high-functioning. She was an event planner, and that's how we met. She said it gave her an excuse to party all day, though she didn't need one."

I lean against the back of the couch. "What happened?"

His gaze slides away from my face, and I know he's only going to tell me half the truth. He's not ready to tell me everything, and I try not to be hurt. That he's sharing is enough for now.

"She didn't want to be in a relationship anymore. She said I never gave her time to herself. It's part of the reason I hid after you moved in. All I wanted was to be around you, but I didn't want to smother you." He brushes a piece of hair out of my face. "Trust me, Talia, when you moved in, all I wanted was to be with you."

"Oh," I breathe. "The night you brought it up, I thought you had a girlfriend who wouldn't leave you alone."

"No. I'm the guilty one."

I let out a shaky laugh. "Thank God. I thought I was going to have to figure out how to give you more space." I crawl into his lap. "All I want is to be with you too."

"Really?" he asks, doubt in his voice, his lips skimming over my jaw.

"Really." I pause. "I have a question for you." Now that we're talking about Serena, her church, and NA, I don't want to forget to ask. I promised her, and it could make a real difference to their church and the people they're helping.

"What's that?" Under my tank top, he presses his hand to my skin, and I shiver.

"Does M&H have a foundation set up for nonprofit organizations to apply for grants?"

"Yeah. I don't handle any of that, though. Why?"

"I told Serena I'd put her in touch with a place that could probably help her church out. They run on a pretty tight budget, but they do a lot of good work there." I rub my fingers over his scruff. Just home from work, he's always so sexy. He changed out of his suit, but I like this casual side of him too.

"She doesn't have to do that. I can write them a check, Talia."

"I appreciate that, but I think they'd accept it easier if they went through the normal process. Though, I wouldn't tell you no if you wanted to flag their application and push it through."

He nods. "I can do that. Come to my office. I'll email you the form, and you can forward it to your friend."

"Right now?"

"Sure. It's January. They can apply for enough to set them up for the year, then they can reapply next January."

I wiggle off his lap and follow him into his study. I've never been in here, and I stare through the wall of windows that shows off what seems to be all the lights in the city. "If you can look at this all the time, how do you get any work done?"

"I've gotten used to it," he says, sitting behind his computer.

Bookshelves take up the other walls, and the same bluish-grey carpet that's in the living room and guest room covers the floor in here too.

"Don't you get lonely?"

He flicks a glance at me. "Sometimes. It was especially hard when you first moved in and I knew you were in your room or sitting at the kitchen table by yourself."

"Soon I'll have a lot of homework," I say, wandering around, my toes sinking into the soft piling.

"I'll be sure to leave you alone," he mutters, bringing up a document and scrolling through the pages.

"That's not what I was getting at, but okay. Can I have a

desk in here? Would you be able to do your work if I was in here too, doing my homework?"

"That's not necessary. I can turn one of the guest rooms into a study."

I sag. I suppose I'd be too much of a distraction. Beau never stops talking about how much work he has to do now that Rick's in Old Harbor for good. I stop in front of a bookshelf and look at a framed picture of Beau and Rick shaking hands in front of a building. I can't tell which building—the picture's too cropped. They look young and happy. It's strange to see Rick's face without his scar. I wonder if this picture was taken before or after the girlfriend that broke up with Beau.

"That's okay," I say, trying to sound like I'm not going to cry. "I can work in the kitchen, or I'll go to the library."

He stands, and I feel him come up behind me. "Talia?"

I shrug and pretend he didn't hurt my feelings. "I wanted to be with you, that's all."

Nudging my shoulder, he asks me to turn around. "Nina taught me the value of personal space. You need it, and I need it. I don't want you to get tired of me, love."

"What if you get tired of me? I used to be an addict. What if you get tired of that? What if you get tired of me living here? Therapy, meetings, school. I'm high maintenance, Beau."

Scowling, he says, "That will never happen."

"How can you be sure?"

He shakes his head. "We can't be sure about something like that."

"And we can't be sure that if we're always together whenever you're not at work and I'm not online taking classes that we'll get sick of each other. I want to be with you."

"I want to be with you too. You really want a desk in here?"

"I really do."

"Okay. I'll have one delivered. Any special requests?"

I wrinkle my nose, and he laughs. "Lots of drawers. A big blotter. I'm an office supply junkie, but I was trying to keep you from finding out."

"An office supply junkie who has big plans if you need a big blotter," he says, a smile playing with his mouth.

Since he's in a good mood, I'll chance one more request. "Speaking of big plans, I did have something else to ask."

"I don't know if I can handle anymore," he says, chuckling, sitting behind his desk again. "Grants and desks and office supplies."

"Well, it does have to do with my stuff."

"What's your email address?"

"TaliaJeanScott@gmail.com."

"Nice and simple. I like it. I sent you the grant application, and you can forward the information to your friend. There are instructions on the last page that will tell her what she needs to do once she has it filled out."

"Thanks."

He turns to me. "Now, what stuff are we talking about?"

"My stuff from our house in Portland. Devyn sent me some of it, but most of my things are in storage in Old Harbor."

"You want your stuff?" he asks, and his eyes are so bright. If I had known this would've made him so happy, I would have asked a long time ago.

"I want my stuff." I crawl into his lap and wrap my arms around his neck. "Because I have closet space."

He searches my eyes, like he can't believe he found me. "How did I get so lucky?"

"Yesterday, Serena and I were talking about reasons to stay sober. I told her about you, and she said God sent me to you when you needed me. Now that I know about Nina, I think maybe that's true. The first week I stayed here, I searched for you online, and seeing you with a different woman every night—"

"Talia—"

"No, let me finish. I looked at the pictures, and your eyes, they were so empty. You'd be going somewhere glamorous, a beautiful woman on your arm, but you weren't feeling anything. Serena said that, and I realized she's right. You need me, and I will do whatever I need to do to be here for you. No matter what."

He swallows. "What can I give you?" he asks, his voice raspy. "Besides closet space?"

"Everything." I want it all.

"No one's ever asked me for that before."

I brush a kiss over his lips. "Then I'll be the first person you give it to."

He clears his throat, and holding me in his arms, he stands. "Let's start with the closets. How many clothes do you have?"

"A lot," I say, thinking about all the clothes Devyn hasn't sent me yet, "but a girl could always use more."

"Then I'll make sure you have more. I went to the bank today after lunch with Rick and added you to my accounts. I had to text Devyn and ask for your social security number and birthdate. I hope you don't mind. I have a debit and credit card for you. You have complete access, so please don't clean me out." He laughs and sets me to my feet in his, I mean, *our,* bedroom.

"You didn't have to do that." I never want him to think I'm with him for his money.

"I should have a long time ago. I don't ever want you to need anything, Talia. Whatever is mine belongs to you now. And that includes all my office supplies."

"Thank you." I can barely get the words out.

"You're welcome."

Beau doesn't have to do much rearranging to make room for me. The suite was designed for a couple, and his suits, though he has many, only use a quarter of the walk-in closet. Twenty minutes later, my clothes are hanging next to his, and my beat-up suitcase is shoved in a dark corner along with the promise of a matching luggage set as a replacement.

He can't stop staring at one of my dresses, a long-sleeved emerald green, that hangs next to one of his black suits. I think it looks nice, like they belong together. Like Beau and I do.

Squeezing his hand, I tell him I'm going to clean up the kitchen, and he's still standing there, half an hour later, his eyes damp. I ask him to take me to bed, and he does.

CHAPTER TWELVE

Beau

I made love to her all night. Didn't leave her alone for one second, and she didn't mind.

Sitting on the edge of the bed, I brush the hair away from her face. She didn't get much sleep last night. I didn't either, but I still got up and got ready for work. Rick stayed in the city until quitting time, and we figured out what we'd do with M&H. I thought he wouldn't be a part of this branch anymore, and I have a few business moves I need to take back.

"What are your plans for the day?" I ask, and then wince. Nina hated it whenever I asked her that. She'd accuse me of checking up on her. Took an innocent question and turned it into something threatening. I want to give Talia all the space she needs, but so far, whenever I take one step back, she takes two forward.

I won't lie to myself and say that it will last.

She lifts onto an elbow. "I want to try to find my mom."

"Do you know where to look?" I don't like that she goes into that part of the city alone, but I can understand why she does. She has a better chance of finding people who will talk to her if she's not marching Camden Way with Mack behind her or cruising the streets in a bulletproof SUV. I want her safe, but I'm not stupid. A bodyguard shadowing her won't help her find answers. Talia has the same grit and determination as her sister, and Devyn's stepped into more than her share of trouble.

She lowers her gaze. "Yeah."

I lift her head with my finger under her chin. "I can't keep you here. All I can do is ask you to be careful, and if you need anything, call me. I'll be right there, no questions asked, no matter what."

Nodding, she says, "Okay."

"What are you going to do if you find her?"

"I don't know. Devyn says she's a lost cause. She paid for Mom's apartment and was willing to help her, so maybe I should believe it's true, but I can't let it go until I see her for myself. I can't put this behind me until I know for sure."

Naked, she crawls into my lap and wraps her arms around me.

I brush my hand down the soft skin of her back, and she rests her cheek against my shoulder. "If you think she'll take the help, we'll talk about it. I'll pay for rehab and whatever else she'll need."

"I think I'm the lucky one," she whispers, tightening her grip.

"We don't give up on family, but I have to make this clear, Talia. All I care about is you. I love you."

"I understand, and when the time comes that you want me to stop, I will. Because I love you too."

She's Devyn's sister one hundred percent, and I might admire Devyn's tenacity, but I don't want Talia to push this aside. It's too important. I put my hand over her belly. "We've been having sex without protection. A lot. We haven't talked about it, but you've started some of it, so I assume you understand what that means."

She covers my hand with hers. "Do you want us to stop?"

"I don't want you to get pregnant if you don't want to be. You're in school, and you're young." *You might want to find someone your own age,* I think, but I don't say the words out loud. Would never give her that idea.

"You think we're not ready for babies," she whispers.

"I think *you're* not ready for babies, and I've been selfish."

Looking up at me, she says, "I have been too. I keep thinking that if I get pregnant you won't leave, but that's dumb. It would never stop you from leaving me."

"And a baby would never stop you from leaving me, not if you really wanted to go. We can't do anything about what we've already done, but if you're not, we'll talk. Do you know when your period is due?"

She shakes her head. "Not really. I'm not regular. It could be tomorrow, or I could skip January completely. I won't know until I get it."

I blow out a breath. "Then we'll have to wait and see. This wasn't a conversation I thought we'd have this morning, but it's good we did. I never want anything I've done to make you unhappy, love. I know I can't make you as happy as I want you to be, but I don't want to make you sad because of the choices I've made."

A corner of her mouth lifts. "Would you want it if I am?"

It's my turn to smile, and I answer without a moment's hesitation. "Yeah. A little girl who looks like you? Yeah. That's why I'm asking you to be careful out there."

"I'll stay here if you ask me to."

It took a lot for her to say it, but it doesn't make me feel better. I'd never ask her to choose between me and her family.

"And hate me for it." I kiss her forehead. "I'll see you tonight. Good luck, Talia. I hope you find her."

I don't give her a chance to respond. I stand and walk out of the room, tempted to take her up on her offer. We can't lock them up, I think, Rick's words coming back to me, but I'll never stop wanting to.

———

It's early, but I ask Mack to stop at a little florist's shop, and I buy a bouquet of baby pink roses.

Jasmine's at the gallery, directing a maintenance man who's hanging a large painting of a dark forest lit with fireflies. She's been a good friend for a long time, but lately, the friendships I've had with the people who knew Nina are fading. Rick had Renata, and because of that, he didn't keep in touch with the group after Nina's death like I have.

Sometimes it's better to move on, even if it hurts. Meeting Talia and falling in love with her, I started a new chapter of my life, and this time, the old won't live with the new.

"Beau, what are you doing here?" she asks, catching me staring at her.

"I wanted to apologize for the other night," I say, holding out the bouquet.

"You didn't need to, but thanks," she says, taking the flowers and inhaling their scent. "I have a vase in my office. Do you want a cup of coffee?"

"Do you have decaf?" I ask, following her down a brightly lit hallway to a spacious office. I've been here a few times, but not many. Jasmine landed this gig long after Nina passed away.

She wrinkles her nose. "No. Why did you start drinking that? Do you have heart problems? I've always told you that you work too hard."

"Talia drinks it, and so I started too. Caffeinated stuff gives me the jitters now."

She scoffs. "How much more of your life are you going to change for her?"

"I'd change it all if she would stay with me." I know how dangerous it sounds, but this is Jasmine. If I can't tell her the truth, I can't tell anyone.

"You know how fucked up that is, right?" she asks, dropping the flowers on her desk and shoving her fists onto her hips.

"I love her," I say, like it's a legitimate excuse. Putting my hands in my pockets, I walk around her office. A framed photo of Jasmine, Nina, and me standing outside a bar laughing sits on a bookshelf full of art books. I remember that night. Bart took the picture. Nina looks happy, but she was angry I showed up. I'd told her that morning I would have to work late. In a normal life, the woman who loved me would have been happy I made it out, but not Nina. One more night she hadn't had to herself, she said bitterly, but all I wanted was to see her after a long day.

"You loved Nina too," Jasmine says, walking up behind me, her heels clicking against the tiled floor. "Look how that turned out."

"She told you, didn't she? That she wanted to break off our engagement."

"Yeah. I told her to give it time, that she was just nervous."

"Why did you defend me?" I can't stop staring at Nina. Even though the photo's in black and white, she glows. She was so full of life. Boozy, sparkling life. I was drawn to that. Her laughter, her energy. She brightened my world, and I wanted to consume her. I needed her light to bleed into me, until there was nothing left of her but me.

"Why wouldn't I? You loved her. You would have given her anything." Her voice is clipped and bitter. "I loved her. I truly did. She was my best friend, but she didn't deserve you."

I turn to her in surprise. "Then why would you tell her not to break it off?"

Her eyes fill with tears. "Because I knew if she had her way, I'd never see you again. I've been in love with you since the day we met. Nina brought you to our apartment, and that was it for me. I was stupid and after the accident thought that I had a chance, but you never stopped loving her. Never stopped loving who you thought she was."

"Jasmine, it's been ten years. You've wasted ten years." I brush my thumb over her cheek. "I'm so sorry."

"Yes, I guess it has been a waste, hasn't it?" She jerks away. "Waiting for you to look at me, but instead, all you do is fall in love with another addict. What is it with you and druggies, Beau? You choose women who can't give you everything they have because they've already given it to their addiction. You think Talia will never relapse? Sweet is all over this godforsaken city."

"She's been sober for a long time. Nina didn't want to stop drinking, wouldn't, even though I asked her several times to dry out. Talia fought to stay in rehab for longer than they wanted to let her. It wasn't her fault she was hooked."

"And that makes it okay?" She shakes her head. "I told Nina to think about it. Ask you for a long engagement instead of the few weeks you needed to wait for the license. She didn't want to marry you at all. She should never have said yes."

I tell her the truth. "She was drunk when I asked."

"Yeah, well, I believe that. Nina had two settings: drunk and hungover. If you'd waited until she was hungover, you might have gotten an honest answer." She studies my face and starts laughing. "You knew what she would have said. Why did you bother to ask her if you knew?"

"She didn't tell you?" I grip the keys in my jacket pocket, and the metal bites into my skin.

"Tell me what?" She frowns.

"That I asked her the day she found out that she was pregnant. I wanted us to be married when she had the baby. She didn't want to get married. She didn't want the baby either." I picture Talia with a bump. I don't learn. I take what I want, consequences be damned, and I don't learn, no matter how many people get hurt in the process. "It's why we were arguing that night. It wasn't about the breakup. She wanted an abortion. She told me on Valentine's Day that she didn't want my baby."

Jasmine covers her mouth with a shaking hand.

"I should have let her go. I should have let her do what she wanted. She'd still be alive."

"I . . . I didn't know. If I had, I would have tried to talk to her—"

"There was nothing you could have said. It's over, and I've moved on the best I can. I didn't know how you felt about me, and you can call me all the names you want. I didn't see it, and I'm sorry. But even if I had, I wouldn't have done anything about it. I don't feel that way about you. You were Nina's best friend, a buffer in a lot of ways, and I'll always remember that."

She freezes, and her voice is just as cold. "You didn't come here to say you're sorry. You came here to say goodbye."

"There's no point in staying in touch. Find a life for yourself, Jasmine. Find a nice guy, someone who will treat you right, and settle down. You deserve that. Your friendship reminds me of everything I want to forget."

I step into the hallway and walk out of the gallery. I pause beside the truck and take a deep breath of cold air. I'm still shaking, but Mack's holding the door open for me, and I slide into the back seat of the SUV.

I'll miss her, but I won't miss the baggage I carried being her friend. I only kept up with Bart and Kindra because of Jasmine, and they won't even realize I'm gone.

Mack lets me out in front of M&H.

Resting my hand on the door, I say, "Shadow Talia today, please, but stay out of sight. She's trying to find her mother, and I think she'll be going to Arrowhead Alley and around in that area. Don't step in unless she needs help."

"I understand, sir."

"Good. No need to keep me updated. That she's safe is my only concern. I'll get myself home."

"Yes, sir."

"Thanks."

Mack nods and takes his place behind the wheel as I trot up the stone steps toward the building.

I told Talia I wouldn't interfere, and this is fine for now. Mack will keep an eye on her. If she finds out, she'll hate me, but I'm doing what I think is best.

I'd rather she walk away because I cared too much than let her think I didn't care enough to keep her safe.

When I break for lunch, I order her a beautiful dove grey desk. It has several drawers and a cream blotter that covers the entire surface.

I'll never get any work done if I can watch her do her homework, but unlike the view of the city, that is one picture I'll never take for granted.

CHAPTER THIRTEEN

Talia

After Beau leaves, I start the shower. I can't help but stand sideways and study my reflection, my hand skimming over my flat stomach. It's stupid. I wouldn't show for months yet.

It's not something I'm ready for, and Devyn would be disappointed. But I'm a woman, a woman in love, and the idea I'm carrying Beau's baby puts a dopey smile on my face all morning.

I get ready for the day as usual, and by nine, I'm sitting in front of my laptop with a cup of coffee and a buttered English muffin.

Using the password Devyn gave me, I open the folder that has Mom's information in it.

There's a Word document inside that's full of dates and times when she saw Mom, beginning the day I was arrested. That date will be seared into my brain forever.

I didn't know Devyn kept such a close eye on us. The cops busted that party and arrested me and several others, but I didn't use my phone call. I didn't think I had anyone to call. I wouldn't have been in that mess if I'd gone to live with Devyn like she wanted. Living with Mom, I had no reason to stay home, but Devyn would have made sure I was doing my homework, helping with the chores, and all the other things she encouraged me to do in Portland. I won't blame my addiction on my mother or the fact that she hasn't been one since her first taste of Sweet, but it's a possibility that if I had been living with Devyn, I wouldn't have gone to that frat party. Anyway, I hadn't called her, but she knew. She knew about me getting arrested, and she hired an attorney who talked me out of jail time and into rehab.

She's always been careful not to act like my mother, but from the night Mom went to that dinner party, that's all she's been.

There are pages and pages of all the times she saw Mom and the money she gave her. Envelopes she left with a priest named Father Will. Until one day, the entries stop. Just like that.

The day we moved out of Cedar Hill.

Only one more date was written after our move. She drove into the city to celebrate Thanksgiving with us, and she looked for Mom on her way out of town and left money at the Catholic church.

She never stopped caring about our mother. She only cared about me more.

I skim through the pages. Arrowhead Alley is where she found Mom the most often, but maybe once out of every five times she looked there. Those aren't great odds, but maybe this Father Will can give me some ideas on where else to look. It hasn't been that long since Devyn spoke with him, and if something happened to Mom, she would have told me or noted it in the file.

While I finish my English muffin, I look over the list of our friends Serena gave me. I'd love to find Jessie, and Tasha too, but after seeing Jensen, I don't think talking to the other frat boys will do any good. They won't remember me, and being drunk at the party, I won't remember them either.

I still have an account on a popular social media site and search for Jessica Norton. We're still "friends," but I haven't talked to her since I dropped out of school. She looks strung out in her profile picture. Lines crease her puffy face, and stress shadows her eyes. Her hair's brittle, and the brunette color is already turning grey. I'm still logged in, though I can't remember the last time I was on here, and I can see she's active. I message her in chat. *Hi. How have you been?*

The tiny picture of her face drops down to my message. She read it. I don't know if she'll answer, and I chew on a fingernail while I wait.

Three waving dots appear, and then: *Hi. I'm okay. How are you?*

Better than I have been. Can we meet up?

I don't want to chat online. I want to see her, ask if she's addicted to Sweet, and if she is, where she was when she got hooked. If she knows.

OK. I live with Foster Dawson. Do you remember him from school?

No, I don't know who he is. He might have been in one of my generals, but 101 classes at the university were huge, and unless you introduced yourself, getting to know someone was impossible.

No, sorry, I don't. Are you busy? Can I come see you today?

She doesn't respond for over five minutes, and just when I

think she decided she doesn't want to talk to me after all, an address pops up that's not far from Jensen's. *I'm home all day.*

I'll leave now. See you soon.

OK. TTYL

TTYL, I reply.

I click out of the social media site, go back to Mom's file, and I write down the Catholic church's name and Google the address. It's too cold to wander around without knowing where I'm going. The picture that pops up with the search results is of an old church, but a real one, unlike Haven Presbyterian. Made of stone with a tall steeple jutting into the sky, it's located on a rundown street. At the moment the photo was taken, a down-trodden man sat hunched on the concrete steps, perfectly capturing everything that church does and the area in which it was built.

I don't know how I'm going to find Jessie and Foster. I mean, I know where to find them, but will they be in the same situation as Jensen, or will they both be sober? They have a roof over their heads, but in that part of the city, that roof could be full of holes. I want to give them something, but I don't know what. Money? I can't save everyone. I already rescued Jensen's dog, asked the police to check on him, and forwarded the grant form to Serena. I can't find all the people in my old life and give them what they need. Without Devyn and Beau, *I* wouldn't have what I need. It's only because of them that I'm in a better place than any of the people in my past.

I change into jeggings and a sweater, and put on my black boots and Beau's jacket. Mack isn't parked on the street, and I'm glad I don't have to try to avoid him. I gave all my cash to Serena, and I stop at an ATM. I want to keep some with me just in case.

Before Beau left for work, he left the bank cards out that he told me about last night. I don't want them, and they're still on the counter near the toaster. I don't need his money. The debit card Devyn gave me has more than enough on it, and once classes start, I decided that I'm going to stop investigating. If I'm on the streets, I won't give my classes the attention they deserve, and I can't be like Devyn, sneaking out in the middle of the night. Beau would know, and now that I've moved into his room, I don't want to miss a single second sleeping next to him.

There's a bus stop on the corner near Jessie and Foster's building, and I don't have to walk far before I can step inside the warm entryway. Glancing up at a light fixture that has a bunch of dead bugs in it, I send up a quick prayer of thanks. Arrowhead Alley is a couple miles away from where the bus will let me off, and I'll be walking for a while to get there.

The security door's lock is broken—that's nothing new in a building like this—and I walk up the six flights of stairs. When I reach the landing, sweat's dripping down my back, and struggling to breathe, I catch the scent of Beau's cologne. I miss him, and he's only been at work for a few hours. I knock on the door of apartment 602, my heart pounding.

Jessie answers, and it drops to my feet.

"Oh," I gasp.

"Hey, Talia," she says, smiling faintly, her hand on her baby bump. I'm not an expert on pregnancy, but it looks like she could go into labor any second.

"You look amazing," I say, leaning around her stomach and giving her a sideways hug.

"Thanks. I don't feel amazing. Come in. Foster's passed out in the bedroom. I doubt he'll be up in time for you to meet him." Pink stains her cheeks.

"You're sober," I blurt out, stepping into her little apartment, but the moment I say it, I smell the sickly-sweet scent of Sweet in the air. She might be clean, but Foster isn't.

I focus on Jessie's bump and swallow back the saliva pooling in my mouth.

"Yeah. I heard you and Serena got hooked on Sweet at that frat party, and I was so glad it didn't happen to me. Here, let me hang up your coat, and if you don't mind, will you take your boots off?"

There isn't a foyer, only a large black mat that they put in front of the door. The apartment is almost identical to Jensen's. A kitchen to my left, with a half wall separating the kitchen area from the living room. Framed photos of Jessie's sonograms sit on the ledge. To my right is a closet and a hallway that will lead to a bedroom or two and a bathroom. The layout's also similar to the apartment Devyn rented for Mom and me. Unless you're rich, most apartments look the same.

"Sure." I take off my coat, and Jessie hangs it in the closet. I tug my boots off and follow her into the tiny living room.

"I straightened up a little after you caught me on chat. I can't believe how long it's been since I talked to you last."

I sit on a couch that's in much better condition than Jensen's. "I'm not on social media much. My account is left over from the year I was at the university. After I got out of rehab and my sister took me in, I've been too busy with school and work to care about that stuff."

Carefully, she lowers down onto the couch, wincing. Despite her obvious aches and pains, I'm jealous. She's not in a situation where having a baby could be a good thing, but I'm still jealous.

"It's pretty much all I do," she admits. "I didn't graduate. Foster and I started dating, and we moved in together. I had to drop out and get a job so I could help pay the rent. This pregnancy hasn't been the best. I'm sick a lot, and I'm high risk for pre-eclampsia. A social worker helped me apply for disability until the baby's born, and Foster gets some unemployment. I didn't get hooked on Sweet that night, so whatever was at that party, it missed me, but Foster's in and out of rehab. He'll never be clean for good."

"Are you going to stay with him?" I ask, my fingers itching to feel her belly.

"Yeah. I love him. He's Harry's father—we're having a boy. He's not aggressive or violent."

No, he wouldn't be. Sweet makes a person high, light. Sweet. Another reason they call it that. Until you start to go through withdrawal because you can't afford it, or you can't find a dealer. But then, when that happens, you don't hurt anyone but yourself. Physically.

"I understand. I would never judge you, Jessie. I've done my share of things that I'm not proud of."

"None of that was your fault. Tasha didn't get hooked at that party either. It was a real shock, you know? You and Serena getting hooked that night."

"Do you remember how we did? My sister thinks we might have eaten some tainted candy from Stevie's store. Serena brought her dipping sticks to the party and we had some. Did you?"

"Yeah, I did. It wasn't that."

Disappointed, I lean back against the cushion. That would have been too easy of an explanation. I'm not saying Devyn isn't right, that maybe there *are* people who buy candy from Stevie's candy stores and come out hooked, but it didn't happen to me.

I was hoping. I didn't want to take the blame for the past six years of my life, but now I have no choice. I was at a party, drunk, and that's completely my fault.

"Ever wonder how you got here?" I ask, tears burning my eyes.

She looks around her living room at the threadbare carpet,

the grimy walls, and the chipped TV stand. Rubbing her belly in slow circles, she says, "All the time. When we started our freshman year, I never thought this is where I'd end up. All you can do is make the most of it, right?"

"Yeah." I pause. "Do you need anything for the baby?"

Jessie scoffs. "Only all of it. Being broke sucks."

"Do your parents help? Or Foster's? Serena's not in touch with her parents anymore."

"My mom said after the baby's born she'd help a little. She's afraid if she gives me any money now Foster will steal it for Sweet. He wouldn't do that. On sober days, he'll go to my appointments. We named him Harry, short for Harrison, together. He doesn't want to be hooked, Talia, but it's such a hard and lonely fight. Especially at night. I'll wake up to go to the bathroom, and he'll be sitting in here, crying."

I nod. I know how true that is. I had some of the most hopeless nights of my life when I was in rehab. When I moved in with Devyn, I had my own room, but one night I wandered into hers and crawled into her bed. I was so lonely. I needed someone. Human touch. A hug. She wrapped her arms around me and held me all night. In Portland, we had our own rooms too, but I slept with her a lot anyway. The first night I slept in Beau's bedroom, I've never been so relieved. I need someone with me at night, and I doubt that will ever change. It's why when Beau told me I could go to Old Harbor whenever I want, I said I wouldn't go without him. I'd miss him, but I need him at night. I'll always need him.

"Can I throw you a baby shower? Before Harry's born? Serena might come, and you can meet her boyfriend. You said Tasha's sober, and we can invite her, and your parents. Foster's, if they're willing."

Jessie blinks in surprise. "You'd do that for me?"

"Of course I would. We used to be good friends, and I'm

sorry we lost touch. I've been scrambling to stay clean, but I'm in a good place now, and it doesn't take so much energy."

"That would be amazing. Really. I don't know how to thank you."

"Then don't. It'll be fun."

Jessie struggles to her feet. "I'm due on Valentine's Day. The chances of me having him on that day aren't great, but I think it's cool. Do you want to stay for lunch? I can make ham and cheese sandwiches, and I have chips."

I doubt Jessie can afford to feed me, but this might be my only meal until I go back to Beau's tonight. "Sure, that'd be great."

We sit at her tiny table and eat ham and cheese sandwiches made with cheap white bread and a handful of generic chips. She points out the ultrasound pictures and chats about Harry. He's healthy, and she's determined to keep him that way.

When I throw my paper plate and paper towel away, I notice the trash is full of Sweet Stuff candy wrappers, and the sugary scent of Sweet floats up to me. "Foster has a sweet tooth when he's high, huh? Serena put me in touch with Jensen Anderson, a guy she knew from the fraternity, and he did too. These wrappers were all over his place."

"Yeah. Whenever Foster goes out, he brings it back. I was going to have some, but it smells funny. I think it's my pregnancy hormones. I go to parenting classes, and the teacher said it's my body's way of telling me to stay away from something that could hurt the baby."

"There are better things you can eat than candy," I say, letting the lid drop over the garbage and the scent that sends a sick craving slithering over my skin.

"I get my sugar fix with fruit," Jessie says, and she walks with me toward the closet and my boots. I don't want to eat and run, but I want to look for Mom for the rest of the day. I don't want to be out after dark anymore. Beau likes it when I'm home in the evenings, and I don't want to disappoint him.

"Good. I'll message you later, okay? And we'll plan that party. We need something positive to look forward to." I pause. "You know that living with Foster, you risk getting addicted, don't you? Cross-contamination is real. When I got hooked, the first thing my sister did was blame our mother. I lived with her while she used, but she never brought it home."

She shakes her head. "Foster doesn't bring it home either."

I tip my head in doubt. I can smell it in their apartment.

"He doesn't," she says firmly. "He gets high on the streets, and then comes here and sleeps it off. I can't do this alone, Talia. I can't."

"You're already doing it alone as long as he's addicted, but I can't tell you what to do. God knows, you won't listen anyway. I didn't listen to a thing my sister said either, but your baby's safety is important and I know what it's like living with an addict. It won't be a good environment for Harry, and you know it. If you kicked him out, he'd have a reason to clean up. If he loves you and Harry, he'd have something to fight for."

She looks away. I know she'd never kick him out, just like I never would have left Mom alone.

"I'll think about it," she says, but her tone is flat.

Maybe after the baby's born she'll change her mind.

"Can I?" I ask, giving in, my hands hovering over her belly.

"Yeah. Go ahead. He's not moving around much though. He always falls asleep after I eat."

I rest my hands on her bump, and she puts her hands on top of mine. A little foot glides under my palm, and I gasp in delighted surprise. "Are you scared?"

"Of the birth?" she asks.

Reluctantly, I move my hands away. "No. Of being a mom."

"Sometimes. I wish I would have done more with my life, but how can I regret this? Bringing another human into the world. He's not even here yet, and I love him so much. We'll make it work. I'll never give up."

I put Beau's jacket on. "I envy you."

"One day you'll meet a guy and fall head over heels in love. You're so pretty, it won't take long for you to find someone. Then you'll have all the babies you want."

"Maybe one day. When I get home, I'll give you my cell phone number over chat."

"Sounds good. Thanks for coming over. I feel cut off, and it was nice to visit with a friend."

"Yeah, it was. Thank you for lunch. Bye," I say, twisting the doorknob and opening the door.

"Bye," she says softly, and I step into the hallway.

Jessie turns the deadbolt and engages the security chain behind me. I don't know how she walks up six flights of stairs, but by the sounds of it, she doesn't go out that much.

I lean against the wall and sigh. She had some of the candy Serena brought to the party. I can call Devyn and tell her that this time, her suspicions weren't true. I don't know if it's worth it to look for anyone else on Serena's list. It will be impossible to figure out where the Sweet came from. Anyone could have brought it to the party.

I take out the hat and gloves I put in the hood of Beau's jacket and step outside. The wind's picking up, and my ears will start hurting in the cold. I should have asked to use the bathroom at Jessie's. The next bus won't be here for twenty minutes, and I walk down the block to a convenience store. I use their restroom that's kind of clean, wash my hands, and walk down the candy aisle. Stevie doesn't sell her candy anywhere except her own stores, and there's only a generic version of Sweet Stuff here. I feel bad, but I don't buy anything. The bored woman behind the counter doesn't care.

The bus is full, and I stand, holding on to a pole as it chugs down a back street full of potholes toward Camden Way. Many of the passengers won't get off unless they need to use the bathroom. This is the warmest place they have to stay, and like the bored woman at the convenience store, the bus drivers don't care. They're paid to drive, and with their faces blank, that's all they do.

I get off alone at the last stop on the route, and the bus turns around in a cloud of exhaust.

I'll look for Mom along Arrowhead Alley first. If I don't find her, I'll talk to the priest at St. Joseph's and leave her money like Devyn did.

I'm tempted to stop in and see Serena, but I can't visit every time I'm in this part of the city. She works at the church, and I'm not in the mood to sit in on another NA meeting. The next time I go, I want to bring Beau with me. I want him involved in as many parts of my life as he wants to be.

We haven't had any more snow, and I trudge over the thick crust on the sidewalk.

My clothes aren't nearly warm enough, but walking keeps my blood pumping. After several blocks, I'm cold but sweating at the same time, and my breath comes out of my mouth in white puffs.

I don't pass anyone on the sidewalks. It's too cold to be out if you have somewhere warm you can stay.

For many years, people who had nowhere else to go have used the alley and the abandoned buildings for shelter. The old buildings have been scheduled to be torn down for as long as I can remember, but I doubt the city would ever take refuge away from a group of people they don't want to help in any other way.

It's a little past one o'clock, and I start scanning the worn and weary faces looking for my mom. Gazes flick in my direction, then away. One old woman steps toward me, her hand outstretched, but she hesitates, her thin frame shaking. "How can I help you?" I ask, meeting her eyes.

"You look like someone who would come here," she says, her lips chapped from the cold.

"Who?" Maybe she's seen my mom. Devyn and I both have her blonde hair.

"I don't know her name. She would give us food and money. Clothes, sometimes."

Swallowing a lump of disappointment, I unzip my pocket and pull out a twenty dollar bill. "You met my sister, and her name is Devyn. I'm Talia. Here. I hope it helps."

Her skin is dry and cracked, and she wraps her hand around the money. "God bless you."

"And to you," I say automatically in return.

I keep going. I ask anyone who will talk to me if they've seen my mother, and I look for her in every group of people that I pass. If she's as bad as Devyn said she was, I wonder if I'll recognize her.

For hours, I introduce myself to people, and surprisingly, some of them remember me from my own time on the streets.

There's still another mile of the alley to search, but the cold has started to seep into my bones. The sun is already setting, and the buildings cast the alley in shadows. I'm hungry, but I don't want to stop and come back.

I don't know how Devyn did this, night after night, looking for evidence against Stevie, and trying to find Mom to see if she needed clothes or something to eat.

Needing a break, I make my way toward a group huddled around a fire flickering out of an old barrel. I hold out my hands like the rest and lean in, letting the flame thaw out my face. I'm tired, and I miss Beau. I want to be warm and safe at his penthouse, and guilt swamps me, just knowing I have a place like that to go. These people live here, and this is their only way of life. Tears trickle down my cheeks, but they don't bother anyone. The number of tears that have been cried in this alley could fill an ocean, and I bet my sister added more than her share.

Next to me, a woman sways on her feet, and mixed with the acrid odor of ash, I smell the sugary scent of Sweet.

Saliva floods my mouth. I sat too long in Jessie's apartment, and my skin crackles with a craving I can't push back.

I could buy some off her. I have the money. I wouldn't need much. Barely a hint would send me flying for the rest of the night.

Moving closer, I inhale. Bubble gum, cotton candy, the pink powder from a package of Sweet Stuff. I can taste the ghost flavor on my tongue, as if I had a hit just yesterday. My blood fizzes with need, and my hands start to tremble.

I have to get out of here.

Backing away, I hold my breath, but it doesn't help. The scent is in my nose, in my memories. I can taste it, and I crave it.

Leaning against a brick wall, I stare at my boots and breathe in and out over and over again until I think I have it under control, then I search for another quarter mile. Sweat drenches my skin, and I can't stop licking my lips. My throat works, swallowing powder that isn't there. The flavor's in my mouth, but my body knows I haven't had any, and the shakes set in.

The sun sinks behind the buildings, covering the alley in dark. Fire and faces blur in my vision, and I stumble into someone who pushes me away. I land face-first in the snow, and I crawl down the alley, once again praying someone will sell me some Sweet.

I need it more than anything.

I picture Beau's face. No, not more than anything.

Crawling through the dark around piles of garbage, I find an alcove, and I squeeze into it, pressing my face against my knees. I don't know where I am. I don't know how to get home. I don't know where home is. Tears soak my jeans, and I don't know how long I'm sitting there when Beau says my name.

CHAPTER FOURTEEN

Beau

It breaks my heart to see her like this. It breaks my heart that she'll do this again and again until she finds what she's looking for, and I won't, can't, stop her.

Dropping to my haunches, I say her name. "Talia."

She lifts her head, and in the glow of the SUV's headlights, her eyes widen. "B-Beau."

"Do you want to go, love?" I ask.

Her eyes dart around, looking behind me, but there's nothing except Mack waiting in the SUV. When she broke down, he called me, afraid to approach her, but he didn't have to worry. She would have been okay with him, but I'm glad I'm here to talk her down.

Slowly, she nods.

"We can go to the penthouse, if that's what you want. Or I can call Devyn." I'll never assume she wants to be with me. "She can be here in an hour."

A wail screeches out of her throat, and she covers her head

with her arms, curling in on herself. "You don't want me like this." She sobs into the crooks of her elbows, my jacket muffling her cries.

"Talia." I sit on the cold stone step next to her. "Talia."

I'm quiet as she cries, and Mack sits patiently behind the wheel waiting to drive us home.

I still haven't touched her, but I do now, putting a hand on her knee. "Talia."

She looks at me. Her cheeks are covered with tears, her makeup is smeared under eyes that are full of fear, and her lips tremble.

"Are you listening to me?" I ask, and the way I speak to her reminds me of talking to Nina during one of her benders. Nothing I said would get through and I had to treat her like a child to make her pay attention.

She nods.

"I love you. I will always want you. The choice to go home with me or not is yours, and it always will be. That's all."

She searches my face.

"I would be happy if you went home with me. I want to take care of you, okay?"

Nodding again, she says, "Okay."

I blow out a breath. "Good. Do you want me to pick you up or can you stand?"

"I can stand up."

"Okay. Let me help you." I hold out my hand, always giving her the choice, and wearing her dirty gloves, she puts her hand in mine.

We stand, and the second we turn toward the SUV, Mack is opening the back door for us. Talia gets in first. "Thank you," I tell him, and he nods. He knows what Everett and Stevie did to Devyn, and he feels just as protective of Devyn and Talia as Rick and I do.

I slide in next to her, and she cowers against the door, as far away from me as she can.

Mack settles behind the wheel, and we start to move.

"Talia."

Her soulful green eyes peer at me. My poor little girl. Always with a monkey on her back.

"Are you scared of me?" I ask, dreading her answer.

"No." Her voice is raspy, and she's still shaking.

I try to relax. I believe her. "Can I hold you?"

She blinks. "Do you want to?"

"I'll always want to, love."

She crawls into my lap, and I wrap my arms around her so tightly I think she won't be able to breathe.

She cries against my chest until Mack parks in the underground parking lot of the building. I carry her up to the lobby floor, but I don't let go as we wait in the elevator. I don't put her down to take off my boots, and I hold on to her, even when I get to the couch. I sink onto a cushion, both of us still wearing our jackets.

My muscles finally relax in relief. I loosen the grip I have on her and try to calm my heart. She's here, and she's safe.

She lifts her head, and there's not one hint of color on her face. "I'm sorry."

"You don't need to apologize, love."

Wiggling on my lap, she takes off her gloves and skims her fingers over my cheek. I need to touch her too, and I kiss her forehead, her skin still cold under my lips.

"How did you know where I was?"

I'll tell her, and she'll want to call Devyn after all. If I'd done something like this to Nina, she would have accused me of stalking her, of not trusting her, and I prepare for the same from Talia. "I had Mack watch out for you today. I didn't want you to go alone, but you didn't ask me to go with you. I trust you, I really do, but the places you have to look for your mom are dangerous and—"

She cuts me off with a violent kiss, our teeth gnashing together. Twisting in my lap, she wraps her arms around my neck.

This isn't the kind of reaction I expected, and surprised, I moan as she slips her tongue in my mouth and cuddles into me. She breaks the kiss and buries her face against my shoulder. "Thank you."

"You're not mad?"

"No, I'm not mad."

That makes no sense. "Why aren't you angry?"

She looks at me and wipes the tears off her cheeks. "Why would it make me mad that you love me enough to protect me? How long would I have sat in the cold until you finished working and thought you should look for me? I would have frozen to death by then. I'm not mad. I'm only thankful that you love me so much that you asked Mack to follow me."

I think about how Rick must have felt finding Devyn zip-tied to a support beam at our site without her jacket. My throat burns and I clear it, trying to hide how scared she made me. "Good. Then we don't have to talk about it anymore. Are you hungry? Is your stomach shaky? Maybe some soup."

She smiles gratefully. "That sounds good."

"Take off your coat and boots, and I'll put them in the closet."

"I lost my hat somewhere," she says, as if only just now noticing, and brushing her hand over the top of her head.

"We'll get you a new one."

She takes her boots and my jacket off and huddles in the corner of the couch, her jeans wet and crusted with grime.

I heat a mug of chicken noodle soup, and while she sips on it, I fill the tub. She's filthy. Not only from crawling through most of Arrowhead Alley, but dirt and tears streak across her face and her hair is a snarled mess.

I step into the living room, and she's cradling the empty mug against her chest, staring into space. I drop in front of her. "I'm running you a bath, love."

"Thanks."

"Do you want help?"

"Will you?" Her green eyes are so sad.

"Anything you need."

She tries to smile, but she doesn't quite make it.

In the bathroom, I help her undress. I added some of the bath salts we soaked in the other night, and the room smells like lavender. I grip her arm and steady her as she steps in. Once she's safely sitting in the water, I dim the lights, letting her soak in the semi-darkness, and kneel beside her.

I lean against the side of the tub and rest my arms along the edge. She does the same and kisses the back of my hand.

"Can you tell me what happened?"

She lets out a shuddery breath. "Devyn checked up on Mom for years, and when I was signing up for classes, I found her notes. It didn't bother me, being there, until I stood next to this woman. She reeked of Sweet. I moved away from her, but I couldn't get the smell out of my nose, and I could taste it. I started shaking, and I felt like when I was going through withdrawal. I wanted some so much."

She stops, but she's not done, and I wait her out.

Her lips move against my hand as she speaks, and the lap of the water against the side of the tub almost drowns out her low voice. "I bumped into someone, and they pushed me. I fell, and just like that, I was back to that summer, literally crawling on my hands and knees, looking to score. I didn't know where I was or how I was going to get home. I don't know how long I sat there until you came."

"Only as long as it took me to get across the city. Mack called me the second you crawled into the doorway of that storefront. He would have tried to talk to you, but he didn't want to freak you out."

"I did that well enough on my own, and I'll thank him tomorrow. Why did you ask him to look out for me?" She lifts her head, and tears shine in her eyes.

"I know that this is something you need to do—for your mom, for yourself, and maybe even for Devyn. I can't stop you, and I know you'll do it tomorrow, and the next day, and the next, until you find her, or find out the information you need to know. I'm trying so hard not to crowd you, love. I did that with Nina, and all it did was push her away. I don't want you to go into those parts of the city alone, but I don't expect you to ask me to go, so I tried to compromise."

Using the edge of the tub to steady herself, she rises to her knees and rubs her lips over mine. "You didn't ask me if I had a taste."

"I know you didn't. You know how I know?"

She shakes her head. She's so beautiful, her skin misty from the hot water and golden in the dim light's glow. Her green eyes spark, and her parted lips tremble.

"Because you said you would do whatever it took to stay with me, and I believe you. Remember, every time you're out there, remember the promise you made."

The water slaps against the side of the tub as she sits down again, and she rests her forehead against my arm.

The water cools as she sits, clutching my hand until my fingers turn numb.

"Don't leave me," she whispers.

And I don't.

———

I wash and condition her hair the way I've watched her do it, and I help her out of the tub, wrapping her in a huge, fluffy towel. She sits on the edge of the bed, cozy in her pajamas, and I brush her hair, easing the snarls out with her brush.

She doesn't speak as she climbs under the comforter, and I turn off the lights. It's still early, but she's exhausted and I don't want to leave her alone.

I slide between the sheets, and she wiggles into me. I spoon her, my arm wrapped securely around her stomach. Seconds later, she's breathing deeply.

I expect her to have nightmares, but she never does.

———

I know what her plans are for the day, and I don't want to tell her goodbye. I'd ask her not to go, but I *can't*. She's still sleeping when I get ready for work, and in a note I leave propped up against the coffeemaker, I remind her to call or text Mack if she wants him to shadow her like he did yesterday. I don't say she can call me for whatever she needs. I hope she knows that by now.

She didn't take the bank cards I made for her, and I push them in front of the note, making it harder for her to ignore them.

I leave for the office without giving her a kiss like I usually do.

Our relationship would go a lot smoother if I wasn't such a needy asshole, having to check myself every goddamned second.

Mack opens the door, and I sit heavily in the seat, shoving my briefcase on the floor. Thank God today's Friday. I want to spend a quiet weekend with Talia, watching movies and eating takeout, but that won't happen. I already know when I come home from work tonight she'll still be out. She starts school on Monday, and I hope going to class and doing homework will keep her inside, but she's just as stubborn as Devyn and won't stop going out to Arrowhead Alley and Camden Way until she finds what she's looking for.

I rub at a headache already forming behind my eyes. She'll either leave me for needing to be in her face every five seconds, or she'll leave like she tried to do the first night we made love, when I was trying to give her space. I won't be able to find balance. I'm never going to get it right.

I should make her leave before she does it on her own.

The idea gnaws at me like hungry rats, its teeth just as sharp.

CHAPTER FIFTEEN

Talia

He doesn't kiss me goodbye. He's not mad at me, but he's not happy, either. I can't blame him. The fool I made out of myself last night. God. I'm lucky he didn't call Devyn, and oh, I'd know if he had. She wouldn't have wasted two seconds calling and telling me how stupid I am, how close I came to throwing everything I've worked so hard for during the past six years in the toilet.

I know it.

What happened last night was exactly what Devyn was trying to keep me from doing by not sharing her information with me. She didn't want me down Camden Way or Arrowhead Alley for exactly that reason. Only, she couldn't have known that Beau would send Mack after me. She couldn't have known that Beau would step in and protect me.

I roll over and bury my face in his pillow.

There are only a couple of days left until classes start, and I won't be walking the streets anymore. What I need to find out,

I need to find out tonight, or it'll have to wait until I don't have that much homework.

Finding Mom has become more important than catching Stevie Johansson selling Sweet. I was dumb anyway thinking I could do something Devyn couldn't. She could find Mom . . . every once in a while. I can too, if I'm in the right place at the right time.

I hope today will be the day, but if it's not, I'll be better prepared. This time before I leave, I'll put money in an envelope like Devyn used to and leave it at the church. I can tell Father Will that my sister doesn't live in Cedar Hill anymore, and maybe he'll call me if he ever sees Mom.

Reluctantly, I roll out of bed. I'm not looking forward to walking in the cold, but if Mom's living in it, I can search for her in it.

The coffee's hot and strong, and sipping, I skim Beau's note. He tries so hard to pretend he doesn't care. I don't know who this Nina woman is, but she didn't appreciate a good thing when she had it. I can't imagine being mad at Beau for loving me. I wonder what happened to her. I wonder if she regrets how she treated him, and all the scars she left behind.

I brush the note, my fingers skimming over the smooth paper, his broad strokes caressing me as if he was here. How would it feel if he let go? If he loved me, and showed me, as much as he wanted to? He said he was fire and he'd leave only ash in his wake, but whenever he's taken everything I can give, I've never felt empty. The more he takes, the more I have.

The black bank cards glitter in the overhead lights, but I push them away. I'll put them in my purse when my last name matches his.

Even though I bathed last night, I shower, get dressed, and do my hair and makeup. I find an envelope in Beau's study, and

I put a hundred dollars in it. That's what Devyn would leave for her, knowing exactly what she would spend it on.

I dig through Beau's front closet for another hat. I'd be stupid to walk the Alley without dressing for it, and I knew I'd find one. You can't live in Minnesota without owning several hats and pairs of gloves. Mine are dirty, but I put them on. I might as well. A new pair won't stay clean.

Near the elevator, I pause. I don't have Mack's number in my phone, but I should. I don't want to have to call him, though. I want to be able to do this on my own, prove to myself I can be around Sweet without being afraid of relapsing or breaking down in a panic attack. Sweet is everywhere. I'll never be able to get away from it.

I sigh. I promised I would be safe. Beau trusts me to take care of myself, and maybe more than only me since I haven't gotten my period yet. I put Mack's number in my phone in case I need the driver's help.

I get on a full bus and stand near the back. The bus driver is starting to recognize me, and he nods, meeting my gaze in his rearview mirror, knowing I'll ride until the end of his route, where he'll need to turn around and start all over again.

The sidewalks are becoming familiar again, and I walk past the same bar toward Camden Way. At this time of day, it's closed, but I pause and watch the bartender put wine glasses away. The sun is shining, and water drips from the icicles hanging off the awnings of several empty storefronts. Surprisingly warm for this time of year, maybe the nice weather will help me find Mom.

The sunshine also lightens my mood, and the past few days of reconnecting with old friends, facing their addictions and personal problems, and searching the streets for Mom, are that much more manageable.

I take my phone out of my pocket and text Beau. *I love you.*

He replies immediately. *I love you too. You didn't take the cards, did you?*

I smile. He knows me so well. *No.*

Why not?

They have the wrong last name.

There's a pause, and then he answers. *Be safe.*

My good mood disappears. I don't answer him and put my phone back in my pocket. He doesn't want to marry me.

Well, why would he, I think, as I walk down the sidewalk. Nothing can hide the buildings' need for repair, just like I'm sure nothing hides what I am, what Beau saw in me last night.

I walk Arrowhead Alley all day, this time keeping my distance from everyone looking for shelter in the old buildings or warming their hands near fire burning in the barrels. I can still smell it. The sugary scent hangs in the air, and it calls to me just like it always does. If Beau doesn't love me enough to marry me, why should I stay clean? What do I have to live for?

My thoughts take a dangerous turn, but I've felt like this in the past. I'd sit alone in rehab, trying to make sense of my life. Trying to make sense of why I was an addict and looking for a reason to keep moving forward even though it was so hard.

My therapist would ask me to write down a list of people who would miss me if I gave in. I'd only have Devyn's name to put on the list. I knew Mom was too far gone to care about what happened to me. "That's one person, Talia," she'd say, "and it's enough. What would you do to her?" It always *would* be enough. I couldn't leave Devyn alone, even if at that point I sometimes felt like my existence was more of an inconvenience than my death could ever be.

I keep walking, breathing shallowly through my nose. I decide to stop and take a break, but I have to walk over a mile to find a diner that's decent enough to use their restroom and order a bowl of soup. Once I'm warm and have something in my belly, I go out again, but to my disappointment, the sun starts to set. I promised myself I'd be home in time to have dinner with Beau, but just as I'm about to turn around and go back to the bus stop, I spot her sitting near a group of people that are standing around a barrel fire. I walked past that group at least three times, but I didn't see her until now.

She doesn't look the same as the last time I saw her, but it's been six years and those years have not been kind. I can see myself in the shape of her nose and the bow of her upper lip, but that's all. Scars cover her face, and a dirty scarf tied tightly under her chin hides her hair. Like everyone here, she's wearing at least three layers of clothes, and her boots are worn down.

"Mom," I cry, stumbling to her, and I fall to my knees by her side. "Mom."

She stinks of Sweet, body odor, and urine, and I try not to gag. She turns her head and stares at me, but her eyes are blank.

I pat her cheeks, but nothing I do will bring her back.

How did Devyn walk away when she would find her? I can't leave her like this, and I put my head on her shoulder and cuddle into her side. We sit, and as it gets dark, the people move around us.

The cold seeps through my jeans, and I doze against her rough and filthy jacket, pretending we're back at our apartment and Devyn is spending the weekend with us. We were happy then. Sweet hadn't been around. Mom and I would bake cookies while Devyn sat and watched, flipping through a fashion magazine.

The temperature drops, and I think I'm the one shivering, but it's Mom. She needs a hit of Sweet, and like a wolf stalking its prey, a dealer swaggers down the alley, arrogant in his power. He knows he has what every single person in this alley wants. He also knows that few will be able to afford it.

He stops a couple of feet away and makes his deals. I want

to get up in his face and tell him to fuck off, to leave these poor people alone, but it wouldn't do any good. Even if I managed to make him go away, he'd come back.

I curl into Mom's side and watch him trade his poison for cash. He stops at our group, and his gaze slides over me. I look like I belong here because I'm one of them.

Two people standing near the barrel buy from him. The packaging has changed since I've been on the street, and I don't recognize it now. You don't need much to get high, but the price . . . a sprinkle would cost fifty bucks, and to an addict without a job, fifty dollars was a fortune.

When he's done, he turns his attention to us. I remember what Devyn said about clean dealers, and she's right about this one. His eyes are sharp, like his smile, and he's wearing a new leather jacket layered over a grey hoodie. He kicks Mom's boot. "Looks like you girls could use a little something to warm you up."

"Whatcha got?" I ask.

"Whatcha think?" he shoots back, taking a white package out of his jacket pocket. He holds it out, like he wants me to admire it, and I do. Oh, I do.

I sit up, and he steps back, my face not familiar.

"Are you a cop?" he asks.

Lifting my chin, I say, "No. Are you?"

I know he's not. He doesn't look like any undercover narcotics cop I've ever seen, and I've seen my share. No matter how smooth a cop tries to look, there's a certain awareness about them that nothing can hide. Cops don't know this way of life and can't imitate it. This guy's too slick to be a cop, and he knows I'm too tired to be one.

He lifts his hand, two packets tucked between his fingers. "Two hundred bucks."

I scoff. There's no way Sweet costs that much. No one would be able to afford it. "Fuck off."

Chuckling, he says, "Fine, fine. A hundred. You caught me on buy-one-get-one night."

I don't appreciate his humor, but I bet he doesn't get a chance to show off very often. High-functioning Sweet addicts don't hang out in the alley. They still have apartments. Addicts like Jensen who live off Sweet, pizza, and unemployment checks.

I turn away and unzip my pocket. I'd be asking for trouble if I showed anyone here how much money I'm carrying around. I pull out a hundred dollar bill and zip my pocket back up. Carefully, I reach toward him with the money. We swap quickly, and I scoot away, pressing into Mom's side and hiding my face in her shoulder.

"Freak." He walks off, shoving my money in his pocket and taking out another packet of Sweet, ready for his next customer.

I look at the packets I paid for. "What the fuck?" I murmur, skimming my fingers over the pink Sweet Stuff letters on the front. I paid a hundred dollars to get ripped off. I bought candy. Powdered candy and dipping sticks made of sugar.

Mom grapples for the packets in my hand, and I let her have one. She tears it open while the others standing around the barrel watch with violent envy. She licks her finger and shoves it inside the envelope, her movements eerily familiar.

As she licks her finger, the scent of Sweet drifts to me. The drug seeps into her body, and she sighs in relief, the symptoms of withdrawal fading.

I wet my lips, the potent and sugary smell clogging my nose.

Craving it, I reach out for the envelope in Mom's grip, but she yanks it away, defending her unexpected score and jolting me out of my hazy need.

She doesn't know me, doesn't recognize me. She only cares about the Sweet in her hands, the pink powder sparkling on her finger. I understand now how Devyn could walk away from her again and again. This woman isn't our mother anymore. That woman was lost a long time ago, and no matter how many years of rehab she went through, it would never be enough. Sweet is a part of her. She's never coming back.

I thought Devyn was cruel and heartless, but she only saw what I didn't see.

"Mom." She doesn't acknowledge me. "Mom."

She's too busy licking the inside of the Sweet Stuff package to look at me.

Slowly, my legs cramping from sitting for so long on the frozen ground, I stand up. Not once does Mom look at me.

I bought my mother drugs. What would Devyn say?

Nothing. She'd say nothing. She left money at the church for her, and she knew that's where it would go. To a dealer, to Stevie Johansson, making her a little bit richer day by day, addict by addict.

I shove the packet of Sweet in my pocket. I don't want it anymore. Beau might not think we have a future, but I'll never convince him if I give in. I'm stronger than that. He always knew it, and now I know it too.

Walking away from Arrowhead Alley, I whisper, "I love you, Mom," but only the moon hears me.

The sidewalks are empty, the winter chill forcing people who can find a place to go inside. A light snow falls, shimmering in the orange streetlights, and I check my phone. Beau hasn't texted me or tried to call. I missed dinner, using that time to sit with my mom, and it might be the last time I'll see her. I don't know.

I want to send him a message, or call, something, but he's complicating this so much. He's giving me space, but I don't want it. I never asked him to come with me because he doesn't belong here and I don't want him to see how easily I fit in. How easily that dealer assumed I was one of them. I had been, in another life, and it's still a part of me, like Sweet will always be a part of my mother. She didn't recognize me, but I saw myself in her. I saw what I would have become if I hadn't been strong enough to fight, if Devyn hadn't been there to take me in.

The church is open, and I walk down the long aisle toward the altar. I'm not religious and I don't believe in God. My parents never brought us to church, and I've never been baptized or taken communion. Maybe if I'd had Faith—not plain faith I would beat my addiction, but *Faith*—it might have been easier. I'm not looking for God now, only peace. I walked away from my mother. Walked away from her as she licked Sweet off a piece of paper, and she didn't know I had been there and gone. All she cared about was the package and the high it had inside.

I sit on the front pew, the candles flickering like the barrel fires, and slide the packet out of my pocket. It's easy to hold. It doesn't feel like Sweet to me, and it doesn't look like it. The wrapper looks exactly like the dipping sticks Stevie sells in her stores, like the candy wrappers in Jensen's and Jessie's apartments. I hold it up to my nose and take a deep breath. I can smell it. Only an addict would be able to tell the difference.

I press the wrapper to my lips as tears run down my cheeks. I have to face the truth that Devyn saw so long ago. We'll never get Mom back.

An older man wearing a black suit steps into the sanctuary. "Can I help you?" he asks, his voice quiet and kind.

Wiping my eyes, I say, "I'm Talia Scott, Devyn's sister. Are you Father Will?"

"I am, yes. You look like her. Have you been looking for your mother?"

"Yeah. I found her."

He nods and sits next to me. "Devyn would come here after walking the streets. Sometimes she'd find her, sometimes not. She would pray for forgiveness."

"For Mom?" I ask, discreetly pushing the Sweet packet up the sleeve of Beau's jacket. I don't think Father Will would be impressed knowing I brought drugs into his church.

"No. For herself."

I rub the tears off my cheeks. "Why? Devyn's done the best she could. There's nothing she needs forgiveness for."

"Why are you here?" Father Will asks. "Because you found your mother, and you walked away. You pray for the same reasons your sister did. I haven't seen her since Thanksgiving. Is she all right?"

"Yes, she is. She's getting married and they're trying for a baby."

A corner of his mouth lifts. "I'm happy for her. When we spoke last, she was torn between living in Old Harbor and staying in Cedar Hill to take care of your mother. I told her I would do the best I could, the way I did when she lived in Portland, and that she should live her own life."

I blink in surprise. "She never told me she thought about staying here for Mom."

"Devyn thinks about everyone but herself. If she's getting married, she found someone who will put her first, and I'm glad. I miss her, and so do some of the others. We'd gotten used to seeing her while she was doing her research."

"How did she make peace with her choices? How did she convince herself that it was okay to stop trying to help?" I picture Mom sitting on the ground wearing ragged clothes that came from only God knows where, skin and bones. She'd rather buy Sweet than food.

"She'll never stop trying to help your mom. Devyn has

done the best she could for years, but she grew tired, like any person carrying a heavy burden would. Sometimes, Talia, you need to put it in God's hands and trust He'll pick up where you leave off."

"I don't believe in God."

Father Will huffs a laugh. "It's difficult to believe when things are at their worst and all hope is lost. You've been to Arrowhead Alley. Not one of those people believes in God either, yet they come to find refuge here. There's peace, and forgiveness. Not because God gives it to them, but eventually, they find it within themselves. You had to walk away, but that doesn't mean you've given up on her. In your own way, in the only way you can with the resources you have, you'll always take care of her. If you're like your sister, you have an envelope you'll leave here for her?"

"Yeah," I whisper.

"I'll give it to her when she comes. She always does, looking for proof someone still loves her, even if she doesn't realize that's what she's doing. You don't have to give up on her to live your own life. Devyn may not visit in person as often as she used to, but she sends money, for the church and for your mother. Are you going to stay in the city?"

"Yeah. Not long ago I met the man I'm going to marry."

"Bring him by. Devyn told me a little about him, and I'd like to meet him."

"I will."

He pats my hand. "I'll take the envelope. It's getting late, and you should find your way home."

"Thank you." I pull the envelope out of the pocket of Beau's work jacket and give it to Father Will.

He pauses, and then says, "Talia, I can see that you're troubled, and I won't try to turn you into a believer or try to convince you that you would find peace with God if you opened your heart. But whether you find comfort in God's arms or the arms of your fiancé, you are loved, and you're worth loving. You love your mother, and it's okay to mourn who she used to be. You can mourn who you used to be, too, before addiction took hold of you. You'll never be that young, innocent woman again, and you'll miss her, but allow yourself to appreciate who addiction turned her into. You faced a lot of demons coming here tonight, and that should be celebrated. God bless you," he says, turning toward the altar.

"And to you," I say softly as he walks away.

The Sweet packet up my sleeve scratches at my arm, a reminder that I'm not the girl I used to be.

I can put this all behind me now. I found my mom and I don't have to give up on her, but I won't be able to rescue her. Not the way I wanted, and not the way I thought Devyn should have been able to. That's something I'll have to come to terms with, starting with an apology. I wanted her to do things she's not capable of doing. Not because she didn't try, but because Mom doesn't have it in her to give us what we need from her. Not anymore.

I step out of the church and into the dark.

It's time to go home.

CHAPTER SIXTEEN

Beau

I decide to call it a day an hour past quitting time. I can't put off going home to an empty penthouse and eating dinner alone, and I stuff my briefcase full of files. I've been good. I haven't texted Talia all day, except for this morning when she texted me first, and it's been hell not to think about what she said.

She won't be home until late, and I'll use the time to get more work done instead of staring over the city, wondering where she is and why she's thinking about getting married.

Before I leave, I call the Cedar Hill Police Department. I haven't heard about the candy I found in the outhouse, and I want to know where it came from, and why they think it ended up at the site.

"Cedar Hill Police Department, how may I direct your call?"

"This is Beau Hendrickson. I found some stolen property

on my construction site. The officers said they would get back to me, but they never did."

"One moment please," the woman says, and an instrumental version of an old song plays in my ear.

"Lost and Stolen, Detective Watts," a gruff voice answers, cutting off the music.

"Detective Watts, this is Beau Hendrickson."

"What can I do for ya?" he asks, a hint of caution in his voice. He knows who I am—most people who live in the city do—and with my connections in the mayor's office, I could have him strung up by the balls in two seconds after we say goodbye.

"A few days ago, I called in a duffel bag full of candy found on my construction site. Two officers retrieved it. I was wondering if there was any more information. It was found on our property, and we'd like to cross it off our list of things we have to worry about."

Papers rustle in the background. "The Sweet Stuff? Black duffel?" he asks.

"Yes, that's it."

"It wasn't candy. An officer brought the bag to the lab for testing and the dogs went nuts, but," he says, sighing, "it went missing and we couldn't run the tests to be sure."

"What do you mean, it went missing?"

"That's what I mean. We've got cops working with the gangs . . . better payday, ya know? Some kid probably thought he could hide the stash on your site until he could figure out where to sell it, and after you found it, a cop was nice enough to give it back."

I catch up to what he says. "It wasn't candy. It was—"

"Sweet. Yeah, from the way the dogs were howling."

Tapping my fingers against my desk, I say, "I don't understand. Only Stevie Johansson sells Sweet Stuff. That's her brand."

"Sure is. A creative kid swapped them out. Nobody's gonna question a bag full of candy. Real go-getter," he says sarcastically. "You get a look at the packages? Just for show, right? People in this shit city are hard on our asses to get Sweet off the streets, and the dealers are getting more creative every day. Like I said, the bag's gone, nothing can be done about it. Sorry." He hangs up.

For fuck's sake.

We had Sweet sitting on the site for God knows how long, and I'm angry all over again that I let Rick have his way with the hotel. I should have insisted we clean it up. I should have done it behind his back.

"You stood me up," Everett says, striding into my office like he owns the place, and well, he probably wishes he did.

"My apologies," I say, leaning back in my chair and giving absolutely zero fucks. "Rick came into town and I got caught up."

"When are you going to do something with the site?" he asks, sliding his hands into the pockets of his pants and wandering around my office. His jaw is still bruised, and my knuckles haven't healed either. I'm lucky Talia's been so preoccupied looking for her mother that she hasn't pressed the issue since I put her off the first time.

I scowl. "It's too cold. You know that. You can't do anything until April either. Is that why you're here? You're bored?"

He flicks a glance at me. I should call security.

"No. I offered you a business proposition, and I was following up."

"Follow up somewhere else. You're delusional if you thought I'd do business with you after the shit you pulled—"

He opens his mouth to speak.

"I know, I know. There's no proof, it was Stevie, blah, blah, blah. That's such bullshit, Everett, and you know it. You didn't come here for that. I already showed you what I think of you. What are you really doing here?"

Everett lifts a shoulder. "Word is, your girlfriend's been down by Arrowhead Alley."

I narrow my eyes. Everett's already hurt Rick and Devyn, and if he touches Talia, all bets are off. "What's it to you?"

"Nothing. Just a dangerous place, that's all."

"It can be," I say carefully, watching him. "But Talia's spent more time there than you and me put together. She'll be okay."

"That's what you'd like to believe, and I want you to keep on thinking it. I was hoping we could trade," he says, staring out the window at the city lights. Rick and I own more of them than he does, but not by much, and that small number has always pissed him off.

"A trade for what? It's only because of a good attorney you're not in prison. There's nothing you have that I want."

Everett cocks an eyebrow. "What about Talia's safety?"

I grit my teeth. "She hasn't done anything to you or Stevie."

He laughs. "You're kidding, right? You think she'll leave this alone? My connections on the street say she's looking into Sweet, same as Devyn. I promised Stevie I'd handle this, and I will. Sign me over the property, Hendrickson, and I'll promise not to hurt a hair on her pretty head."

I'm shoving him against the window before he can blink. "If you hurt her, you son of a bitch, I guarantee you, I will not stop until you're dead. I'm not Rick. He might have walked away after what you did to Devyn, but trust me, we have a different way of dealing with things and you won't be so lucky."

He jerks out of my grip, straightens his tie, and holds up his hands. "All right, all right, I thought we could negotiate like adults, but have it your way. Don't blame me if something happens. A little Sweet goes a long way."

Whistling, he swaggers out of my office, and I have no choice but to let him go.

I call Talia and get her voicemail. I don't leave a message. I call again, but I don't leave a message this time either. Agitated, I call Rick, and he answers on the second ring.

"Is Devyn okay?" I ask before he can say hello.

"Yeah, why? She's right here."

"Everett was just here, at the office, and he threatened Talia, mentioned Devyn."

"Is Talia with you?" He moves the phone away from his mouth and murmurs something to Devyn that I can't hear.

"No. She's out looking for her mom, and she's been gone all day. I wanted to give you a heads up that Everett and Stevie think Talia's snooping around, the way Devyn was."

"Do you want us to fly in?" Rick asks.

I pause. "No. If Stevie knows Devyn's here, that'll only make it worse. When I find Talia, I'll keep an eye on her twenty-four seven."

"You don't know where she is now." It's not a question.

"No. I've been trying not to—"

"I know. Call when you find her."

"Okay, okay." I rub at my forehead, a headache pounding behind my eyes. "Thanks."

"Yeah."

Rick hangs up, and I stare at my home screen, a picture of Talia sleeping that she doesn't know I took.

Fuck.

She'll hate me if I do this.

I close my eyes and picture Nina, her face twisted in anger. I can feel her yank her hand away, her fingers sliding from mine as she turns to run.

The light changing to red.

The slippery streets.

The second she steps off the curb.

I remember it all.

She's going to hate me as much as Nina did, but I still make the call.

"Hey. It's Beau. I need you to track a phone for me."

CHAPTER SEVENTEEN

Talia

The buses won't stop running for a couple more hours yet, and I have plenty of time to catch the last one. It feels later than it is, but the cup of soup didn't last very long, and I head toward Camden Way, my stomach rumbling.

It's almost a relief that I won't be doing this again, at least, not anytime soon. There's nothing I can do for Mom except make sure she has some money, and I won't need to come out this far very often. If I visit Serena and Aaron, I can ask Father Will about her, but I don't want to walk Arrowhead Alley anymore.

"Devyn! Devyn Scott!"

I hear someone shout my sister's name and I turn around. A man about my sister's age jogs toward me, his breath white in the air.

"Hey, you're not Devyn," he says, skidding to a stop in front of me.

"No, I'm not," I say, though I can understand how he could think that from a distance.

"You're Talia, her sister." He holds out a hand.

I eye him without shaking it. "Who are you?"

He chuckles, grabs my arm, and tugs me down the sidewalk. I don't like that he's handling me, but he doesn't give off any dangerous vibes.

Huddling against a building and giving his back to the street, he says, "I'm Detective Lucas Chaney, Narcotics. You can call me Luke." He pulls out a badge that's hanging on a chain hidden under his jacket and a thick sweatshirt.

I nod. I know a real badge when I see one, and apprehension slithers down my spine. Did he see me buy Sweet off that dealer? Beau would never want me if I was arrested for possession. "What do you want?"

"I thought you were Devyn. She was looking for evidence against Stevie, and I got to know her a bit. We helped each other."

I don't remember seeing Luke's name in Devyn's notes, but there were so many, and I didn't skim them all. "I was looking for my mom."

"Can we grab a cup of coffee and talk? She must have told you about what she was doing."

"She did, but that doesn't have anything to do with me," I say, except, it does. Devyn started looking into Sweet because of Mom and me. Sweet destroyed our family, and she wanted to stop it from doing the same to other families. She wanted Stevie Johansson to pay for all the harm she's done.

"Just a few minutes," he says, his dark brown eyes shining in the streetlight. "Then I can give you a lift home and you won't have to ride the bus."

That sounds appealing—riding in a warm car instead of

standing in the back of a packed and drafty city bus. "Okay," I agree, "but I don't have much I can tell you."

"That's okay."

We walk in silence to the same diner where I ate my small lunch. Even though I'm hungry, I only order coffee. Luke orders a BLT and fries, and I push back my frustration. I don't want to sit here while he eats. Maybe I'll walk to the bus stop after all.

Adding to my aggravation, he doesn't start talking until the waitress serves his sandwich. The greasy, salty fries smell delicious, but queasy hunger churns my stomach. I don't want to eat until I'm home with Beau.

"I was hoping you could give me Devyn's notes. She disappeared off the face of the earth. I've tried contacting her, but I can't get a hold of her."

"Stevie ran her out of town," I remind him, cupping my hands around the warm mug. For a trash diner, the coffee's good.

"Yeah, I know. She won't answer my calls. She left everything behind."

"Not everything," I whisper. She had every reason to leave me behind, but she didn't.

He tilts his head. "She brought you with her. Where'd you two end up?"

"Portland. A little town north of here, about five hours. She worked for the paper there. You couldn't have searched that hard if you didn't find her."

Luke munches on a fry and says with his mouth full, "I had other things on my plate. When she was on the streets, she collected a lot of info, and I was hoping she'd give me what she had. Do you have access to it?"

"I do, but it's two years old now, and I don't think she'd want me giving up her sources. She's an honest reporter."

"Yeah, one of the few left, from what I hear. No, I get it, but she didn't give you any leads? She told you how to find your mother."

"No, she didn't. I knew that from before." I blush, embarrassed.

"Oh, right. I heard about you getting busted. You're brave to be out here. That shit's everywhere."

"I know. Listen, I don't have anything for you. I'm gonna take off." I twist to get out of the booth.

"Wait a minute. I said I'd give you a ride, and I'm good for it."

I sigh. "Fine."

The Sweet packet scratches my arm, and taking a chance, I wiggle it out of my sleeve. "Can I ask you something?"

Luke eyes the candy wrapper. "Sure."

"How long have you worked in Narcotics?"

He drags a fry through a blob of ketchup on his plate. "A few years."

"Okay, so, when did Sweet start looking like candy? When I was hooked, it came in clear plastic baggies, like coke and meth."

"How do you know that's Sweet?"

"Besides a dealer selling it to me? I can smell it. I'm sure any addict could."

Luke rolls his shoulders and his eyes turn into slits. "That's interesting. But, to answer your question, a couple of years ago. Right around the time you and Devyn moved out of the city."

"If you know that, why hasn't Stevie been arrested?" In frustration, I squeeze the Sweet Stuff wrapper in my fist. The answer is right in front of their eyes, and the cops won't do anything about it.

"Can't prove it. We bust dealers on the streets, but no one will rat her out. The wrappers aren't enough—we need proof of the source. Her delivery trucks, we can't tell one load from the other, and she screams about her rights if we let a dog get too close. Not to mention, she's probably turned more cops crooked than we have straight in the department. They look the other way."

"That's why she's been able to get away with it for so long," I say, tapping the packet against the chipped tabletop.

"Yeah, mainly. One day, she'll switch it up again. A different candy, a different wrapper. She's got a few others that only she sells. She chose Sweet Stuff because she's been selling it for so long, no one would think to question it. The thing is, the DA and the DEA won't touch her with a ten-foot pole if we don't have hard evidence." He pops the last of his BLT into his mouth and chews.

I take a sip of my coffee. "What do you need?"

"Pictures of her supply. While I was asking around, I found out the wrappers with Sweet in them are different from the Sweet Stuff candy she sells in her stores. See?" He takes out his phone and brings up the website for Stevie's candy stores.

Comparing the wrappers on his phone with the one in my hand, I say, "Sweet wrappers have hot pink lettering, and real Sweet Stuff candy has blue and light pink."

"Exactly, but we've accused Stevie before, and she says the color tells customers what flavor it is. Hot pink for strawberry, light pink for bubble gum, and blue for blue raspberry. Every time we think we have something figured out, she can brush it off."

"Then what would pictures do? There's no proof in a picture."

Luke nods. "True, but we've never had a recovering addict in her warehouse before. You say you can smell the Sweet through the wrapper, so you know what's inside. She won't let us run dogs through there, that's not a surprise, but we never thought to have a person tag the pallets that aren't candy."

"And then what?"

"You swipe a few, we test them, and bam, we have ourselves a witness."

"I could do that," I say slowly, skimming over the risk. I couldn't tell Beau about it, or Devyn. They'd never allow it. All I would have to do is poke around Stevie's warehouse, take some pictures, and grab a few packets like Luke said. I could be in and out in fifteen minutes. Do it at night when she's not there. I'd bring him the packets that I knew had Sweet in them, and with my testimony, there would be more than enough evidence for a search warrant.

His eyes widen. "Are you sure? It'll be dangerous, Talia. Stevie has that shit guarded around the clock. Devyn knows she doesn't fuck around."

I know how dangerous Stevie can be. My sister disappeared right in front of my eyes, and it was only Rick's love that found her. Without him, she would have frozen to death.

But that's only another reason why I need to do this. Stevie has hurt so many people, and if I can help bring her down, then I should. I think of Jensen, Jessie, Serena . . . their lives will never be the same. Stevie Johansson brought Sweet to the streets of the upper Midwest and made a fortune off other people's misery.

"I know," I say, "but Devyn wouldn't let it stop her. It didn't, so if she can do it, I can do it, too."

Luke nods and lifts his hand for the check. "Then let's go."

"Tonight?" My grip tightens around my mug.

"Right now. The sooner the better. If I let you take off, you'll get cold feet. You in?"

I don't hesitate. "Yeah. I'm in."

He grins at me. "Sweet."

CHAPTER EIGHTEEN

Beau

Cecilia answers, and I purr into the phone, "Mayor Ramsey."

"Beau, what a pleasure to hear from you tonight. What can I do for you?" she murmurs.

In the background, cutlery clinks against china. Cecilia's already out celebrating a hard-earned Friday night. I should have thought of that, and I'm surprised she answered her phone. Even for me. To her, everything's a game, and she's ignored me a time or two thinking it gave her the upper hand. That's why she thrives in politics. No one plays the game better than Cecilia Ramsey, and I need to remember that. If I lose, my loss will be bigger than hers.

"I need to pull in a favor, love," I say, wincing. I don't use the endearment lightly, and since Talia came into my life, she's the only one I talk to that way.

"Oh, really?" she asks, curious, and the sounds in the background fade. "Do tell."

Cecilia and Stevie are friends. About as friendly as two women can be who are on opposite sides playing to win. Cecilia looks the other way when it comes to Stevie's "business," and Stevie supports City Hall in return.

"My fiancée's stepped into a bit of trouble," I say, pacing my office. I don't have time for this, Everett's threats buzzing in my ears.

"She's your fiancée now," she says, amused. "Congratulations. I didn't see the announcement."

"We haven't told anyone."

"Good for you, Beau. You deserve it, though, I am sad to say it wasn't me."

"Our relationship has been beneficial in other ways."

"That is true. Well, what is it?"

"What would you say if I could tell you how to beat Stevie Johansson at her own game and turn yourself into the Sweetheart of the Midwest?" It's exactly what she'd be if she cleaned up the streets.

Her voice drops to a vicious whisper. "There's no way you can do that. Devyn Scott was the best there was in this town, and even she couldn't do it. Stevie has too many friends."

"Including you?"

"I didn't say that, but I know where my butter comes from, and it hasn't been from you."

"I could change that," I say, holding back a growl. We're wasting time, but if I go in without a plan, we'll be back to where we were when Stevie ran Devyn out of the city. This needs to stop, or Everett and Stevie will never leave Talia and Devyn alone. Ever. I can't do this without Cecilia's help. Because she's right. If it was possible, Devyn would have done it.

She scoffs. "How?"

"You're not Devyn Scott. You have more power behind you than she did."

"Because of Stevie," she says.

"That proves my point. You want to owe her for the rest of your career?" Like any big-time mayor, Cecilia has political aspirations—ones she won't be able to claim as her own if someone else keeps handing them to her.

"No, but I can't go in half-assed. You saw what she did to Devyn, and she got off lightly. Stevie won't be so soft with me."

"You won't. You have my word." My word actually means something in this city. If it didn't, Cecilia wouldn't give me the time of day if I asked.

"What do you have?" She sighs.

"Declan Everett and Stevie Johansson kidnapped Talia. I tracked her phone, and she's at Stevie's warehouse on 190th and Pike right now. Never mind the drugs you'll find when you raid it—that's a bonus. Talia's there, against her will, and they're doing God knows what." I clear my throat. "You send in SWAT, and it will be all over. You'll come out on top, and you won't have to depend on Stevie, ever again."

"*Pfft*. You could have called that in yourself. Why did you bother to call me?"

"Because you know the dirty cops from the clean ones." I mean that in every way that could be taken. "*And* you know she still keeps Sweet at that warehouse." I don't know if Stevie moved her entire supply to her new distribution center near Highway 65, but when Cecilia pauses, I know my hunch paid off.

"How do you know Talia's there? Besides tracing her phone?"

"Everett was here, barely an hour ago, and he threatened her. The security tapes will show him in the lobby and in the elevator."

"Why would he show his hand like that?" Cecilia asks, and I push back a string of swear words. All we're doing is wasting time.

"Because he's an asshole. Because Rick and I have always had everything he wants. Because if he can put his hands on Talia, he knows he's sticking it to me. You know what he did to Rick and the site, CeCe," I say, not too proud to use every weapon I have to get her to fucking *move*. "He likes playing dirty. He's engaged to Stevie, for Christ's sake."

"You know she's there. Without a doubt."

"Yes. She's there." And it scares the shit out of me.

"Does Everett know you know?"

I'm not too proud to admit to my mistakes. I'm just too fucking dumb to learn from them. "No. He knows I've been letting Talia look for her mom. She's been searching Arrowhead Alley, and I think that's where they picked her up. I didn't want my relationship with her to turn into what I had with Nina." *It will anyway.*

Cecilia knows what happened—Christ, the whole city does. It was all anyone could talk about for months. She might not have been mayor then, but she heard about it just like everyone else.

"Fuck. If this goes south, you're going down with it."

I sigh and close my eyes. "Thank you."

"I'll call it in. If you want to be there, go."

"Cecilia, I don't know how to thank you."

"If things go the way you say they will, it will be thanks enough. Go."

She hangs up, and I don't waste another second.

CHAPTER NINETEEN

Talia

Luke's car smells like peppermint, and even though he was walking the streets, it's warm inside. A plain sedan, there's more than enough space in front, and I melt into the cushion, drained. I shouldn't be doing this, but Devyn didn't ask permission to go after Stevie either.

He glides away from the curb not far from Haven Presbyterian, the headlights cutting through the dark and the falling snow glinting in the glow.

Flicking a glance at me, he says, "Thank you for doing this. We've been after her for a long time."

"It's smart, isn't it? Making Sweet look like candy? No wonder she's never gotten caught," I say, watching the crumbling buildings go by. I pull out my phone, but Beau still hasn't texted or called. If I was sitting on the bus and checked, it would have made me sad. Now I'm glad that I don't have to answer a text or call him back. I don't want to lie to him, but it doesn't keep tears from burning my eyes.

"Anyone wondering where you are?"

I put my phone to sleep and slide it back into the pocket of Beau's jacket. "No. Devyn lives in Old Harbor now, and the guy I'm seeing . . ." I shrug. "He can't decide if he wants to be with me or not."

Luke briefly touches my hand. "What's his problem?"

I think about last night. What a fool I made out of myself and how Beau had to rescue me. Sliding down in the seat, I say, "I'm too much trouble, I guess."

"Then he's not the right guy for you. I'm a cop, and I still like to find a little trouble now and then." His mouth quirks in a smile. "You're gorgeous. You can find someone better."

We stop at an intersection, and I stare at the red light. I don't want to find someone else. I want him to love me like he loved Nina, but there's something wrong with me and he keeps holding himself back.

We don't talk for the rest of the ride.

Stevie built her first distribution center in an industrial park that has slowly turned into a rundown part of the city. Gangs have made this area their territory and it's not safe to be out—day or night.

I don't see any guards, but that doesn't mean they aren't there.

Luke parks a couple blocks away and turns the car's lights off. "Are you familiar with the building at all?"

Twisting in my seat to face him, I say, "No. I've never been here before."

"Okay. There's a main entrance, but right now it'll be locked. I heard from someone that the lock on the east door is broken, and you can get inside that way."

"What if it isn't?" I bite my bottom lip.

"It is. That's why I wanted to do this tonight. I didn't want to give Stevie time to fix it."

"Oh."

He studies my face in the car's dim interior. "Are you okay? Still on board?"

"Yeah." We've come too far to turn back now.

"Okay. You know what the Sweet wrappers look like. All I need you to do is find the pallets and take some pictures. Swipe a few of the packages for evidence, and then come back. I doubt you'll need more than twenty minutes. In and out, okay?"

My hands start shaking, but I say, "How do I get past the guards?"

"I brought along a few fireworks that I'll set off a block from here. Once they start popping, run for it."

"No one's in there, right?"

He looks me straight in the eye. "There's no one in there."

I climb out and quietly shut the door, and Luke drives away. He doesn't turn his headlights on again, but the street-lights don't let him disappear until he turns a corner and a building blocks my view.

The sidewalks are empty, and I relax. I pictured thugs carrying huge guns walking around her warehouse, but I don't see anyone. I hurry down the street, my boots leaving tracks in the fresh snow. I suck in a breath of cold air hoping it will clear my head and help me focus. I've never been in this part of the city, and I pause to figure out where I am. Luke said the east side of the building, and I trot in that direction.

I hear the *pop! pop! pop!* of the firecrackers echoing through the dark, and I break out into a run. The guards will want to know what's going on, but they'll see it's nothing and come back. I find the door easily enough, but there isn't a handle on this side. Luke didn't warn me, and I stare, heartbroken I failed, but my brain starts to work and I take my gloves off. My fingers fit in the crack between the brick and the door, and I pry it open, my fingertips going numb against the frozen metal.

The hinges squeal and I freeze, hoping no one heard it. When nothing happens, I slip inside. The door bumps shut leaving me in the dark.

Sagging against the wall, I wait until the pounding in my head stops. There's a faint light near the floor several feet away from me, and my eyes slowly adjust to the dark room. I don't want to risk using the flashlight on my phone, and sliding my feet hesitantly across the floor, I inch my way toward the glow. There aren't any pallets stored in this area that I can tell, though there could be some tucked into the shadows along the walls. I don't have much time to find what I'm looking for, and I keep moving.

A door is the source of the light, and I open it. The sudden glare blinds me, and I block it out with my hand.

"You're right on time," a woman says.

Though I've never met her in person, I know who the voice belongs to. I lower my arm.

"Come in, sweetheart," Stevie Johansson says, gesturing for me to step farther into the room.

I turn in a panic to run, but a hulking giant steps in front of me, his grip loose on a silver handgun. I can't get around him. His body takes up the entire doorway.

"Do you want the red or the white?" a man asks as he steps into the room holding two bottles of wine. He looks my way. "Talia Scott. This is quite a surprise. Hendrickson would be disappointed to know that you didn't tell him your plans. We know how much he loves to keep track of his girl-friends."

I recognize Declan Everett. "You son of a bitch."

He laughs. "For a little thing, you have a mouth. Don't worry, you didn't hurt my feelings. I've been called worse."

A door on the other side of the room opens, and Luke shuf-fles inside.

"They got you, too," I say, my heart thudding dully in my chest.

He smiles, showing all his teeth. "Sorry, Talia. Stevie paid me to bring you here. You were so easy, and you really should be more careful. You trust the wrong people."

"But . . . you're a cop."

Stevie laughs. "Didn't your sister teach you anything? Chatting up my dealers and writing list after list of the pig scum who'd rather follow the money than serve and protect. Why do you think I've been able to sell Sweet all this time? Life's hard, little girl. Not everyone dates a billionaire. Come, we're being rude. Let's find a more comfortable place and sit. Luke, do you mind taking care of your pet?"

Luke grabs the collar of my jacket and jerks me across the room. We follow Declan and Stevie down a dim hallway and into another room that's full of pallets.

I don't need to ask if there's Sweet in this room. I can smell it, the scent thick and heavy, like sticking my face in a bag of powdered sugar. The desperate craving zips through me, and it makes my skin burn. This is worse than being in Jensen's apartment. Worse than when I was visiting Jessie. It can't compare to sitting next to Mom in the alley. My heart skips a beat, and I stumble.

Luke hauls me up and pushes me forward.

"Do you want some?" Stevie teases, looking over her shoulder at me.

Violently, I shake my head.

She laughs. "You won't have much choice, sweetheart. Not after I'm done with you."

Luke forces me to follow Declan and Stevie into a large office, and he shoves me down onto a metal chair.

"Don't let her move," Stevie says, taking a roll of grey duct tape out of an old desk and throwing it to Luke.

"Devyn didn't know you hid Sweet in candy wrappers," I say, knowing it's useless to fight Luke who tapes my wrists to the armrests of the chair.

Stevie lifts a shoulder. "I had to figure out a different way to package it. She was getting too close, but I couldn't let her stop me. I've been selling Sweet and running the money through my stores for *years,* and that isn't going to stop anytime soon. Especially when you crawl out of here so addicted that's all you'll be able to think about for the rest of your pathetic life. And Devyn. Well, if she starts sticking her nose into my business again, who's going to help her? Rick Mercer? Please. What a useless piece of shit."

I realize at that moment no one is going to rescue me. Devyn and Rick are in Old Harbor, and Beau, he thinks I'm out looking for Mom. I didn't ask Mack to shadow me, hoping that after last night I had it under control.

I'm too scared to cry. The scent of Sweet hasn't faded, and my skin crawls.

The shakes set in, and my vision blurs. If I go into shock, maybe I won't know what they do to me. Stevie's plan is clear. She's going to torture me with Sweet until I go crazy.

"Just like his business partner," Declan says, laughing. "You know, I went to see Hendrickson. I offered to trade you for the property, and he didn't even blink. I wouldn't count on him saving you."

Kneeling, Luke finishes taping me to the chair. He squeezes my thigh, his eyes hot. Maybe Stevie told him he could have me when they were done.

"Find her phone," Stevie orders him. "She won't need it."

He knows exactly where I keep it, and he unzips Beau's jacket. As he reaches inside, the back of his hand brushes my breast. I flinch and try to lean away, and he chuckles. He takes my phone out of my pocket and flips it across the room to Stevie. She snatches it out of the air.

"Ah, Dec's right. No texts. No calls. No voicemails. Too bad." She shows Declan my phone, and he smirks at the screen. "I understand how it feels to be unlovable. My mom never loved me. She was like yours. Decided drugs were more important than anything else. Including her only daughter. She left me with a bastard who liked to beat on me, and I promised him he'd get what he deserved. He did, too."

She pries the phone out of its case, drops it on the floor, and stomps on it, the sharp heel of her boot cracking the glass. Kicking the broken pieces out of the way, she rounds the corner of the desk and drops to the floor in front of me. Gripping my chin in her hand, she says, "What you don't realize until it's too late is that nothing can ever fill that hole in your heart. Nothing can replace love, and when you're told over and over again that no one will ever love you, it hurts. It hurts, until one day, you don't feel it anymore."

Over my shoulder, Luke hands her the packet of Sweet I gave him at the diner. She's going to hook me using the Sweet I bought in the alley. I was able to resist, but it will still kill me.

"I'm not like you," I say, but I know I am. Beau doesn't want me as much as I want him, and he's shown me that since the day Devyn went back to Portland.

"You're not?" She looks around and fakes surprise. "I don't see anyone here who will save you. Your mother's high in a ditch, your sister traded you for a lover, and Beau would rather keep his precious land than protect you. Tell me again, sweetheart, how you're not like me."

She rips the packet open and takes out the white dipping stick made of sugar. She licks it and covers the tip in Sweet.

Declan leans against the desk and sips a glass of wine, enjoying the show.

"Hold her head still," she says to Luke, and he twists his fingers in my hair and grabs my throat.

"Do you smell it?" Stevie coos, tracing the bow of my lip with the dipping stick.

The sugary scent is overwhelming, and I try to hold my breath. It doesn't work, and my heart slams in my chest and all my nerves tingle. I can taste the phantom bubble gum flavor, and my throat burns.

"All it takes is just a little, tiny, taste," she whispers, skimming the candy stick over my lips. "Don't you want it? Don't you want to fly? Take it, baby, and let go."

Tears fill my eyes. I can't help it. If it somehow gets in my mouth, I'll never recover. The need would too strong and even Beau's love wouldn't be able to save me.

A tear drips down my cheek. Silently, I tell him how much I love him and wish my sister and Rick all the happiness in the world.

She's about to push the stick between my lips, but suddenly, she freezes.

"What was that?" she asks, standing. She shoves the dipping stick into the wrapper and puts the packet of Sweet in the pocket of the cardigan she's wearing over her black dress.

Luke lets me go, and frantically, I rub my lips against the collar of Beau's jacket. The material still smells like his cologne, and I inhale, trying to breathe in anything to cover the scent of Sweet before I have a panic attack.

"What was that?" Stevie asks again, her eyes locking with Declan's. "Who knows we're here?"

Faintly, I hear a dog barking. No, not one. Several.

"I don't know!" Everett says, setting his wineglass on the desk and moving toward the door.

She turns on Luke. "Who followed you here?"

"No one, I swear," he says, defending himself.

"Someone knows we're here. You stupid—"

The door slams open, and two law enforcement officers inch into the room, their weapons aimed at Stevie and Declan. Another follows behind them, his sights set on Luke. He raises his hands in surrender.

A detective wearing a rumpled suit walks into the room, his face covered in whiskers. He looks old, but there's a glitter in his eyes that could only come from taking down the Sweetheart of the Midwest. "You have the right to remain silent . . ." he begins.

Two officers cuff Declan's and Stevie's hands behind their backs.

"What are the charges?" she screams at the detective, her eyes wild.

"Drug possession with intent to sell, money laundering, kidnapping," he says, nodding at me. "For starters. We got a nice tip that panned out. You're going away for a long time."

My muscles strain against the tape, and my stomach quivers. I want to get out of here, find Beau, and tell him how sorry I am for being so stupid.

"I want to call my attorney. I'm not saying shit to you!" She steps toward Everett and snarls, "When did you talk to Hendrickson? It's always been about that fucking property. That goddamned, *fucking* hotel! You stupid son of a bitch."

The detective laughs, dry and raspy. He hands another officer a pocketknife. "Cut her loose. What are you waiting for?"

The young officer hurries past the desk and starts cutting the duct tape off my wrists.

An angry voice echos down the hallway. "I'm not waiting another fucking second! Let me see her."

"Beau," I whisper, hope flaring so bright I lose sight of

everything but him. He strides into the room, his anger zapping like electricity.

His gaze flicks to me and the cop ripping the tape off my jacket's sleeves and then to Declan. "I told you, if you hurt her, you'd pay for it." Beau rams his fist into Declan's jaw, snapping his head back.

"All right, that's enough. He'll get plenty of that where he's going," the detective says, stepping between them.

Shaking out his hand, Beau turns to me. The officer's done cutting the tape off my ankles, but I sit, watching him. I will always have this weakness. This crack in my armor. I will always fight this addiction.

He knees in front of me, his eyes wary. "Are you okay?"

"Yeah. Thanks to you."

He leans in to kiss me, but I turn my head.

"I understand," he says, backing away.

I shake my head, confused. "You understand what?"

"Everything." He stares the floor.

I don't know what he means. "Beau."

He lifts his head, and his eyes are full of shadows and secrets he hasn't told me.

"I have to wash my face. I have Sweet on my lips. Please."

Brushing his thumb over my cheek, he says, "I'm sorry, love. There's an ambulance outside. We didn't know what they were going to do to you. Will you let them do it? And take a look at you?"

"Okay."

He picks me up, and I cuddle into his chest. He walks me outside while the police swarm the warehouse, dogs going crazy over the pallets of Sweet Stuff, and I have never felt more loved.

———

Beau never leaves my side, and the medic cleans my skin several times with disinfectant. The scent is harsh, and it gets rid of the sickly sweet aroma that was stuck in my nose.

I talk to the cops, and he's there, his arm around me the whole time, while I tell them what happened and how I ended up at the warehouse. I trusted Luke and almost paid with my life.

It's close to midnight when the detective gives Beau permission to bring me home, and he helps me into an SUV that's parked near the warehouse next to several law enforcement vehicles. He drove himself, and he climbs into the driver's seat and rests his forehead against the steering wheel.

"Beau, what's wrong?" He's trying to find a way to let me down easy, but nothing about this will be easy. I try to breathe through this other kind of panic.

He's tired, and he forces a smile. "Besides all that?" he asks, tipping his head in the direction of Stevie's warehouse.

"Yeah. How did you find me? How did you know where to look?"

Holding my hand, he brushes his thumb over my knuckles. "I tracked your phone."

"How? Stevie broke it. The cops will probably search that office, and they're going to find it on the floor somewhere. She stepped on it."

He lets go of my hand.

I can feel him withdraw, like he always does whenever he talks about watching over me, as if it's the most horrible thing in the world to have someone care about you so much they want to know where you are every second.

"Isn't it enough that I did?"

"Yeah. Sure." I buckle my seatbelt, and he drives out of the lot.

"Devyn and Rick are at the penthouse. I told them Everett

came to the office and threatened you, and they flew in. I want you to go back to Old Harbor with them."

He stares straight ahead, the streetlights streaking across his hard features.

"Okay," I agree softly.

He flinches and presses his lips together.

Like hell I'm going to Old Harbor with Devyn. Beau and I are making a life together here, in Cedar Hill, and if he thinks I'm going to give that up because a woman in his past taught him his love is an inconvenience, he's going to be unpleasantly surprised.

"Can I have the weekend?" I ask as we drive toward his building.

"Talia . . ." His voice is raspy, full of anger and resignation.

"What? If you're breaking up with me, at least give me the weekend."

His eyes snap with annoyance, and he turns the vehicle sharply into the underground parking. Slamming on the brakes, he parks and turns the engine off. The inside of the truck is quiet and tension vibrates around us. I unlatch my seatbelt and crawl into his lap, wedging myself between his body and the steering wheel. I trail kisses over his jaw, his stubble scratching my skin, and he shudders.

"I just need the weekend to settle," I say, hoping he's listening to me. "Stevie rubbed Sweet on my lips. If you wouldn't have come when you did, she would've hooked me. You saved my life. If you don't want me in yours anymore, that's fair, but give me the weekend to settle and breathe. Please."

I straddle his lap and nibble at his lips.

He groans and pushes his tongue into my mouth.

He's warm, and his arms are tight around me. I'll wear him down. I'll need a long time to convince him that what he wants to give me is exactly what I want too, but I'll be a recovering addict for the rest of my life. Planning that far ahead doesn't scare me.

"We need time to say goodbye," I whisper. I'll break his heart because he thinks he deserves it, but I'll fix it and we'll come back stronger than we ever were.

"Fine."

"Thank you."

We don't speak in the elevator, and he stares straight ahead, his shoulders tense. He doesn't try to hold my hand, but I hold his, tangling our fingers. The doors slide open and he jerks away, but Devyn's waiting, pulling me into her arms and not giving me a second to say anything to anyone.

Rick hugs me next, and I hug him back, just as tightly.

Stevie was wrong. I am lovable, and I am loved.

Maybe her mother abandoned her, and maybe our mother abandoned Devyn and me, but I won't do it to the people I love.

In the living room, I sit in Beau's lap and tell everyone what happened. He's angry I'm pushing, but he doesn't let me go, cuddling me to him and resting his chin on the top of my head.

Devyn's glowing, almost bouncing in glee on the couch next to Rick. She's happy that I'm safe, but nothing can compare to Stevie in prison and her drugs off the streets. There will always be Sweet in the city, but the DEA will keep anyone else from taking her place in Cedar Hill and it will definitely be harder to come by.

It's late, and reluctantly, they leave to spend the night at Rick's. The elevator doors slide shut, and Beau stomps into the bedroom, changes, and crawls into bed. I could let it hurt my feelings, but I won't.

In a hot shower, I wash the street, diner, and Stevie's touch off my skin. If I take a shower whenever Beau's home, he'll lean against the vanity and talk to me, but he doesn't tonight and I miss it. I'm eager to jump into bed, but I don't rush, putting lotion on and brushing my teeth. I dress in warm pajamas and crawl in next to him, but he rolls over, giving me his back.

His stubbornness is amusing and I want to laugh, but it scares me, too. I can't let him have his way, but if he really thinks breaking up is for the best, there's nothing I can do to force him to let me stay here.

Holding in a whimper, I roll off my side of the bed.

He stiffens, waiting for me to leave and sleep in the guest room. Instead, I crawl back in on his side, and wiggle into his arms.

"Make love to me, Beau. I'm so cold," I murmur against his lips.

He does, and like fire, he devours everything I have, and never stopping, I beg him to take more.

CHAPTER TWENTY

Beau

I wanted to stay and be there when Talia woke up, but Rick asked me to head out to the site, and I reluctantly agreed. Devyn will be there, and I'll have to be okay with that. I didn't let Talia fall asleep until close to five this morning. When I kissed her forehead, I noticed a bruise forming on one of her wrists. I held her in place all night, pinning her to the mattress while I had my way with her. If only keeping her in my life would be as easy.

We stop for coffee on the way.

The street's empty, and I park where I usually do on the days I have to drive out. It's too cold, and I'd rather not do this here, but Rick and I have unfinished business and I don't want to talk in front of Talia and Devyn.

He holds my coffee cup, and I open the padlock that keeps the fence door locked. The sound of the keys jingling interrupts the quiet of the morning and annoys the birds perched in the trees along the street. I push the door through the snow on the ground, the hinges squealing, and we both step onto the site. He hands my coffee back to me, the paper cup warming my palm through my leather glove.

"A lot has changed since October," he murmurs.

There's no arguing there. "Yeah."

He kicks at some snow. "I don't think things are settled. Not here at the site, not in the city, and not between us."

Uneasily, I shrug. Things aren't right between us, but I don't think they ever will be. "It's fine. Let it go."

"I tried that, and you were so angry you didn't want to be my friend anymore. I've always taken our friendship for granted. Men do that, I guess. We're not like women, checking in with each other, going for coffee all the time. The feelings part of it. I apologized once, but you were too mad to listen to me. I *am* sorry for not being there for you after Nina died, and I'm sorry the site is still like this—" he gestures to the hotel with his coffee cup— "and I'm sorry I got so caught up with Devyn that I didn't see the damage me hiding in Old Harbor caused."

I'm calmer than I was the morning he tried to talk to me at the office, and I nod. "Thanks. I learned a lot about myself when I met Talia. Well, maybe it wasn't that, but I buried a lot of things that came back up. I'm needy. I can't be a coward and not admit it, because it's true. I need the people I care about around me. We're good friends, and the time you've spent in Old Harbor has hurt on a level that I didn't want to tell you about. You have a right to live your life without me hanging on your leg like a little kid. It's okay."

Rick scoffs. "You've always been able to express yourself better than I have, and I think it's saved our friendship more than once." He sips his coffee. "The two years I've lived in Old Harbor hurt you, but I also hurt myself. This hotel isn't important, and the Cedar Hill branch isn't important. I want you and Talia to move to Old Harbor. I'm settled, and Devyn has a job that she likes. You can work with me if you want, or get into something different if that's a direction you think you'd like to go. Talia can go to school anywhere."

I shake my head. "I'm sending Talia to Old Harbor with you and Devyn."

Rick raises his eyebrows. "Why?"

"It hasn't sunk in yet that I tracked her phone to find her. Once it does, she'll realize the type of guy I am."

"You saved her life. You think she's going to get angry about it?"

"No, maybe not about this, but about something else. When I want to go to the store with her, when I follow her all over the penthouse. If she goes for a walk, and I want to go too. I'm so in love with her, I can't see anything, can't feel anything else when she's around, and when she's not, all I can think about is being with her again. I'm suffocating, and I can't be any other way. The way I am killed Nina, and it's better if Talia leaves with you. When she first moved in, I thought I could be different, but I can't. I'll finish the hotel. I made that promise, and I'll stick to it. After that, I'll figure out what to do. The company doesn't mean as much to me as it used to."

"You're right. You *are* needy," he says.

His agreement hurts as much as it validates me. Rick knows me better than anyone.

"And so am I," he continues, stepping toward the building, "so I guess I better end it with Devyn."

I follow. "It's not the same, and you know it."

"No. It's worse. My back hurts all the time. I'm lucky Devyn already knows how to massage the knots out, or she'd probably have to learn. In fact, I woke up last night in pain, and at two in the morning she was trying to get me to loosen up. I'm having surgery on my shoulder soon, and she's going to be doing all the cooking and cleaning. I told her we could hire a housekeeper, but she didn't seem to like that idea very much. If she gets pregnant, she'll be doing a lot of the parenting on her own. We probably shouldn't have a kid, but I'm a selfish bastard and want one with her. I'll try to do as much as I can, but she already knows that won't be a lot. She's hanging in there, but I shouldn't let her do that. She can find someone else. Someone who doesn't need a pain management appointment every six months, right? We'll send them both back. We'll be doing them a favor. Thank God we haven't gotten married yet. I already lost a shit-ton in a divorce. Don't need to do it again."

"I know what you're doing, and it's not funny."

"No, it's not funny. That shit goes through my head, all the fucking time. *All the time.* Why do you think I left her after Stevie and Everett dumped her here? This fucking site. I hate it. I was pinned in this spot for three hours." He points angrily to the ground where the boom fell. "I will never recover. What you see, right now, is the best I am ever going to be. The best I am ever going to feel is after Devyn rubs me down and I have two fingers of Glenlivet and a handful of ibuprofen in me. How is that fair to her?"

Rick's voice cracks, and I blink. This is a side of him I've never seen before. Not after the accident, not even after Renata left him, did he show me his true feelings.

He rubs his hand under his nose and clears his throat. "But for some dumb-assed reason, she loves me, and I'm not too proud to take it. It took a lot for me to get there, and I almost lost her. If you send Talia to Old Harbor, there's a really good chance she'll listen to what you say, and she won't come back."

"I don't know what to do." I don't want to send her away. The thought of her not coming back if I changed my mind chills me to the bone.

Rick sips his coffee, but I'm caught up in our conversation and mine is forgotten in my hand. "You negotiate better than any businessman I have ever met. You handle deals in your sleep and always come out on top. Why is Talia different? Explain what you need, then listen when she tells you how much of that she can give you. You reach a happy medium you both can live with. Nina didn't listen to you, but you didn't listen to her, either. She wanted to do her own thing, and her own thing didn't include you. Period. Maybe the words didn't come out of her mouth, but she showed you, and you ignored it. How does Talia act, and what does that say? Did you tell her you were sending her to Old Harbor with Devyn?"

Heat crawls up the back of my neck. "Yeah."

"And what did she do?"

I lift a shoulder, but Rick's too smart for that.

"She didn't let you get any sleep last night, that's what. We're all needy. You can't be human and not be needy. I need our friendship, and I'm sorry I've never been clear about it. I need it, and I wish you'd think about moving to Old Harbor. We can promote what's his name, and he can do the CEO thing for a while."

My mouth quirks in amusement. "You want to promote a guy to CEO of a billion-dollar company and you don't even know his name?"

"Andy, right? Andrew. Andrew Milner. Miller? Something. We wouldn't be that far away if he needed our help." He turns and his gaze sweeps the site. "What did Everett want with this place? Why is it so fucking special?"

"It wasn't the land," I murmur, and the wind that's picking up snatches some of my words. "It was all of it. Everett was alone until he met Stevie. He's done business alone, never had a partner. He didn't want the land. He wanted our friendship. He wanted our success. Success we had *because* of our friendship. He sabotaged the lift, hoping to get us back, and he did. This property symbolizes everything we have that he wanted."

Rick stares into the distance, but he's not seeing the hotel or the snow covering the ground. I'm not sure exactly what's going through his mind, but he nods thoughtfully, squinting against the bright morning sun. "Then let's not give him the satisfaction. Move to Old Harbor, Beau. You and Talia. We'll raise our children together."

I swallow around the lump in my throat. "You know something I don't?"

He laughs and slaps me on the back. "No, but I know you. You'll get your shit with Talia straightened out, and it won't be long." He pauses, and then he says, "You really want to see this through?"

"She's caused a lot of pain," I say, nodding at the metal and wood, "but she'll be a beautiful bitch. I want to finish, and we'll throw the biggest party the city has ever seen."

"We'll dedicate the old girl to that asshole Declan Everett. May he find the friendship he was looking for in prison."

I chuckle on the way to the truck, but I feel sorry for Everett, too, in a way. If he *is* in love with Stevie, he'll never see her again, and that will hurt him more than doing time in the state penitentiary. I want Talia in my life, but I can't suffocate her. I can only tell her what I need and hope she understands.

I walk into the foyer and she steps into my arms. Cuddling her close to my chest, I think maybe we have a chance.

I should have known nothing in my life would ever be that easy.

CHAPTER TWENTY-ONE

Talia

I open my eyes and blink against the sun streaming in through the gauzy curtains. I know I'm alone. Through a haze of sleep, I felt Beau kiss my forehead and roll out of bed. I heard him turn the shower on, and I let exhaustion pull me back under.

The alarm clock on the nightstand says it's after ten, and I groan. The faint scent of coffee perks me up, and I shuffle into the kitchen hoping to find Beau at the table reading the *Times*.

Instead, my sister's sitting behind her laptop, her fingers clicking a mile a minute.

"Good morning," I say, yawning.

She pushes back a grin. "Good morning. Did you get any sleep last night?"

Helping myself to a mug of coffee, I say, "Barely, but I'm not going to complain. He probably kept me from having nightmares all night. Where's Rick? Is Beau with him?"

Her smile fades. "They went out to the site. To talk, I think.

They have a few things to hash out." She gets up and brushes her hand down the back of my head. "Are you okay?"

I'm not, but not in the way she's referring to. Beau saying he wants to send me to Old Harbor scares me more than the Sweet Stevie brushed over my lips.

I stare into my coffee cup. "I'm sorry. I was stupid. I thought I could pick up where you left off. All it did was get me in trouble."

"I found plenty of trouble," Devyn says, leaning against the counter and resting an elbow near the coffeemaker. "It's not your fault."

"I found Mom," I whisper, tears filling my eyes.

"How was she?"

"You know."

"Yeah, I do. I didn't want you to see her that way, but I don't think you ever would have believed me if you hadn't."

"I blamed you for a long time, for a lot of things. I didn't know you paid for Mom's apartment. I didn't know you left money at the church and that you made arrangements with Father Will to give it to her. I thought you didn't care, and I'm sorry."

She wraps me in her arms, and I put my head on her shoulder. "I didn't want you to know. One of my biggest fears was you searching for Mom and getting hooked again. When Bill fired me, I was devastated. I never wanted to stop paying her rent. I always wanted her to have a safe place to sleep."

"I found the church, and last night, I talked to Father Will. He told me it's okay to let her go. Beau offered to put her through rehab, but she's too far gone. I sat next to her, Devyn, sat right next to her, and she didn't know me. She looked right through me. I bought her a packet of Sweet, and that's all she cared about."

"She loved us," Devyn says, rubbing my back in the same

soothing circles that helped me sleep the first few weeks after I left rehab. "Before she went to that dinner party, she loved us. Dad left her, and she still took care of us. She did the best she could on her own for a long time. You can still love her. I do. Remember the good times . . . they don't let the bad hurt so much."

"You still give her money." It's not a question. Father Will told me she does, but I want to hear it from her.

"Yeah. I mail cash to the church and he passes it on to her. Rick knows I do. He offered to buy her an apartment, but she wouldn't understand she could live there, that there would always be food in the fridge. She's been on Sweet for too long, and her mind is gone." She pauses. "Will you tell me more about last night?"

I sip my coffee. Maybe one day I'll go back to the regular kind. In some ways, I'm getting stronger every day. In others, I still feel like a little kid scared of her own shadow. "There's nothing to tell, really, that I didn't tell you last night. I trusted the wrong person—a narcotics cop who thought I was you at first." I scoff. "Now that I think about it, that must have been his way of getting me to talk to him. I shouldn't have trusted him, but who wouldn't trust a cop? I underestimated how much Stevie hated you, hated *us,* for snooping around. I'm lucky Declan Everett went to Beau's office and threatened me. I'm lucky Beau tracked my phone, and that he was able to before Stevie broke it. I'm lucky the police came when they did. I was two seconds away from living the rest of my life like Mom."

I breathe in the scent of coffee and remind myself where I am. Bubble gum will never smell the same to me—the sweet, sugary scent will always bring me back to that warehouse where I was taped to a chair and watched Beau stride into the room like my guardian angel.

"Stevie threatened you with Sweet."

"Yeah. Scared the crap out of me."

"Before we moved to Portland, she did the same to me."

My lips part in shock. "You never told me that."

"I didn't want you to know how serious the whole situation was. You were already dealing with so much. When I woke up in the hospital, I thought she followed through with her threat and hooked me. You can ask Rick how bad I freaked out. You're so brave, Talia. You're a lot braver than I ever gave you credit for." She squeezes my hand.

I shake my head. "No. I wasn't brave, not back then. Not in rehab, not the year we lived here, and not in Portland. I want to spend the rest of my life with Beau, and that makes me brave now. I'm brave for him, and I promised." I pause. "He told me to go with you and Rick when you go back to Old Harbor."

"Do you know why?"

"He thinks he's too needy, too stifling. He thinks I'm going to get tired of him watching over me and wanting to spend time with me. He dated a woman who didn't like it. That's all I know, and I don't want to know any more unless he tells me. The thing is, I need that. I want to be with him too, whenever and however I can. I don't know. Maybe I should go and let him think about it."

Devyn grabs her mug off the table and pours more coffee into it. "I let Rick push me away, and it worked. He needed time to realize he loved me and didn't want to live without me, and eventually, he came back. I think, from what I know about Beau and what you've told me, if you left, he'd think it just proved him right. No, I think you should stay here and show him that you're not going anywhere, no matter what he says."

"I asked for the weekend to give us time to say goodbye."

"Oh, honey. What did he say?" she asks, frowning in sympathy.

"He agreed. That's it."

"He doesn't want you to go. I'll tell Rick I need to get back to Old Harbor to submit an article for the paper, and you two can have the rest of the weekend together alone. You're starting school soon, right? Winter break is almost over?"

"Monday."

"Then ask him for another week or two for classes to calm down. He'll give them to you, and then when those weeks are up, ask for more."

I laugh. "He's not stupid. He'll see right through that."

"So what? You're not hiding anything. You want to stay here. Tell him often, and eventually he'll believe it. I tell Rick all the time his injuries don't mean anything to me. I care if he's hurting and always do what I can, but I'd never leave him because of that." Tears shine in her eyes. "Renata left him for exactly that reason, and he was certain no one could love him the way he is. I suppose that's the way Beau feels, too, if a woman left him because he only wanted to be with her. You're different people, and what she hated, you'll love. Hang in there. It's all we can both do."

"Do you know about Nina?" I ask, pouring more milk and coffee into my mug.

"No. Rick hasn't said anything about her. I've trusted Beau since the day we met him, and that hasn't changed. He won't hurt you."

"No, he won't. Hey, I have a question for you," I say, grateful to change the subject. I've been wondering about this for a long time, and this might be one of my last chances to ask. Now that Stevie's in jail waiting for her sentencing, Devyn will be free to think about other things. We both will. Soon she and Rick will have a baby, and this will all seem like a dream. No, not a dream, a nightmare.

"Sure."

"The night the cops busted that party and arrested me, I

didn't use my phone call. Did a police officer contact you, or social services? How did you know that I got arrested? When I had to go to court, the deputy at the jail told me I had an attorney to represent me, and I was shocked. I saw you in the courtroom the day the judge ordered me to go to rehab."

She drags in a breath and rubs her hands over her cheeks. "I did my damnedest to do well in school. I always wanted to be a journalist, a reporter who told the truth, and I think I've done that. But that doesn't mean when I left, I walked away from you and Mom. I knew about the frat party, and I knew about the six months you were hooked. I checked in at the apartment, but most of the time you and Mom weren't there. I looked for you on the streets, and if I didn't see you, Father Will would tell me how you were. I didn't want you to live the rest of your life like that, and the night you went to that party with Serena, I was looking for you. I was the one who called the cops. I knew you were arrested for drug possession because I was there."

I step into her arms and cry.

"It was all I could think of to do," she says, her shoulders shaking with sobs she won't let go.

I can't speak for several minutes. "Thank you," I finally say.

"You don't have to thank me for loving you," she says, letting me go and wiping the tears under her eyes. "You'll always be my sister, and I'm so proud of you. In the spring, when Rick and I get married, I'd be honored if you stood up with me."

I rub the tears off my cheeks. "Of course I will. If you stand up with me, too. I will get Beau to marry me. I need him just as much as he needs me."

"Then don't back down."

"I won't."

The elevator doors open, and Beau and Rick step into the foyer. Devyn rushes through the kitchen and wraps her arms around his neck. She presses her lips to his, and chuckling in pleasant surprise, he kisses her back.

I don't give Beau a chance to push me away and cuddle against his chest. After a moment, he sighs and pulls me closer, and I take it as a good sign.

I'll stay strong. I've faced addiction, rehab, and looked Stevie Johansson in the eyes as she threatened me with Sweet. I can face whatever comes my way.

Little did I know how heartbreaking Beau's past is, and what that meant for our life together.

———

"I need to shower. Will you keep me company?" I ask, looking up at him.

His eyes flatten, and I catch Rick glare, his fingers still tangled in my sister's hair. Beau forces a smile. "Sure. Let me hang up my coat."

I'm naked and in the shower by the time Beau steps into the bathroom holding a cup of coffee. He leans against the vanity like he always does.

"Devyn has to go back to Old Harbor today for work," I say, shampooing my hair, my heart beating a mile a minute. "I know I asked for the weekend, but because she has to leave and school starts on Monday, I was wondering if I could stay here for the next week or two, just until classes settle down and I have more time to move out."

The shower stall's glass is blurry, and I can't see the look on his face.

He doesn't say anything, and I add, "I can move into the guest bedroom again, if you want."

He'd never let that happen.

"I promise I won't be in your way," I say, knowing full well all he wants is to be around me as much as possible.

I poke my head out of the shower. He's staring at the floor, and his jaw is clenched so tightly I'm surprised his teeth aren't cracking.

"You won't even know I'm here," I say brightly.

He snaps his head up and narrows his eyes. "What are you doing?"

I wrinkle my nose. "Giving you what you want?"

I finish my shower, and to my surprise, he stays in the bathroom, sipping his coffee. Normally, we talk about our plans for the day, but it's enough that he's here.

He hands me a towel as I open the door. "Thanks. All I need is a little time. The beginning of a semester is always so busy. I might not have a lot of stuff here, but I'll still need to pack it up and find a place to live."

"Talia . . ."

Stepping out of the shower, I say, "I'm not living with Rick and Devyn. The second I move into their spare bedroom, she'll get pregnant and need it for a nursery. There's no point in that. I'll live somewhere in town close to campus. It will be fine."

I start to dry off, and he notices the bruises he gave me last night. He can say whatever the hell he wants, but his touch says something different every time.

I'm proud that my voice is steady. If I thought for one second he'd let me move to Old Harbor alone, that I would have to live by myself after six months of addiction, three years of rehab, three years of living with Devyn, and four months of living with him, I would be *freaking out*. There's no way I'm prepared to live alone.

He lingers, and I put lotion on and brush my hair. Awkward in his own suite, he stands in the middle of the room, his hands shoved into the pockets of his khaki pants. I like it when he dresses down, and I tell him so. "You look nice."

He stares at me.

I shrug. It was only a compliment—he can accept it or not. I wrap the towel around myself and step into his walk-in closet. "I'm going to miss all this space," I say over my shoulder, pulling a pair of black yoga pants and a sweatshirt from the University of Portland off their hangers.

Once I'm dressed and my towel's in the hamper, he follows me into the living room where Devyn and Rick are cuddling on the couch. They look comfortable together, and I'm glad my sister found someone who makes her happy.

"We're going to fly back this afternoon," she says, her body curled into Rick's side. "Has there been any news about Stevie?"

Beau sits in a recliner near them, and I crawl into his lap, tucking myself against his chest. He hugs me, slipping his hand up my sweatshirt and splaying his hand over my ribs. His jaw brushes my cheek as he speaks.

"I talked to someone at the mayor's office this morning. The raid went as planned, and Cecilia did a happy dance all night. They searched the building where I found Talia," he says, his fingers digging into my skin, "and there was over two million dollars worth of Sweet in that warehouse alone. Another five million in her warehouse on Highway 65. All of it packaged in Sweet Stuff candy wrappers. There was never enough evidence for the cops to find a judge who would sign off on a warrant to search with dogs, and the cops who were able to poke around thought they found product for her stores."

"I can't believe with all my digging, I didn't put two and two together," Devyn says, scowling.

I speak up. "Luke told me Stevie had just started packaging it like that when you and I moved to Portland. It was too risky for her to keep selling it in plain sight. You couldn't have known."

She quirks a corner of her mouth. "I guess you're right. Did you look up any of your friends from that frat party? Did they get hooked on Sweet eating candy from Stevie's store?"

I link my fingers with Beau's under my sweatshirt. "I talked to a couple of people who were there. One guy said he got hooked eating out a girl who put it you know where."

Rick grimaces and turns to Devyn. "Don't do that. You're sweet enough as it is."

Wrinkling her nose, she says, "Definitely not my thing." She sighs. "That's too bad. She ruined his life."

"That's he what he said. After I left his place, I asked the cops to do a welfare check. Maybe he'll be okay. I found Jessie, one of the girls who went shopping with us that afternoon. She said she had some of Serena's candy, and she was okay. Serena and I got hooked at that party, but we can't blame the candy she bought at Stevie's store. I was just being a stupid kid."

"It could happen to anyone, any time," Devyn says, always defending me. "Your therapist told you that, and your story about that guy just proves the point. You can't blame him for being intimate with a woman and getting hooked on Sweet, and no one blames you for being a nineteen year old girl looking for a little fun. It's what you do with the rest of your life going forward that matters."

"Yeah, I know." Talking about it embarrasses me, and Beau understands. Giving me a quick squeeze, he changes the subject . . . kind of.

"You *were* on to something when you thought people were getting hooked on the candy from her stores," he says to Devyn. "With similar packaging, some of the wrappers that had Sweet in them did accidentally make it onto her shelves. Talia and her friend might not have gotten hooked that way, but other kids probably have."

Devyn nods, a little surprise and a lot of satisfaction gleaming in her eyes. "It wasn't my theory—Barney, the editor-in-chief at the *Herald*—mentioned it during my interview. He'll be angry he was right. Now his niece will be fighting an addiction that never should have happened."

I feel sorry for her, and I tuck the idea in the back of my mind to meet Barney's niece and offer her support and friendship if she wants it. When you're dealing with addiction, you can never have too many people in your corner wanting the best for you.

Beau continues telling us what he knows. "Stevie's looking at a lifetime in prison for drug possession, intent to sell, money laundering, and kidnapping. Talia needs to go to the police station and officially press charges. I put them off—I wanted her to have the weekend to calm down—but we won't let her get away with it. Everett, though, he's a slimy bastard."

"Fuck," Rick mutters. "I knew him being there was too good to be true."

"He'll be charged with kidnapping, but just because he was at Stevie's warehouse doesn't mean he was selling Sweet or helping her launder the money. Any attorney who has a brain won't be able to make those charges stick, but he'll get time for what little we can pin on him."

I snuggle into his chest, and he kisses the top of my head.

"The newspapers will be writing about this for months. Has anyone from the *Times* called to interview you?" Devyn asks me.

"I don't know. Stevie broke my phone. If Beau had waited to look for me, he wouldn't have been able to find me." He stiffens, but I will never believe him tracking my phone is as horrible as he thinks it is. "I'll give you an exclusive interview, and the *Herald* can print it."

Devyn smiles. "That's perfect. Barney will be thrilled."

We order Chinese takeout for lunch and talk for the rest of the afternoon. I don't leave Beau's lap until it's time to say goodbye to my sister and Rick.

In the foyer, she nudges me aside, and Rick and Beau have a last-minute conversation, too.

"Call if you need," she says, tugging on her gloves. "He looks like he's doing okay, but if you want to get out of here, I'll come and get you, anytime. You're not alone. Remember that."

I can't hug her tight enough. "I will. Thank you, for everything."

"The next time I'm in the city, we'll go see Father Will together. We won't give up on Mom and we'll do what we can, okay?"

"Yeah." After seeing Mom and how she is, what we can do won't be much, but it's a lot easier for me to understand.

She kisses my cheek. "Good luck with your classes. I miss it."

"I'm excited. I've already been going over my assignments." I look at Beau and Rick. They're slapping each other on the back in that gruff way men have when they're showing affection.

"Let me know what you think about what we talked about earlier. The offer's always open," Rick says, putting his hand on Devyn's lower back to walk her into the elevator.

"Yeah. I will. Can't do much about it right now," Beau says, glancing at me.

"Never hurts to make a plan," Rick says, sounding a lot like my therapist.

Devyn steps into the elevator. She wiggles her fingers at me. "Bye."

I feel like I did the first time she left me here, and my throat burns. I'll always miss her when we have to say goodbye.

The doors close with a soft bump.

"What do you want to do now?" Beau asks. He's still uncomfortable, and I wish he'd relax. He's waiting for me to tear into him for tracing my phone.

"Will you help me clean up?" I ask, heading into the living room where our takeout boxes are still sitting on the coffee table.

"Yeah, sure." We put leftovers away, Beau standing so close to me that our arms brush. I feed him little bites of his chicken and broccoli as I dump it into a storage container. He laughs over his fortune, and he reads me mine. By the time the kitchen is clean and the coffee's dripping for our usual evening cup, things feel like normal.

"Do you want to watch a movie?" If he's going to want to spend every second with me, I'll make it easy. He doesn't need to follow me around the penthouse when what he wants, I want too.

"That sounds good." He looks so relieved I'm not going to lock myself in the guest room or hide behind my laptop, my heart breaks.

"You choose this time, and I'll find the popcorn. I bought some microwave stuff when I put that food order in. Our groceries are getting low. Will you sit with me tomorrow and make a list?"

He presses his lips together but after a moment, he nods.

I pretend that I didn't notice. "Thanks."

He doesn't say anything, only goes into the living room to start the movie.

I pour coffee into mugs, dump the popcorn into a bowl, and after putting everything on the coffee table, crawl into his lap. I curl myself into a little ball and he wraps his arms around me.

His heart thumps under my ear, and I feel so safe. Nothing can hurt me as long as he loves me.

I need him so much.

During the end credits, I start sniffling.

"Are you okay?" he asks, meeting my eyes.

Forcing a laugh, I say, "Yeah. Just thinking about how much I love you." I slide off his lap and kiss his cheek. I don't wait for him to respond. His eyes soften, and maybe he'd say it back, but I don't want to hear him say that he loves me too but that it's not enough. I carry the empty popcorn bowl and our mugs into the kitchen and wash them. He stands next to the sink and smooths his hand over my hair.

"I know it's early, but do you mind if we go to bed? Were you planning to do a little work?" I ask, tangling my fingers with his.

"No. I'm tired too."

He follows me to the bedroom, and we change into pajamas and brush our teeth together.

I stand uncertainly at the foot of his bed, but I don't give him a chance to tell me to sleep in the other room. I crawl in, and he turns off the lamp. He gets in next to me, and I lie halfway on top of him.

"What did Rick mean? What offer was he talking about?"

He rubs the backs of his fingers up and down my spine. "He wants to promote someone to CEO of this branch, and he asked us to move to Old Harbor."

He doesn't sound happy, and my eyes widen in surprise. "I thought that's what you wanted."

"I thought I did too, but now I don't know. There's so much unfinished business here."

"I know what you mean. When Devyn and I moved to Portland, I didn't want to leave Cedar Hill, but we didn't have a choice. I didn't tell her because she was doing what she had to, but I didn't want to leave Mom. I was born in this city, and I grew up here." I pause. "Are you talking about the hotel?"

He sighs. "That's part of it. There are things I'm not ready to forget."

"You mean Nina," I whisper.

"Yeah."

"You miss her."

He doesn't say anything, and at any other time, with any other man, I would have gotten out of bed and slept in the guest room. But this is Beau. He expects me to do that. He's been waiting for me to leave since I moved in. No, that's not exactly true. He's been waiting for me to leave since the first night he made love to me.

I lick at his lips. "Maybe I can help you not miss her so much."

We make love, but he's different than he has been. He lets me have control, and I go slowly, my lips never leaving his skin. "I love you, Beau." I repeat it like a prayer. My hands in his hair, his cock deep inside me, I whisper it until I'm hoarse, and even then, I never stop until we're slicked with sweat, lying in the damp sheets, panting. He didn't use a condom, and I don't care. After what happened last night, I needed him close to me, filling me with everything he's willing to give me. Maybe that's not much. Maybe it will never be what he gave Nina, but I'm so in love with him that I can't leave.

I start to tremble, and he holds me to him. "What is it, love?"

"I'm scared to live in Old Harbor alone," I say, my lips brushing his arm as he spoons me. "I've never been on my own, and I'll miss you. Will you visit me?"

"Fuck." He growls low and deep. "Don't go. I don't know what I was thinking."

I turn over and search his eyes in the dark. "You don't want to need me, but you don't understand. I need you enough for both of us."

"One day you'll regret you said that," he says, gently tugging a piece of hair out of my mouth.

"For as young as I am, I have a lot of regrets, but I know that won't ever be one of them."

We fall asleep, my heart pressed against his.

I traded my addiction to Sweet for an addiction to this man. Sweet killed me, lick by lick, but Beau's love will bring me back to life.

———

Sunday is the same as any other I've spent with Beau, but different too. We sleep in, make love and shower together, and later sip on coffee while we flip through the Sunday *Times*. We write down a list of things we need from the grocery store, and instead of filling a virtual cart, we shop in person, arranging for it to be delivered.

We walk downtown, the sidewalk empty on an early Sunday afternoon, and we replace my phone at a wireless store near a little café where we decide to eat lunch. While we wait for our food, I cuddle into him and take our picture to test the camera. Beau bought me something better than what I had before, and the picture's sharp and clear.

The storefronts are decorated for Valentine's Day—hearts, flowers, candy, and jewelry—but Beau doesn't look at any of it. I pause at each window, pressing my nose against the cold glass. I've never celebrated Valentine's Day with a man before. In high school, we could pay for candygrams and send them to our secret crushes, and during my freshman year of college, I went to a dance on campus, at the non-alcoholic dance club. But in rehab we didn't celebrate, and in Portland, Devyn and I didn't have a reason to. The day after Valentine's Day meant cheap chocolate, and we were more interested in that than complaining about the fact that neither of us had men in our lives who cared about buying us jewelry.

I gaze at the diamond necklaces and rings and bracelets, and he waits patiently, checking his phone, his disinterest clear.

Maybe Nina didn't like to celebrate Valentine's Day.

On the way back to his building, we stop at a red light. I step off the curb a moment too soon, and Beau jerks me back onto the sidewalk, a speeding taxi nearly running me over. "Be careful," he snaps. "The roads are slippery."

"Sorry," I murmur, but he doesn't hear, yanking me across the street toward his building.

"I need to do some work for a few hours. Will you be all right?" he asks in the foyer, taking his jacket and shoes off.

"Yeah."

He turns away.

"Beau."

He stops and looks over his shoulder.

"Kiss me."

That makes him smile, and he cuddles me, nuzzling my lips with his. "Why?"

"Something happened while we were walking downtown. I'm sorry if I did anything to make you mad."

"It wasn't you, love. Valentine's Day brings back bad memories, that's all. If you want to go out, I'll reserve a table at a fancy place. I'd like to see you dressed up."

"Yeah, sure," I murmur as he lets me go, but I already know I won't want to go if he doesn't want to be there.

He walks down the hallway, and a moment later, I hear a door shut. The groceries that we shopped for are delivered, and alone, I put them away. Instead of coffee, I bring him a cold bottle of lemon Perrier.

"Thanks," he murmurs, looking over a spreadsheet.

I kiss his cheek. "You're welcome."

My desk hasn't come yet, but Beau said I could be in here, so I settle on the loveseat with my laptop, a pen, and a notebook.

He glances at me, then turns in his chair. "What are you doing?"

There's no way he wants to be alone or he never would have said I could have a desk in his office in the first place. He's not complaining about me being here, he's fighting against the relief he feels that I'm spending the afternoon with him because I want to. "I'm going to start reading my textbooks. Everything I need is online, and I want to get a head start. And I have to message Devyn and let her know I got a new phone. She emailed me this morning to ask how things are, but I would rather she text and be able to call. I won't bother you, I promise."

"I don't need you around every second."

Yes, you do, I think, but I'm learning that if I don't want us to fight, this needs to be about me. A lot of it is, and I'm mostly telling him the truth. "I know you don't, but I don't want to sit in the kitchen by myself. I've already done enough of that, and it will bring back bad feelings that you don't want me here."

He winces. "Fair. And I'm sorry about that."

"I know. We worked it out, and it's not a big deal."

He nods and turns back to his computer, and I start a chat with Jessie, planning her baby shower. She wants to have it before the baby's born, and I completely understand. Hoping she doesn't go into labor early, we decide on a date just before Valentine's Day, and I ask her to put together a guest list with their mailing addresses. I still don't want to let Jessie or Serena know where I live or who I'm dating, and I tell her I'll use her address for the return on the envelopes. We say goodbye, and I order her a simple white crib and blue bedding from a department store near her apartment. She'll need it, and I doubt anyone will buy her one.

"I'm throwing a friend a baby shower next week," I say to Beau as I close out of the website. "Will you go with me?"

I hate picturing Beau sitting in Jessie's little apartment or going to NA meetings with me at Haven Presbyterian, but I can't hide who I used to be. I have friends there, and they mean something to me.

"Sure. Who's the friend?"

"A girl I used to hang out with at school. She's the friend I told Devyn about. Jessie didn't get hooked on Sweet at the party we went to, but her boyfriend, her baby's daddy, he's hooked. High-functioning, but he doesn't have a job. She won't leave him."

Beau frowns, and the skin around his mouth tightens. "Can you be around that?"

"I'm getting better, but it would help if you were there."

"I'll support you however I can."

"Thanks."

At six, he starts to stretch, and I mark my place in the textbook I was reading. "Do you want to help me make dinner?"

"What were you thinking?" he asks, putting his computer to sleep.

"Homemade macaroni and cheese?" I close my laptop.

"Sounds good."

We spend a pleasant evening in the kitchen. We chat about Jessie, and he lets me know that the director of M&H's foundation is processing Serena and Aaron's grant application. I sip water, and he pours a glass of Glenlivet. I'm glad he's starting to be more himself around me. I don't ever want to stop him from doing what he wants to do, and that includes drinking in the evening.

After we eat and do dishes, we watch another movie, and I lie on the couch with my head in his lap. I want to ask if he feels like he's missing out because we spend so much time at his penthouse, but I'll save it for another day.

It's a little early, but we get ready for bed. We have to get up early anyway, and I'm looking forward to starting classes in the morning. I don't want to sit here by myself, and I try to figure out a way to ask him if I can go with him to his office. He turns out the light, and I snuggle into him. "Does your building have internet?" I ask.

He laughs, and in the dark, he rubs his nose against mine. "Yes, Talia, my work has internet. I'm not sure I could do my job if we didn't. Why? What's going through that pretty head of yours?"

"Well, I was thinking, since I don't like being alone, maybe I could attend my classes in your office? I'll use earbuds and be quiet. I don't have to participate much. Just answer a question every now and then."

"You want to go to work with me?" he asks, surprised.

I'm glad I thought of it because it's a good compromise. I don't want to be alone, he doesn't want to ask if I'll spend time with him, and we both get what we want.

"Do you mind?"

"No, but we have to leave early. I have an eight o'clock meeting."

"That's perfect—I have an eight o'clock class."

"Every day?"

"Mondays, Wednesdays, and Fridays. Tuesdays and Thursdays I have a ten o'clock class, but I'd still like to go with you every day, as early as you need to. Devyn and I talked while you and Rick were at the site on Saturday, and she reminded me that I'm at my best if I stick to a schedule. These past few months have thrown me off, and if I can plan on going to work with you, I can make the most out of my classes."

He turns on his side and brushes his thumb over my cheek. "I haven't been supportive, and I'm sorry. I've been dealing with my own shit, and you've been paying for it. Of course you can go to work with me. We can eat lunch together and come home together if that's what you want. Call your therapist. You've been saying you will, but you haven't and it's important. If you want to have privacy during your sessions, you can use an empty conference room. If you want me to sit in on some of them with you, I will. Lord knows, it couldn't hurt me. I forgot about what you need, and I'm sorry. I'm sorry we haven't talked about Stevie. I was so scared, Talia. So scared when I saw you taped to that chair. And then you didn't want me to kiss you . . . Christ."

"You know why I didn't want you to kiss me," I say, my lips close to his.

"I only understood after you said something. You turned away, and it dredged up a lot of painful memories. I need to put those aside. You need me, and I haven't been there for you. I'll do better."

"That you want me at all is a miracle," I say, burying my face in the curve of his neck and breathing in the scent of his cologne that has already helped me through so many tough times.

"From the second I saw your face," he murmurs.

We stay up talking most of the night, but when the alarm goes off at six, I'm not tired.

Mack drives us to Beau's office, and he holds my hand on the way. By seven forty-five, I'm logged into the university's online program, a cup of decaf near my laptop and a new notebook and pen waiting for notes.

Beau leaves for his meeting, his suit jacket hanging on the back of his chair.

The last six years were rocky, but finally, I found my place.

———

Sitting at the conference table in Beau's office, I attend all my classes. It feels normal, it feels right, to meet my teachers and classmates, listen to lectures, and take notes. Over the weekend, word spread Stevie Johansson kidnapped me, and I'm the center of attention for the first five minutes of each class. Everyone wants to know what happened, and they beg me to tell them about that night and my role in Stevie's arrest.

Every time Beau comes back from one of his meetings, his eyes sparkle when he sees me. He leans over my shoulder and kisses my cheek. My laptop's camera catches him, and my classmates laugh. I blush for the rest of the hour. My professor playfully fans herself, and half an hour later, she closes out the class and tells me to be good.

We work in comfortable silence, and at noon he asks if I want to go to lunch. My classes are done for the day, and I say sure.

In the SUV, I sit in his lap, and every so often, Mack shoots us amused glances in the rearview mirror.

"Italian okay?" Beau asks, nibbling at my lips.

"Yeah. You don't care we had macaroni and cheese last night?"

"No. Do you?"

"No." I tilt my head and part my lips, letting him slip his tongue inside my mouth. I'll never get enough of his kisses, never get enough of the way he wants to touch me.

He tugs my blouse's hem out of my dress pants and caresses my breast through my lacy bra. "You're gorgeous," he murmurs.

I moan and straddle his legs, pressing against his cock. "What are you starting?"

Mack stops in front of a casual Italian restaurant and clears his throat.

"Something I'm going to have to finish at home," he says, glowering playfully.

I laugh. "I love you."

He holds my face in his hands.

"Stop," I whisper. "Stop being sad when I say it."

"I'll try."

While we eat, he asks about my classes and I ask him what other plans M&H has going on besides the hotel. He describes a couple of his pet projects, and I'm glad he and Rick reached a truce and that he's happy to talk about the things he'll be working on this summer. Toward the end of our meal, I ask if we can stop by a stationery store on the way home. I need to buy the baby shower invitations and mail them as soon as I can. I'll also create an event on social media, but sometimes it's nice to do things the old-fashioned way. It feels good to talk about something other than Sweet, addiction, Nina, and Old Harbor. I can see us falling into a lovely routine of work for him, school for me, lunch dates, and then going home, cooking dinner, and ending the day with a movie.

"Will you get bored?" In the truck, I rest my cheek against his shoulder.

"With what?" he asks, cuddling me close.

I look up at him. "With me. With what I need."

He kisses my forehead and says, "What you need is what I've been looking for all my life."

I hope he always feels that way.

He helps me through security, never stepping more than an inch away from me as we wait for my bag to move through the x-ray machine. Most of the security guards know who I am, and one asks how I'm doing. The lobby's full of employees coming back from their own lunch breaks, and in the packed elevator, Beau wraps his arm around my shoulders, shielding me from the crowd.

We step out, and Beau turns toward his office, but I pause. "I'm going to go to the bathroom, then I'll start on my homework. I have a paper to write, and I don't want to have to get up again," I say.

He holds out his hands. "Let me hang up your coat and purse."

"Thanks."

With my coat draped over his arm and my purse dangling from his hand, he walks down the hallway, and I turn toward the ladies' restroom. It's empty, and after I go, I stand in front of the long mirror and finger-comb the snarls out of my hair. I shouldn't have let him take my purse—I could have freshened up my lip gloss. I straighten my blouse and brush my hand over my belly. I still haven't gotten my period, but the number of times we've had sex without protection makes that more and more unlikely as the days pass. Beau wants a baby, and I want to give him one. There's no point in denying it or putting it off, even if it would be nice to graduate first. Women do it all every day, and I can be one of those women too.

I step into the hallway thinking of baby names, topics for my paper, if Beau would prefer to have a boy or a girl, and if I should stop at the library on the way home. No, we have to go to the stationery store. I won't have time to go to the library too, but that's okay—

An elegant brunette stomps out of Beau's office, and she slams the door. The *crack* echoes over the entire floor.

She's gorgeous. Tall and willowy, her features are petite and refined. She's wearing an expensive black sheath dress, and her black cashmere coat hangs open showing off a beautiful diamond necklace and her tiny waist. Four-inch heels are strapped to her feet, and she towers over me. She's just the type of woman Beau would be photographed with before he met me. Ten years older than I am, has worked toward a professional career. She's more suited for him than I will ever be.

Comparing myself to her sophistication, I feel like what I am: a young girl who used to be addicted to Sweet, struggling to get through school and find her way.

"You're Talia Scott," she says, her voice matching her figure. Smoky and lithe.

"I am," I say, tilting my head. "Are you Nina?" It would make sense for this woman to be the love of Beau's life.

The blood drains from her face. "Nina? No. I'm not Nina. Beau didn't tell you what happened to her."

It's not a question, but I answer anyway. "No, he didn't."

"Nina's dead, darling. He killed her."

I suck in a startled breath. "What? I don't understand."

Beau steps out of his office, and he slumps against the wall. Shoving his hands in his pockets, he watches us.

"He wouldn't leave her alone," she says, her lips twisting into a frown. "He had to be around her every second. All she wanted was a little space, a little room to breathe, but no. He had to know when she was working, and he was always there to pick her up. She was a party planner, did you know that?"

I remember him telling me that's how he met her, but I don't say anything.

"He would go to the parties she put together, following her around while she tried to do her job. She couldn't have a girls' night out. She couldn't spend the weekend with her parents without him. He had to be everywhere she was, until one night, on Valentine's Day, no less, she got so fucking sick of it, she ran away. He killed her. Only a technicality kept him out of prison. Get him to explain that to you, and then we'll see if all his money is worth your freedom." She flicks a glance over her shoulder. She knew he was standing there.

I meet his eyes. I've never seen him look like this.

"You're young and pretty," she continues. "Find yourself a man who doesn't need to be with you every fucking second of every fucking day."

I lick my lips. "Who are you to Nina?"

"I was her best friend. Trust me, I know exactly how he treated her."

Her brown eyes are lovely, flecked with gold and framed by long, dark lashes. A blush stains her cheeks the longer I stare. "How long have you been in love with him? How long have you wanted what Nina had?"

"Fuck you. He killed my best friend."

"And when she died, you thought you had a chance," I say softly, feeling sorry for this woman who's been in love with Beau for so long and had nothing to show for it except bitterness because he didn't feel the same way.

She steps forward, but she doesn't scare me. She's never walked Arrowhead Alley, she's never bought Sweet off a dealer in the middle of the night. She's never been taped to a chair and teased with one of the most addictive drugs in the world.

"He was so obsessed with another woman, why would you think he would love you?" I ask. She takes another step toward me, but I don't move. "You wanted him to live and breathe for you like he did for Nina, but love doesn't work like that. He still loves her. He told me just the other night how much he misses her."

"Talia!" Beau barks, but I ignore him. Nothing I'm saying is a lie.

"He's given me pieces," I murmur, not knowing if I'm getting through to her, "but Nina will always have all of him. I don't know your name, but you're wrong. He'll never do the things to me you say he'll do, not when he'll always be in love with another woman, living or dead. You should go. You don't belong here."

Gently, she touches my cheek. "If what you say is really true, then neither do you."

She presses the call button, and her dramatic exit is saved when the elevator doors open. She steps inside without looking at me again. Slowly, I turn around and face Beau.

His skin is an ashy grey, and his hands shake.

I walk by him, and he closes the door behind us.

"Talia—"

"It's okay, Beau. It makes sense now."

He frowns. "What makes sense?"

"How you act. How you treat me. Nina's dead, and you'll never get another chance with her. Do you want to tell me about it?"

He doesn't. That's the last thing he wants, but I love him and I believe that underneath everything, he loves me too.

Standing in the middle of his office, I wait.

CHAPTER TWENTY-TWO

Beau

She's waiting for me to speak, but I can't force the words around the ball of misery in my mouth. The truth would have had to come out eventually. I couldn't keep running hot and cold, but to have Jasmine talk to her, accuse me of murder right in front of my face, that's not how I wanted this to go. I wanted to control the situation so that maybe after Talia hears the truth she wouldn't leave. There's no chance of that now. Jasmine wiggled under her skin, and Talia looks at me, wary and suspicious.

"Everything Jasmine said was true. I met Nina and fell completely in love with her the second I saw her." I shrug and shuffle to the window. It will be easier to get it out if I'm not looking at her, if I don't have to see the accusation in her eyes. "A lot like I did with you. I saw you, and your eyes and fragility blew me away. Nina wasn't like you—you're beautiful in a different way. Quiet, reflective. You're peaceful, and at this point in my life, I need that, but back then, when I met Nina, she was like a sparkler. I wanted to hold her, but all she did was burn me if I got too close."

"You don't have to tell me anymore," she says, stepping toward me.

I shake my head. "No. I've owed you this for a long time. When I'm done, I'll drive you to the airport."

She doesn't say anything, and I sigh.

"Nina was an alcoholic, and Jasmine and Rick were a little concerned when they found out you had been addicted to Sweet. You handled it. Nina didn't. She didn't want to. She loved drinking, the buzz it gave her, and I tolerated it. Hell, I would have tolerated anything. I *did* tolerate anything. Everything. We dated for two years, if you can call it that."

"What do you mean?"

"The closer I wanted to be, the more she backed away. I would go to the parties she planned to watch her work—Jasmine was right about that—but I wasn't stalking her. I just loved watching her. She had such a fire, she would blaze with the energy. I spent every second I could with her. It's not that I didn't like her spending time with her friends or family, I just couldn't leave her alone."

"Is this the real reason you ignored me when I first moved in with you? It wasn't about sex."

I huff a laugh, but it sounds cold and hostile. "Oh, it was about sex too. You remember that night."

She nods.

It would be difficult to forget how I went at her. Her threat to leave broke down my last remaining defenses, and I never gave her a second to rest the entire night.

"I couldn't keep my hands off her, but she didn't feel the same way I felt about her. She consumed me, but to her, I was just a toy. Something to play with when she was bored. I always felt like I could lose her at any second, and I tried like hell to stop it. I asked her to marry me, and she said yes. She was drunk when I asked. Jasmine accused me of doing that on purpose, and maybe I did. I didn't want her to say no."

Talia flinches. I didn't want to talk about us getting married. I couldn't. She didn't know what happened, and she couldn't say yes without knowing the truth.

"How did she die? I don't believe it was your fault," she says, rubbing her bare ring finger.

"Nina got pregnant."

"Oh, Beau," she whispers.

"You can say I got what I deserved. I knew how she felt about me, and I wasn't careful. Didn't want to be. I thought she'd stop drinking, that we'd get married and be a family. That was a dream I wanted, but it was never hers. It was on Valentine's Day, ten years ago now. We went out to dinner, and she told me she didn't want it, that she was going to get an abortion. We fought, and she left in a rage. I followed her, of course I followed her, and I grabbed her hand. I should have just let her go."

I rub my eyes, hoping to blank out the memory, but nothing will make me forget that night. I lean my arm against the window, the city spread out in front of me. Everything I have is because I worked so hard to make up for Nina's death.

Talia waits for me to keep going, her arms wrapped around herself.

"Nina jerked away and ran. The streets were slippery, and a truck sped through a red light. It hit her, and the impact killed her instantly. Jasmine said it was my fault and she wasn't wrong, but witnesses told the police it was an accident. It wasn't, though. I'd been killing her for months. I just didn't want to see it."

"You said you still miss her," she says, tears dripping down her cheeks.

"No. *You* said I still miss her. It's been ten years. I have a lot of regrets, a lot of things I would have done differently, but I don't miss her. She was never mine to miss."

"What happened after that?"

"Nothing. Her parents didn't know we'd been fighting, and they didn't know we were arguing that night. They didn't know she was pregnant. They didn't ask for an autopsy, and no one knew except me. They buried her wearing my ring and treated me like the grieving fiancé I was. Rick helped me through a lot of it. Jasmine hung around, but I didn't know why until a few days ago. I went to the art gallery where she works and told her I didn't want to be friends anymore, that I needed to leave things in the past or I'd never be happy in the future with you."

I don't know why I added that last part. It's not going to happen. I have no future with Talia, and I knew from the moment we met that my relationship with Nina would stand in my way. In some way or another, we always get what we deserve, and this is Karma paying me back for my part in Nina's death.

"I tried to give you space, but I'm not built that way. I'll never be in a normal relationship. I'm too needy, and one day it'll push you away just like it did to Nina. I'll drive you to the airport. The plane will be ready to fly you to Old Harbor when we get there."

She lifts her chin. "No."

"What do you mean, no? Didn't you hear anything I just said?"

"I heard it. And do you want to know what I heard?"

She keeps speaking without waiting for me to answer.

"I heard you loved Nina. I heard you loved her with everything you had, but she didn't love you, Beau. Maybe she thought she did, or maybe the alcohol numbed her true feelings. Maybe she was lying to herself because she liked the sex or the money, but she didn't love you. She didn't love you, or she would have wanted to spend time with you. She would have wanted you to visit her at work and asked you to go for weekend getaways with her parents. She would have wanted that ring on her finger and the baby you gave her." She presses a hand to her belly. "If I'm pregnant, you can be sure I want it."

"Talia, love—" I want her to carry my baby, but I've never let myself believe she'd want it too.

"Come sit."

She tugs my arm, and I let her lead me to the loveseat pushed against the window. She sits down next to me and grips my hand with her two small ones. Her eyes are so green, and since the day we met, I've wanted to fall into them and never climb out. She might be young, but she has more wisdom than I could ever have.

"Can addiction ever be a good thing?" she asks, gripping my fingers. "Knowing what it feels like, I'd probably have to say no. Like you found out, it can take over your life. I never had any peace after my first taste of Sweet, and it sounds like you felt the same after you met Nina. Sweet took my family, and it took some of my friends. It took my pride and self-esteem. But there's some good that came out of it. My relationship with Devyn is stronger than it ever was. I learn something new about myself every day. I learn that I'm strong in some ways and weak in others. In the areas where I'm weak, you've been there for me, because you love me and because you care. Nina twisted that into something ugly, but it's not."

I yank my hand away. "You don't know what you're talking about. We've been together for four months."

She lifts her hands. "And in those four months, you don't think I've gotten to know you? You've given me space when I wanted it—when I went to look for Mom and when I found my friends. You've given me space when I haven't wanted it—like the first couple of months I lived with you. You can do it with me, and you did it with Nina. You built this company with Rick, didn't you? You felt like you were hounding her because she made you feel like that. Have I *ever* made you feel like you annoy me? Like you inconvenience me? No. You know why? Because you don't. I like spending time with you, and God help me, I need it too. If you don't listen to anything I just said, fine, but listen to this: *I need you just as much as you need me.*"

She stands up and walks toward the window. I want to pull her back and tell her she could never need me that much.

"It's hard for me to admit," she says, looking out the glass. "I don't want to need you. I don't want to need anybody. But I do need you, and I need Devyn. There might not be anything I can do to help her, but I need to know how Mom's doing, even if I don't like how that is." She turns and meets my eyes. "You're not any different than me. You can need me. I'll give you permission if that's what you're looking for. From the moment you open your eyes in the morning, until you fall asleep holding me, I will always be there for you."

I hold out my arms, and she steps between my legs. "I don't want to stifle you, love. I don't want to smother you."

She scrubs my scruff with her fingers. "That's why people talk to each other. Even if those conversations are hard. Even if they're uncomfortable or embarrassing. There's nothing more awkward than baring your soul to a therapist every Tuesday and Thursday like I've had to do since getting out of rehab. If I can talk to her about the things I did for Sweet, I can tell you that I want to go out for lunch with Jessie alone. If we talk to each other, and listen, we will never have a problem."

I nudge her, asking her to sit on my leg, and she does, comfortable in my lap. She belongs here, and she's felt perfect since the first time she did it. I believed Nina when she showed me the wrong things, but didn't listen to Talia when she tried to tell me the right ones. "I'm scared, Talia. I don't want to lose you."

She holds up her left hand and smiles. "This would be a good start."

"You want to get married. Really?"

"Yeah, I do. When you're ready to ask."

I risk her running away from me for the completely opposite reason Nina did. "I'm not yet. I need a little more time."

She gently presses her lips to mine. "Take all the time you need."

As crazy as it sounds, I'm glad Jasmine came by. I don't know how or when I would have found the courage to have this talk with her, but things turned out better than I thought possible. "I love you."

"I love you too."

We sit like that for a while, her head resting in the crook of my shoulder as she plays with my tie.

"You wanna get out of here?" I ask, tugging the hem of her blouse out of her dress pants and skimming my fingers over the soft skin of her back.

"Sure, but remember, we're stopping by the stationery store first. Finishing what you started at lunch will need to wait a few minutes longer." She laughs, easing my hand away.

She moves to crawl off my lap, but I cuddle her to me. "This is going to work, isn't it?"

Laughing, she murmurs, "Ah, screw it," and kisses me, slipping her tongue into my mouth.

We don't leave early, but we make it to the stationery store just before they close.

Rick understands what I need out of our friendship, and Talia knows my darkest secrets and loves me anyway. Life has turned around in ways I never would have expected, never would have dared to think about, since the day that crane tipped over and caused so much heartache.

I spent ten years believing that loving someone with my whole heart was a lethal addiction, and it took someone who fought her own addiction and won to show me how untrue that is.

She proves it to me every day.

After the stationery store, we go home, make dinner, and watch a movie. Simple things I will never take for granted or get tired of.

This is the life I dreamed of with Nina, but she didn't want it, and I will always be thankful I found a woman who did.

"Thank you," I say as I hold her in bed, tangling our legs and wrapping my fingers in her hair.

"As a wise woman once said, you don't have to thank me for loving you. When you love someone, you love all of them, and I do love you, Beau. I walked into your office with Devyn, and I knew from that moment that I found my place."

She wiggles against me, trying to get closer.

"Took me a second," I say, nuzzling her lips with mine.

"That's okay," she whispers against my mouth. "If you let me, I'll give you all of mine."

Do you know how many seconds are in a lifetime?

I don't either, but all of Talia's belong to me, and I won't waste a single one.

CHAPTER TWENTY-THREE

Beau

The following week we go to the baby shower Talia throws for her friend, Jessie. It's fun to watch her eat pizza off a paper plate and lick the grease off her fingers, chat with Jessie's mom, and coo over baby gifts.

She explained the situation to me a little more, and before the party, I brought Talia to a department store and bought them out of clothes and toys and arranged for a few boxes of diapers to be delivered to their apartment every month.

Jessie and Foster's apartment is tiny, and more than once I think about moving them into a nicer place, but I never mention it. Like Talia figured out looking for her mom, we can't save everyone. But we can support them, and when Foster stumbles out of the bedroom, his eyes bloodshot and his body trembling from withdrawal, I shake his hand.

Stevie's been in jail for close to three weeks while the DA's office collects evidence and she waits for her trial. All her candy stores have closed, and the local DEA's office has been working around the clock to make sure the Sweet Stevie had coming into the city didn't reach her dealers' hands.

The effect was immediate . . . and catastrophic.

People going through withdrawal filled up the rehab centers and hospitals, and the price of Sweet that was already on the streets skyrocketed. Only the rich were able to feed their addictions a little while longer.

The shrinking supply caused a wave of crime and death, and Cecilia has handled it all with competence, compassion, and grace. As I imagined, helping the cops arrest Stevie put her on top, and Cedar Hill elected a new sweetheart to reign over the city.

She never sent me a thank you card, too aware of how easily it could have gone the other way.

"That was fun," I say as we walk down the sidewalk to the SUV. Talia asked if we could drive ourselves, and I agreed.

"Thanks for coming with me," she says.

I open the door for her. "Thanks for inviting me."

She beams, and I have no choice but to kiss her shining face.

The night before Valentine's Day, Talia tells me she got her period, and I hold her while she cries. I'm not sad. I know there's plenty of time for us to have children. I think her tears had more to do with Devyn calling with her own good news than it did with Talia not having any of her own to share. Rick looked a little dazed over the FaceTime call, and I gave him a hard time while Devyn laughed. They're good together, and no matter what Rick thinks, they'll both make great parents.

Talia and I go out for dinner on Valentine's Day. She didn't want to, but I convinced her. It's time to put the past behind me and make new memories. She's gorgeous wearing in a dark green cocktail dress and heels, and we eat at the fancy restaurant I promised her, photographers snapping our pictures through the windows. I've been living such a quiet life while getting to know her, I forgot about the city's interest in my life.

I kiss the back of her hand, and she blushes over a thick slice of chocolate cake.

Tonight would have been the perfect night to ask her to marry me, but I hold off. We talk about babies instead, and sadness glints in her eyes.

"You should go on birth control, love," I say, squeezing her wrist. "I want you to finish school first. Even if that means we wait another two or three years. I'm not that old. I can handle it," I tease, trying to brighten her spirits. I love that she wants to make me happy, but I never want her to regret anything we do.

"If that's what you want." Her voice is soft, and she speaks to the dessert plate.

"Talia, I love you, and we'll have babies when the time is right. Finish school first. You're young and healthy, and we won't need long once we decide it's what we want. Besides, there's no harm in keeping you to myself for a bit. I think you told me once that you haven't been out of Minnesota. I promised to change that."

She smiles, and we talk about where we would go first.

There's nothing I'd enjoy more than showing her the world.

We fall into an easy routine after Valentine's Day. She comes with me to the office every day and uses the time to go to her online classes and therapy sessions. Sometimes Devyn joins in on the Zoom call, and sometimes I do. Talia blossoms, and I've never seen her look more beautiful.

March blows in, and with it, the coldest temperatures of the year. I wait them out impatiently, wanting to get a start on the hotel. Rick doesn't ask me about moving to Old Harbor. I know he still wants us to, but because of the hotel and Devyn and Talia's mom still out on the streets, a permanent move is a ways off.

One cold and dreary Saturday afternoon, Talia and I attend an NA meeting at the small church on Camden Way. We're becoming good friends with Serena and her fiancé, Aaron, and the second we step into the church's little foyer, she hugs me.

"I hear I have you to thank for the grant money. We received the approval email today," she says, her eyes wide.

I can see traces of the Sweet addict she used to be under the lines on her face. Her addiction aged her, and her lack of support added to her hard life. Talia told me about Serena's parents not helping her after rehab, and I appreciate the relationship Talia has with Devyn even more. Meeting Talia's friends and seeing firsthand how Sweet has affected people, I snuggle her to me every time I think about it. Talia was able to beat her addiction, but I'm learning she's one of few.

"It wasn't anything," I say.

"It was more than nothing," Aaron says, coming up behind Serena and pressing his lips to her cheek. "Your foundation is funding so many programs this year, and we're grateful for the offer to apply again next year. Daycare, job search assistance, addiction support, food for the homeless . . . you have no idea what that money will do and how it will bring this community together."

I wrap my arm around Talia. It's a gift she brings me to places like this and shows me the pieces of her life she's not ashamed to hide. Living with me on the other side of the city, she could walk away and not look back, but she visits Haven Presbyterian twice a month, and she always asks if I want to go with her. I always say yes. "Talia's showing me. I have a small idea."

We sit on folding metal chairs during the NA meeting, the room full now that Sweet is harder and more expensive to come by. Talia's proof that having a good life after addiction is possible. There are days—weeks—she's so calm and focused that I forget what she's gone through, but then she has a bad day and I'll find her sitting on the floor in our closet, her head in her hands and tears streaming down her cheeks. I sit next to her and talk her down, just like I did in Arrowhead Alley, and then together, we call Devyn and Rick. I always want Talia to know she has people she can lean on.

She's not afraid to cry and show her feelings, and she's rung out by the end of the meeting.

I hold her coat, and she tiredly slides her arms through the sleeves. Serena walks over to us, the dog Talia found in Jensen's apartment dozing in her arms. "Talia, I wanted to wait until after the meeting to tell you. I have bad news."

"What is it?" she asks, her shoulders stiffening under my hands.

"The Salvation Army's director let me know. They found your mom in Arrowhead Alley. She passed away. Withdrawal maybe, but it's been too cold to stay outside for long. She might not have been able to find somewhere warm to sleep. I'm sorry."

Talia presses her face into my chest, and I rub her back. It was only a matter of time before this happened, and I'm glad I was with her when she heard the news.

She turns to Serena and says, "Thank you for telling me. I'll see you in a couple of weeks, okay?"

"Yeah. God bless you, Talia. You deserve every happiness."

"And to you," she says softly, wiping tears off her cheeks.

"I'm so sorry, love," I say, helping her into the truck. She always asks if we can drive ourselves whenever we meet with her friends. I used to think she was ashamed of my money, that she didn't want them to see Mack driving us, but I realized it's because she doesn't want to make anyone uncomfortable. She's always thinking about everyone but herself.

"She's not suffering anymore," she whispers. "I need to call

Devyn. I guess Mom's body is at the morgue. We'll have to claim her."

"I can handle all that. Don't worry." I slam the door shut and trot around the hood to the driver's side.

"It would be nice, I think, if we had the funeral at the Catholic church. Father Will would want to be in charge of her service," she says as I get into the truck.

I settle behind the wheel and turn the engine on, hoping the vents will blow out warm air as quickly as possible. I haven't been to the church or met Father Will yet. Talia talks about it sometimes—how Devyn would leave money for their mother there, and how she did it herself once, asking the old priest to forgive her for making decisions that never should have been hers to make.

I smooth my fingertips over her cheek. "Whatever you need."

She forces a smile. "I need you."

"And you have me, one hundred percent."

We decided to have the funeral at the end of April. The weather cleared, and the afternoon sun melts what's left of the snow.

The church is full of people wanting to say their last good-byes to a woman who'd been a constant presence in Arrowhead Alley for close to ten years. It strikes me, as Talia tells me the story of her mother going to a dinner party and tasting Sweet for the first time, that it was the same year Nina died. Her mother's addiction and Nina's death put us on the same path. It took ten years for us to meet, but we did, and it changed our lives.

Father Will's message is full of hope, and the casket is covered in cheerful flowers. Rick and I scuffled over who would pay for what, and in the end, we split the funeral and reception costs. After the service, everyone is invited to stay and eat a warm meal. We catered in more than what was necessary and filled the church's kitchen with food.

Looking around the sanctuary, I know for some it will be their only meal of the day.

The service ends, and as people shuffle toward the stairs to go down to the basement, Talia slips outside. We're going to the cemetery together after we eat, and I know she's stealing a few minutes to breathe.

I follow her, just like I always do unless she says she needs time alone. She's always sure to tell me if she wants a minute, and I do the same, though we rarely do.

To anyone else, the amount of time we spend together would be shocking, and Rick warned me about codependency. Talia's therapist likes to talk about the subject too, but I'm not worried. Talia and I have open communication, and we need what we're giving each other. It's not anyone's business but ours.

She's sitting on the stone step, and I come up behind her. She squints up at me and smiles.

I'm wanted, and it took me a while to get used to that. Nina taught me that my presence was a burden, and even after so much time, I needed to smooth out that part of what she'd done to me. I think that's why I couldn't ask Talia to marry me on Valentine's Day. I needed a little more time to see the facts and believe them.

"Hi," I say, sitting next to her and giving her a kiss on her cheek.

"Hi. Thank you for this. We could have had her funeral on the other side of the city, but no one would have come. Mom fits in here, and Father Will is so happy the church is being used for what it's meant for."

"I like him. In fact, there's something I wanted to ask you."

She tilts her head, no hint of expectation on her face. "What is it?"

Talia's been patient since that day in my office and never mentioned getting married again. She gives me room to be who I need to be while not giving me room. It's difficult to explain how I can be with her twenty-four hours a day, seven days a week, and it doesn't crowd me . . . or her.

I don't know how to start. "It's been a good seven months. We're happy. Some would probably say we moved too fast—"

She laughs. "They *do* say that."

I chuckle. "True. They do."

"We didn't move any faster than Devyn and Rick. When it's meant to be, it's meant to be."

"I agree. We had a few bumps, but what couple doesn't."

"Right," she says, still unassuming. "A lot of what I told you, you couldn't believe until you saw it for yourself. I'm happy with the way things are. I hope you are too."

"I am. Rick and Devyn are getting married next month," I say, rubbing my thumb over the diamond ring in my pants pocket.

"Yeah. She's so happy. A little sick, but happy."

She's not jealous or bitter, simply glad her sister found someone who loves her and wants to take care of her.

"You and Rick okay?" she asks, brushing her fingers over my jaw. I shaved for the service, and her touch sets my skin on fire.

"Yeah. It's part of what I wanted to ask you. You don't want to move to Old Harbor full time." I know that. Now that she's finding old friends in the city and making new ones, she doesn't want to go, even if she could see Devyn whenever she wanted.

"Unless you do. Really, I'm fine either way. As long as you're with me, I'll be happy."

"I was hoping you'd say that, but I think we can compromise. What if, the next time we fly out, we look at land and build a house? We won't have to stay at a hotel, and if we want to visit for more than a weekend, we can have our own space."

She crinkles her eyes at me. "I like it."

"I wanted to see what you thought—I know how much you depend on your schedule." I'm starting to get nervous, and I'm drawing this out. The sun is warm, the temperatures in the low seventies, and I'm overdressed. The wind is still cool, but it's not enough to keep sweat from slicking my forehead and running down my back. I've done this once before, and it hurt me to the point I didn't think I'd ever do it again.

"Honestly, Beau, all I need is a heads up and a promise you'll be there. I don't want to go to Old Harbor alone, and you know that. If there's ever a time we plan to visit and you can't go, I'll stay here. It's the way I want it."

"I wouldn't want you to go without me, either, love."

She kisses my cheek. "Then I'm glad that's settled. We should go inside. I want to check on Devyn and make sure she's trying to eat something. I think the fresh air at the cemetery will help her feel better. It's so stuffy in there."

I swallow hard. "Wait."

Frowning in concern, she asks, "What is it? Are you okay?"

"I didn't think I'd do this here. A funeral isn't very romantic, but then I thought, maybe there isn't a better place." I take the ring out of my pocket. It's small and dainty, like her hand. Like she is. The band is gold, the diamond a princess cut. She doesn't wear much jewelry, and I didn't want to buy her something so huge she wouldn't want to wear it while she was hanging out with her friends. Something, now that Jessie has had her baby, she does frequently. With and without me. "I want you to know that I will always be here for you. That you might have lost your mom, but you'll never be alone. I thought when you moved in with me that my needs would suck everything out of you, and I didn't want that to happen. You told me that when I take, it gives you more, but I didn't believe it. I had to see for myself that every second I need to be with you doesn't drain you, but instead, makes you happy. When we're at home, I follow you from room to room, and you know what I noticed?"

Dazed, she shakes her head.

"When you're talking to me and you go to a different room, you don't stop. You know that I'm right behind you, listening. I thought you were taking me for granted, but then I realized you do it because you want me to follow. You'll never understand what that means to me, Talia."

"I always want to be where you are," she whispers.

"I know. I know that now. I also had to learn that if we aren't together, for whatever reason, you aren't leaving me. That if you want to take a bath alone you aren't planning to break up with me, or if you meet up with Serena for coffee and I'm in a meeting, that when the meeting is done, you'll be there because you came back. I had a lot to work through, love, in the past few months, and the only way I could was to go through the motions and see the proof right in front of me. Now that I know how our life is going to be, will you marry me? Be my wife and accept all that comes with it?"

"Yes. Yes, of course." She wipes a tear off her cheek.

Her hand trembles as I push the ring onto her finger. It looks good. Right. It's the perfect fit.

Gently, I kiss her, twisting my fingers in her hair. This perfect woman is mine for the rest of my life, and I will take care of her and give her whatever she needs. Always.

"I have something for you too," she says, taking her phone out of her purse.

"What?" She's already given me everything I could ever want.

"We never talked about you asking Mack to follow me or you tracking my phone when Luke tricked me."

My cheeks heat. "I know. You know why I did those things, and I'm sorry—"

"That's why we never talk about it. I don't want you to apologize. You did it because you love me and care about my safety. Rick won't like this. I know he doesn't like how much time we spend together. My therapist wouldn't like it either, and maybe we just don't tell them."

I frown. "What are you talking about?"

"Let me see your phone."

Confused, I pull my cell out of my pocket. When we replaced her phone, I bought her one like mine. She places them side by side on her lap and wakes them both up. I don't hide my phone from her and it's not protected with a password. She has access to it whenever she wants, and she's asked me to look in her phone for contact information and to look at pictures of Harry, Jessie's son.

She swipes the screens, and there's an app on both that I've never seen before.

"We can talk later about how healthy this is and if you want to keep it, but this is a tracking app. You can find me whenever you want, and I can find you . . . if we have our phones." She smiles wryly. "You don't have to ask a friend, you don't have to order Mack to follow me around. I'm not going to be walking the streets anymore, but I feel like this was the last little thing we needed to take care of. Now we can look ahead without having to look back."

My mouth is dry, and it's several seconds before I can speak. "Are you sure?"

"I have never been more sure about anything. Well, besides this," she says, holding up her left hand, the diamond glinting in the sun. "You need to know where I am all the time. This is my way of telling you that I understand, and that I'm okay with it. I doubt we'll have to use it very often. We're with each other all the time, and when we do have other plans, we always tell each other. Anyway," she says with a laugh, "I hope this makes you feel a little bit better. You saved my life—both times—and I know you will never track me down unless you think I'm hurt or need help. Because, you know. Text me first."

I laugh, and I let go of so much tension. Talia understands me in a way no one else will. "I love you."

"I love you too. We better go inside. We've been gone for a while now, and I want to thank Father Will for the service."

"Oh, that's another thing I wanted to ask," I say, the priest's name tripping my memory. We talked about so much, and my mind is spinning. "What do you think about getting married here? I'm not Catholic, but maybe Father Will can make an exception?"

Her laugh is full of delight, and she covers my mouth with hers, her lips warm. I take her kiss as a yes. Rather than lean away, I pick her up and carry her into the building.

We'll say our vows in this church, and Devyn will become my sister-in-law, and Rick, my brother. They're the family I've wanted, the family I've needed, and I have it now, because of this little girl in my arms.

I carry her down the stairs and into the basement's reception hall.

Rick smirks, and Devyn rolls her eyes, a sad smile on her pale face. Today is bittersweet. She loves how I love her sister, and I love her too, for giving Talia and me the space we needed to figure things out.

Talia might have found her place stepping into my office, but having her in my arms with Rick and Devyn walking toward us through the crowded room, I, finally, find mine.

BLOG SIGNUP

If you loved Talia and Beau, let's stay in touch! Sign up for my blog to stay up to date with new releases, sales, and news. As a thank you, you'll have access to *My Biggest Mistake*, a free, full-length billionaire, ugly duckling novel!

Sign up here! https://vmrheault.com/subscribe/

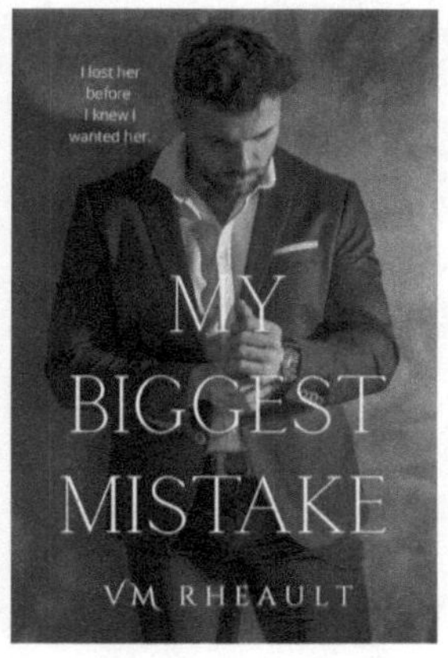

ABOUT THE AUTHOR

VM Rheault writes several subgenres of romance including billionaire, romantic suspense, and small town.

She lives in Minnesota with her two children and their newly adopted tuxedo cat, Pim. When she's not writing, she's working her day job, sleeping, or enjoying the four seasons with a hot cup of coffee in hand.

Find her at vmrheault.com.

ALSO BY VM RHEAULT

Captivated by Her (Cedar Hill Duet Book One)
Addicted to Her (Cedar Hill Duet Book Two)

———

Rescue Me

———

Give & Take (The Lost & Found Trilogy Book One)
Lost & Found (The Lost & Found Trilogy Book Two)
Safe & Sound (The Lost & Found Trilogy Book Three)

———

Faking Forever

———

Twisted Alibis (Ghost Town Trilogy Book One)
Twisted Lullabies (Ghost Town Trilogy Book Two)
Twisted Lies (Ghost Town Trilogy Book Three)

———

A Heartache for Christmas

———

Cruel Fate (King's Crossing Book One)

Cruel Hearts (King's Crossing Book Two)

Cruel Dreams (King's Crossing Book Three)

Shattered Fate (King's Crossing Book Four)

Shattered Hearts (King's Crossing Book Five)

Shattered Dreams (King's Crossing Book Six)

———

Loss and Damages

———

Wicked Games